VENOM BOUND

I. S. BELLE

Kindle eBook ASIN: B0DJHFZ3GV

KDP Paperback ISBN: 979-8-307372-63-0

IngramSpark Paperback ISBN: 978-1-067041-80-9

IngramSpark Hardcover ISBN: 978-1-067041-81-6

CONTENT WARNINGS

Underage drinking (alcohol), consensual blood drinking, nonconsensual blood drinking, parent death, grief, dog bites, burns, murder, gore, emotional abuse, addiction, child abuse, torture, stabbing, brief depiction of a seizure.

You will feel woe, rage, injustice — starve them all.

Nothing matters but the hunt.

— Guide To Hunting The Accursed Vampyre,
volume XXI

———

FEED IT OR IT WILL EAT YOU

— Kade Renfield's t-shirt

FOUR MONTHS after Theo Fairgood died, he snuck back into his bedroom with a pocket full of foraged mushrooms.

It had still been dark when Theo left the house through his bedroom window, but darkness didn't mean much to Theo since he was turned into a vampire. He spent his sleepless nights studying or hunting unlucky woodland creatures to tide over his hunger. And some nights—thanks to a particularly helpful YouTuber who specialized in native Tennessee fungi—he foraged for mushrooms.

He couldn't eat them. But he *did* have someone who was all too happy to take them off his hands.

Theo smiled to himself as he cleaned the mushrooms in his en-suite bathroom and hid them in his backpack. He could already picture Kade's expression: those gray eyes lighting up, how he'd chew on his lip to stop himself from grinning. He would tease Theo for it mercilessly, but Theo was getting better at seeing through Kade's sharp mask. He *liked* it when Theo brought him things.

Theo touched the lighter he'd been keeping in his pocket for weeks. Maybe today would be the day.

A sad whine echoed through the bathroom door. Theo looked over to see Sparky's paw wiggling underneath the door.

"No, you can't come next time," Theo told her, zipping up his backpack. "You're too loud."

He opened the door. Sparky stared up at him, her orange eyes baleful.

Theo sighed, reaching down to pet her short dark fur. "I know, girl. You can't help it. But the one time I let you come, you barked so loud that my parents almost caught us sneaking back in. I can't let that happen. They have to believe I'm a normal teenager and you're a normal dog, okay? Not a vampire and...whatever you are. Hellhound? Familiar?"

Sparky huffed, tail wagging reluctantly.

"You can't come to school with me, either," Theo told her, heading for the hallway. "I got in big trouble last time you showed up. Come on, now."

Sparky fell into step beside him. She was still a puppy with oversized paws and ears, but she'd almost doubled in size since she showed up in the woods several months ago. She barely fit beside Theo as they went down the stairs together.

.   .   .

Carol Fairgood sighed as her son came into the kitchen, dog at his heels.

"Look, honey," she said, stirring her coffee with a Fairgood & Fairgood pen. "The dog's with him."

Theo tensed, waiting for his dad to chime in about how Theo was too lenient with Sparky. How dogs needed a firm hand and to know who was boss. How dogs shouldn't sleep on their owners' beds, because it made them feel like they were equals.

But Victor Fairgood only said, "What a shocker."

Then he looked up from his newspaper to shoot Theo a wink.

Theo couldn't wink. He nodded back, surprised by the good mood his dad was in. Victor had been strange and distracted all summer. Carol said it was because of the case they were working on, but *she* seemed normal, which made Theo think it was something else.

"Coffee's still hot," Carol told him, tugging her crisp shirt collar up.

"Thanks." Theo poured himself a thermos full of it. It was important to keep up appearances. So far he'd been able to get away with saying he'd developed the same stomach issues as Victor, who rarely ate in the mornings due to nausea.

"I'm just glad you can still drink coffee," Victor said, watching Theo push the coffee jug back onto the warmer. "When *I* was your age, I couldn't stomach anything but water until almost midday. Had to absolutely stuff myself at lunch."

Theo nodded, stepping around Sparky toward the dishes drying on the rack. He hadn't used any yesterday—he needed to run some bowls under the faucet when he got home. Throw that raw chicken they'd gotten him into the woods to make it look like he was still eating dinner. Keep up the fiction. Image was everything, as his parents so loved to tell him.

Theo hitched his backpack further up his shoulders. "How's the case you're not allowed to talk about?"

"Not guilty on all charges," Carol said.

Victor leaned across the kitchen island and held up a hand. She high-fived it, and Theo hid a smile at the easy affection. Living together, working together, raising a kid together—Theo kept waiting for them to get sick of each other, but they never did.

He waved at them with the thermos, trying to draw their attention to it. *It's me, your son! Consuming normal human drinks! I totally didn't drain a squirrel with my teeth at two a.m!*

"Hope someone does something absolutely terrible and you get to talk them out of it," Theo said. "See you later."

Carol frowned. "Already? You're early."

"He's a go-getter, Carol." Victor folded his newspaper and stood. "Before you leave, could I have a second?"

Theo couldn't sweat. But if he could, his shirt

would've stuck to his chest as he followed his dad into the hallway, Sparky trotting happily beside him.

This was it. The moment he'd been waiting for since the rest of sophomore year, and all summer after that. He'd never seen any consequences—parental ones, anyway—from abandoning a basketball game for the second time in a month. *My friend's in trouble*, he'd said. Like that would matter to his parents.

He'd come down from his bedroom—clothes freshly changed after killing his transformed history teacher, hiding the deep cuts scoring his torso, Sparky locked in his room while he figured out what to do—and found his parents waiting for him downstairs. Theo had waited to be told to stand in one spot overnight, or kneel with his arms out until dawn, or lift weights until he sobbed, or—thanks to that one time he got caught smoking in middle school—smoke cigarettes until he puked. But his dad had just stared at him with cold disappointment and told Theo to go to bed. It had sent a shiver down Theo's spine, imagining what was to come.

But nothing happened. Which was impossible, because something *always* happened when Theo screwed up. The waiting was worse than any punishment they could come up with. He wanted them to get it over with already.

Sparky whined, bumping her nose into Theo's hand as they walked. Sensing her owner needed comfort.

Theo shushed her. He was suddenly terrified his dad

would do something to *her* as punishment. He was still shocked his parents let him keep her so soon after he ran out of the basketball game. Carol had started to protest, but Victor had spoken over her and said they'd allow it as a lesson in responsibility.

Victor turned to Theo, his face unreadable.

Theo braced himself. Anything was fine as long as they didn't involve Sparky.

"We both know I'm hard on you," Victor started.

Theo waited for the punchline. Victor's *usual* line was that he wasn't hard *enough*. That he was letting Theo off easy.

"I don't know about that," Theo said, anxious to be let in on the game.

Victor shook his head, picking at the sleeves of his button-down. Another uncharacteristic move. Victor wasn't a fidgeter.

"No, I have been. More than your mom. It's just because I worry about you, Theo. I worry you're—"

"Soft," Theo said, ignoring Sparky's wet nose bumping insistently against his wrist. "I know. Dad, I'm so sorry about the basketball game, you know I'll make it up to you."

"No. Hey." Victor put a hand on his shoulder, and Theo forced himself not to tense. "We all have weak moments. You're a kid, it's going to happen. I guess...I guess I expected you to be a hothead. But you're not. Which isn't a bad thing! It just means you know when to drop the nice guy act. Then, when the times comes—you strike. Right?"

He gave Theo a firm shake. He looked proud, like he'd finally figured out a puzzle he'd been working on for a long time.

"Right," Theo replied. He would have agreed to anything in that moment. Relief hovered at the edges of his stomach, waiting to rush in. Maybe this was real. No game, no rug to be pulled out from under him. It would be a first, but it was a year for strange things.

Victor sighed. "I know I've been distant this summer. I've just been...worried. About things happening around town. That's actually something I've been meaning to talk to you about. Can we chat tonight?"

"Sure," said Theo faintly. He cleared his throat. "Definitely. Love to."

"That's great." Victor gave him one last shake, then ruffled Theo's hair.

Theo stiffened automatically. Sometimes it was just a fond hair tousle. Other times it was a hard clench, almost ripping Theo's blond curls out from the roots. Maybe this was where the tide turned. Theo waited, not daring to blink.

"I know it might not seem like it," Victor said. "But I'm proud of you, son. You're a Fairgood, through and through."

And then Victor's hand was gone. He straightened

his tie as he retreated to the kitchen, giving Theo one last nod.

"Knock 'em dead," he called.

"Always do," Theo called back weakly, caught between immense pride—*I'm proud of you son*, like he'd done something incredible—and relief at not getting punished.

Sparky nosed at his hand. Theo finally let himself pat her. He wanted to sag against the wall. Instead, he turned and headed out the front door, still reeling.

"Stay," he told Sparky as he closed the door behind them. "*Don't* jump the fence today. I mean it. I'll be back in the evening, you can wait until then."

Sparky whined but sat down on the doormat.

The blooms lining the front path were rotting. Theo touched one as he passed, shriveled black petals coming off under his hand. He would clip them tonight if the gardener, Russel, didn't get to them first.

Kade was balancing on top of the lidless disabled toilet when Theo came in, blowing smoke toward the open window. He spotted Theo and grinned.

"Took your time, blood boy," he said, playing up his British accent that had faded after so many years in the states.

Theo watched him climb down. Kade was wearing a flowy black shirt with an anatomically correct heart embroidered over the left side. The red stitches were so neat and intricate Theo couldn't help but imagine Kade in his cramped bedroom, leaning over the shirt with a needle and thread, tongue out. He stuck his tongue out when he embroidered, one of the many stupidly endearing facts Theo had learned about him over the summer. The two of them had met every few days in the woods so Theo could feed and Kade could get his venom hit. Sometimes they went to Milly's, going over translations or discussing theories. And sometimes they even went over to Kade's place to hang out.

They *hung out* now. Kade said it was only fair, since they were trapped together. Hooked on each other's blood and venom, staring down destinies neither of them wanted.

Theo strode up, gesturing at the black fuzz over Kade's head. "It's getting thick. Are you shaving it off yet?"

Kade scrubbed his head self-consciously. It was longer than Theo had seen it since Kade rocked up with a buzz cut last year. It suited him better than the buzz cut, and *much* better than the frizzy mop that Theo used to glare at during class, wishing Kade would wise up and start taking care of it.

"No," Kade said after a moment, his British accent back to its usual parameters. "Think I'll let it grow."

Theo nodded. "You sleep alright?"

"Yup," Kade said, popping the *p*.

He was lying. Theo could see the bags under his eyes, even more prominent than yesterday. The nightmares that had started last year were only getting worse, but every time Theo asked, Kade insisted he didn't remember them.

Theo held out a hand. Kade huffed, but fished around in his pocket.

"Smoking me out of house and home," he said nonsensically as he fit a cigarette into Theo's waiting fingers. As always, he was careful not to let their skin touch. If he did, Kade's skin would sizzle with heat and Theo would have to heal the burn. They tried to avoid it.

Theo leaned forward. Kade used to offer his cheap, shitty lighter, but Theo told him not to waste the lighter fluid. He kissed his unlit cigarette up against Kade's lit one, both of them breathing in until it caught.

Theo's cigarette flared to life, the orange glow reflected in Kade's gray eyes.

"Don't even need to breathe," Kade muttered as he leaned back, flicking ash onto the white tiles. "You said you had something for me? Other than the usual."

Theo snorted, pulling his backpack off. He'd give Kade the lighter tomorrow, he decided. Giving him two things in one day was just weird. He didn't want to come off too strong.

He pulled out the plastic bag. Kade's eyes lit up just like Theo imagined.

"Free veg," he said. "Hell yes. And you're sure they aren't magic?"

"Sorry to disappoint," Theo said dryly as he handed them over.

Kade pouted. He held the plastic bag up to the crappy bathroom lights, examining the mushrooms. "Are these puffballs?"

"Yes," Theo said, absurdly delighted that Kade remembered. "So you have to eat them fast."

"Got it." Kade chewed his cheek, trying to hide his smile. He narrowed his eyes at Theo, who groaned.

"They're tasty! I promise!"

"You've never had it! You could be feeding me forest gunk!"

"Well, everyone says it's tasty. And *I* sure can't eat it. And my parents will be annoyed if they think I'm wasting time foraging for mushrooms." Theo sucked on his cigarette distractedly. The exciting part was lighting it—leaning into Kade, watching his face. The actual smoking, he could live without.

Kade sighed dramatically. "Fine! I'll tell you how it goes. You can live vicariously through me and my human tastebuds."

He bent down, stuffing the bag haphazardly into his own backpack: black and falling apart, patched together with fraying gray thread. It was always the least aesthetic thing about Kade's outfit, if he even bothered to bring it to school.

"Speaking of tastebuds," Kade continued, stubbing out his cigarette. He pulled his leather jacket off and stalked forward, baring his neck.

Theo wanted to say something witty. But words failed him as he stared at Kade's throat, the veins fluttering underneath his pale skin, that dark mole right in the middle like a bullseye.

"Bon appétit," Kade said. He sounded wry, but Theo could hear his heart racing as his fangs lengthened in his mouth. He could hear Kade's heartbeat from the parking lot, could smell him from the other side of school if he concentrated. Like all his senses were homed in on him. It had to be because of their strange link, which had let Theo track him down after Hawthorn kidnapped him, but sometimes Theo thought it was just because Kade smelled *that* good.

Theo leaned in. Kade's skin parted under his fangs, sweet blood rushing into Theo's mouth. The world narrowed: blood on his tongue, filling him up. Kade jerked against him, his skin sizzling where Theo's lips touched him. But Kade's pained groaned turned weak with ecstasy as the venom flooded his system, turning everything in him to liquid pleasure.

That was how he phrased it once. *Like I'm a big glass of happy, all sloshing around,* Kade had continued, like that would lessen the impact. Like Theo wouldn't have the phrase *liquid pleasure* bouncing around his head for days after, remembering it every time he bit into Kade, the boy sagging against him and panting.

Theo pulled back. Kade leaned into him, as always, and Theo caught him, rubbing a thumb over the bite mark ringed with burn. The wound healed under his touch. When Kade could stand upright again, his neck was all smooth skin.

Kade picked up his backpack with a woozy wave. "Thanks, sunshine. For the mushrooms, too."

Theo laughed. "Sunshine?"

Kade blinked, startled. Like he hadn't meant to let that slip out. His expression turned annoyed.

"Sure, 'cause you're all..." He waved a dismissive hand at Theo's blond curls, his letterman jacket and jeans, his gleaming sneakers tied in neat knots. "Shut up."

He gave Theo another annoyed wave and stormed out of the bathroom. Theo watched him go, oddly delighted, his gaze stuck on the burn on Kade's wrist: the only wound that Kade hadn't let him heal. It sat right over the knob of bone, shiny and pink as a kiss.

CHAPTER
TWO

NOBODY WAS stupid enough to sit down at a cafeteria table with Kade "Monster" Renfield unless they wanted to get growled at.

It suited Kade fine. He was used to being alone at school. He only stayed in the cafeteria long enough to shove their shitty food in his face. He spent the rest of lunch lurking in the woods or embroidering in the seclusion of a bathroom stall.

But not today. Today he had his earbuds in, the music silent as he eavesdropped on the shitshow unfolding at the table in front of him.

"I'm just saying," Aaron Fletcher snapped, loud enough that Kade didn't even have to strain to hear him over the cafeteria chatter. He dug ferociously into his meatloaf, shoulders as rigid as his gelled hair. "I don't know why you're being such a bitch about this. They're my *parents*."

Felicity Sloan glowered and folded her arms, which were toned with the muscle she'd gained over the summer. Gained *back*, anyway. She'd been an award-winning gymnast until middle school, then gave it up for modeling. All those muscles had withered into nothing—but now they were back with a vengeance. According to Theo, her mom made her train for five hours a day all summer. She was trying to go toned instead of bulky, Theo insisted, for the sake of her modeling career.

"And I'm your *girlfriend*," Felicity hissed, flipping her blond hair over one shoulder with such force Theo had to duck to stop it from hitting him in the face. He was so obviously trying to stay out of it, hunching over a tray of food he would quietly dump in the trash on the way out, that Kade couldn't hold back a snort.

Theo's gaze flickered up, so fast Kade thought he imagined it. But there it was—Theo's exasperated eyeroll, right at Kade. *Can you believe these two?* Then he looked up again, eyes focusing on Kade's meatloaf.

Kade rolled his eyes back at him. He'd scarfed down the energy bar and the disgusting sports drink Theo had given him that morning, but if he didn't eat enough now, Theo would rag on him for it later.

Making sure my blood bag is okay, he called it. He made sure Kade had enough iron tablets and was always asking how he was feeling and if Kade was having any withdrawal symptoms. Which he hadn't. All summer long, the worst Kade got was a vague tiredness and sweating, at which point it was time for Theo to feed and Kade would feel fine again.

Kade took a giant forkful of meatloaf, making sure to chew wetly and annoyingly.

Theo ducked his head back down to his tray, hiding a smile as his friends bickered around him.

"You're supposed to take my side," Felicity hissed, with none of the usual brightness she usually injected into her scathing comments. "You weren't supposed to *tell* them in the first place!"

Theo frowned. "Wait, what did you tell them?"

Aaron ignored him. "What did you expect me to do, Liss? They're my *parents*. I don't even know why they're being so weird about it, but they asked, so I told them!"

"Right," Felicity sneered. "And now you side with them. You pick *them*."

"In *what*?" Theo asked.

Aaron turned to Felicity, a faint smirk gracing his face. He'd been showing more expression in the past year, less of his usual haughty blankness.

"Yes," he said simply.

Felicity glared. For a moment Kade thought her blue eyes were filling with tears. Then she blinked and the wet sheen was gone.

"Then you're stupider than I thought," she snapped, standing up so fast her chair clattered to the linoleum behind her. "We're *done*."

Kade turned hastily back to his food. He wasn't the

only one looking up after that noise, but the last thing he wanted to do was draw attention to himself. They couldn't afford it, with everything that was coming for them.

The back of his neck prickled. Someone was coming up behind him.

"What were you laughing at, Monster?" Felicity whispered.

Kade turned. He expected her to beam at him, that brittle too-white smile that always meant someone was going to get eviscerated with Felicity's vicious words. Her teeth were out, but her smile was...desperate. A little unhinged. There was a scab under her chin, like she'd been picking at a pimple.

Felicity snapped her teeth and flounced off, leaving Kade's heart hammering in his chest, not daring to look over and see if Aaron had noticed.

There had been strange, dark rumors about Felicity over the summer. Some about her mother. Some about the bruises she showed up with, which Theo insisted were definitely from gymnastics practice. *You can tell because she has less of them as time goes on*, he'd told Kade once. *Her body's getting used to hitting the mat.*

The other rumors were the usual high school shit: drugs, DUIs, shoplifting, secret abortions, secret older boyfriends, secret older *girlfriends*. Kade had assumed most of it was bullshit, just like most of the rumors about him were bullshit. Theo certainly insisted they were bullshit whenever Kade brought it up. But he couldn't deny that junior Felicity was more...*unhinged* than her sophomore version. Too eager to fight back. To go crazy at a party. She lashed out at anyone who tried to calm her down. Kade almost expected the next story to be about Felicity launching herself fists first at the next person who insulted her. Just like the stories they told about him.

Kade risked a glance over at the next table. Theo was glaring at the rest of the cafeteria, who quickly turned away and started chatting again.

Theo put a hand on Aaron's shoulder, pulling him close. "The hell was that about?"

Aaron swallowed. "I...don't know. What the hell, man."

Kade raised his dark brows. He'd never heard Aaron so shaken. He'd always assumed Aaron and Felicity were dating for social status, to look good, to make their families happy. But maybe Lock High's power couple really did love each other.

"She'll come back," Theo said hastily. "She's just pissed. She'll cool off."

Theo lifted his head, sending an anxious look out the door Felicity had just stormed out of. They'd drifted apart in high school. She'd tried to reconnect with Theo last year, but Theo had to bow out with all his vampire shit. By the time things settled down and he started texting back, she wasn't interested in talking anymore. Theo insisted he wasn't worried, but Kade saw how he looked at her sometimes. Like he regretted not talking to her when he had the chance.

Aaron cleared his throat hard. "Uh. Are we playing basketball after school?"

"I have a thing. Tomorrow?"

"Sure. As long as you stay late. My parents keep wanting you there for dinner," Aaron said, suspicion evident in his tone.

Kade winced, picking at his meatloaf. The Fletchers kept inviting Theo around to the house. It couldn't be to make sure he was human—they already knew he was a vampire. Which meant they were just doing it to screw with him, make him eat human food that he'd have to throw up later. Not that they'd admit it. And Theo wasn't about to admit he knew they were hunters. Going over to the Fletchers was one big game of everyone acting like everything was normal, while Aaron—still clueless—got increasingly creeped out about why his parents and best friend were being so passive-aggressive about things that made no sense.

"Don't tell them," Aaron said hastily.

"Man, the whole school heard her yelling. They'll know by tonight."

"Shit. You're right." Aaron's voice got desperate, so soft Kade had to stop chewing and concentrate. "Look. You've been...weird. I know we're not talking about it, don't shove me into another wall—"

"I won't if you don't talk about it," Theo said warningly.

Aaron flinched. It was a strange movement to see from the aloof, unaffected asshole who had once laughed in Kade's face for wanting to kiss him after they had a fumble in the woods during freshman year.

"I'm just *saying*," Aaron whispered as Kade ducked back toward his tray. "Something's going on with you. Hanging out with Monster, getting that freaky dog that hates everyone but you—but you're my best friend. Okay? When it comes down to it, it's you and me and... and Liss. Right?"

There was an obvious vulnerability there. A rawness. Even if Aaron was an evil prick, Kade considered as he speared a slice of lettuce onto his fork, he was still a sixteen-year-old kid.

Theo was quiet. Kade fought the urge to look up. Sometimes Theo talked like he was only friends with Aaron for information on hunters. Other times he sounded like he was still on Aaron's side, childhood friends until the end.

"You know it," Theo said finally.

Kade nudged his backpack with his foot. The plastic bag of mushrooms crinkled. They were *friends* now. Friends of circumstance, the two of them trapped in a situation neither of them would choose—but still. It didn't make the bitter pill of Theo ignoring him in public and being friends with assholes any easier to swallow.

Kade kept eating. His phone vibrated.

It was Theo. Or BLOOD BOI, as Kade had him in his phone.

Still doing tree later?

Kade thought about ignoring it. He'd been too *eager* with Theo lately, laughing too much and sharing stories he would regret later. Letting his guard down. Kade couldn't afford it, unless he wanted his heart broken by another rough-hearted jock. At least, a jock who *pretended* to have a rough heart. Kade was still uncertain how much of Theo's roughness was real and how much was a show. On the days where Theo watched him sew a patch onto his jeans, or complimented Aunt Sundance on fish sticks he wasn't eating—two surprisingly common instances this summer—it was usually the latter.

Kade scratched his shirt, the embroidered heart itchy underneath his fingers. Then he texted back three words:

You know it.

Sundance looked up from the couch as he barreled in. She had a book in one hand, the other folded in a sling across her chest. She had another few weeks of leave before her work stopped paying her, and she was spending most of that time parked on the couch in her dressing gown, reading cowboy books.

"Just here for a bit," Kade called as he sped to his bedroom. "You look nice!"

"You're a dirty liar," Sundance called back. "I haven't washed my hair in days!"

Kade grinned as he rooted through his nightstand. Rings, necklaces, lamp, bits of thread, cigarette butts— homework. Bingo.

Kade ran back through the living room toward the front door.

"Hold it," Sundance said.

Kade turned, trying to look less sweaty and pale, panting from the very short run from the next block where Theo had parked the car.

Sundance squinted. "Were you hungover this morning?"

Kade blinked. He didn't get drunk the night before a feeding. He hadn't drunk very much this summer. It was a big improvement from sophomore year: constant puking, blacking out, drinking anything he could get his hands on as soon as he got it, then waltzing out to look for someone to fight.

"Because you've been doing better," Sundance continued, worrying the wrinkled pages of her cowboy book between nicotine-stained fingers. "You've been really *steady* this summer. I was hoping this was the year I could stop worrying."

Kade squirmed guiltily. He'd given her a scare last year: first he went to the hospital for mysterious blood loss, then he went missing overnight. He'd lied and said he passed out in the woods. What was he supposed to say, he got kidnapped by a vampire and then helped Theo kill him?

"I wasn't hungover," Kade protested. "I just...didn't sleep great."

Sundance sighed and adjusted her dressing gown. "Bad dreams still?"

He shrugged, shooting her a lopsided grin. He woke up screaming more than he woke up hungover these days. The funny thing was, he could never remember the dreams. Just a horrible sense of loss and dread and the acrid stink of smoke.

He dug a hand into his pocket, feeling the fire eye he'd been carrying with him since he got kidnapped by his history teacher.

"Heading out," he repeated, tangling the vine around his fingers. "I'll be back for dinner."

She nodded, going back to her cowboy book. "Don't get into trouble."

He paused near the door with a gasp. "Me? Never."

Then he left, the fire eye thorns pricking comfortingly into his hand.

Theo drove them to the woods near his house. He parked off the road, and even held the back door open for Kade.

"Thanks," Kade said sarcastically as he unfolded himself from the backseat. Theo still insisted on his 'can't be seen in my car' rule. Kade knew it made sense

—the fewer people who saw them hang out, the better —but that didn't stop him from bitching about it. It was practically an inside joke by now. Kade would enjoy it if it didn't make him feel a little like Aaron used to make him feel—like Kade was this shameful, dirty secret no one could know about.

They headed into the woods.

Theo looked over at Kade as the tree line faded behind them. "Got your homework?"

Kade groaned. "Yes, Mum. Sorry, I mean *Mom*."

Theo shrugged. "It's not like this time will work, we might as well get some study done while we're there."

"Quit distracting me with school shit," Kade told him. "What the hell was with Felicity breaking up with Aaron? What did Aaron tell his parents about?"

Theo's jaw worked. "I don't know," he admitted. "They won't talk to me about it. I think it's pretty serious. Like, I think Felicity got into real trouble."

"And she didn't tell you?"

Theo ran a distracted hand through his hair, blond curls falling artfully over his forehead. Kade wanted to sketch it. Kade wanted to dig his fingers in it and pull.

"She doesn't tell me anything," Theo said, yanking Kade out of his stupid fantasies. "I'm just surprised Aaron's keeping quiet. That's why I think it's really serious."

Kade hummed. He kicked a rock, sending it skittering into Theo's ankle. Theo glared at him, like he couldn't have dodged it with his vampire reflexes.

Kade asked, "So who gets you in the breakup? Her or Aaron?"

"Neither," Theo said sharply. "I don't know. I have to stick with Aaron to find out if his parents are planning something. Or if we can get them to help us stop the ritual, like Milly said."

"Which I still think is a terrible idea."

"Maybe," Theo admitted. "But...I don't know. I was Felicity's friend first. I've been closer with Aaron for the past few years, but now he's..."

Kade kicked another rock, this one bouncing harmlessly off a tree, and waited. *He's an asshole. He's in a family that wants me dead. He was terrible to you, Kade, my new buddy and beloved blood bag.*

"He's been pissing me off," Theo finished darkly.

For a moment Kade let himself pretend that Theo was angry on his behalf. Aaron hadn't said one word to Kade since everything came to a head last year. Even when Kade bumped into him in the hall and made Aaron drop his water bottle. Aaron had turned around, nostrils flaring—then he'd seen who it was and a strange expression had flickered over his face, gaze jerking toward Theo. He'd almost looked frightened. Then he'd walked off. No insult, no cutting quip. Just a scared glance at Theo and a run for it.

When Kade asked about it later, Theo had muttered something about the two of them having a fight. It was natural for Kade's dumb crush-brain to invent a scenario where Theo was mad at his best friend for the things he did to Kade. That same dumb crush-brain that made Kade stay awake at night, touching the burn on his wrist and imagining Theo kissing his neck, no burns, just sweet pressure. He imagined Theo taking him flying, fighting bullies for him.

He imagined a lot of things. He would rather die than tell Theo about any of them.

Theo started walking faster into the woods.

"I still don't know how you can tell," Kade called as Theo walked ahead. "All these trees look the same to me, and you have super-sight, not X-ray vision. You can't see *through*..."

He trailed off as he stepped into the clearing. The tree they were looking for sat in the middle, gnarled and stooped. The branch where Hawthorn had thrown Theo was still broken, moss growing over the sharp splinters.

Theo stood next to it, waiting.

Kade sighed. "Moment of truth?"

"Probably not," Theo replied.

Kade walked up slowly. No matter how much he knew nothing was going to happen, it still sent a shiver up his spine. This was the spot where Cyth had been set on fire and buried deep in the ground. Somewhere beneath their feet, she was still burning.

"You know," Kade said conversationally as he stepped around the thick tree roots. "I spent *hours* tied to this tree and nothing happened. No visions."

"It's the only thing that's worked so far," Theo pointed out.

"Maybe we should get Fletcher and son back here," Kade suggested dryly.

Theo snorted. It wasn't, Kade thought, a terrible idea. If they were throwing everything they had at the wall, they might as well replicate the only situation where this worked. But somehow Kade knew, deep in his bones, that the Fletchers didn't have anything to do with it. The visions, the tree—those roots were in *them*. Kade and Theo. Knotted together in ways they still didn't understand.

Kade reached out, fingers shaking. Another shudder ripped down his spine. *No*, he thought, unknown horror bleeding into him as his hand neared the tree trunk. *No, no, no*—

His fingertips brushed bark. Then his palm.

Nothing. Kade blew out a shaky breath, the horror leaving him. He *hated* that part. Like there was something crucial he needed to remember, but it kept slipping away every time he reached for it.

"How long are we giving it this time?" Kade asked.

Theo shrugged. "Don't have anywhere to be for a few hours. Where's your homework?"

Kade threw his head back and groaned. "Quit trying to turn me into a good student, Fairgood! It's not gonna work! You'll drag me into the C-plusses over my dead body."

"The only dead body here is me," Theo said. He reached into Kade's jacket pocket.

Kade twitched. He tried to stay still whenever Theo came too close, all too aware that one wrong move meant a burn. Also, staying still meant he had something to focus on that wasn't Theo's sturdy jawline, his deep brown eyes, that smile turning oddly sweet if Kade said the right thing.

"Careful," Kade said. "I have fire eye in the other one."

"Good thing I didn't go into that one." Theo pulled out Kade's cigarette pack and lighter. "I'll trade you for some iron tablets."

"Promises, promises." Kade motioned for Theo to continue, hand still pressed to the tree trunk.

Theo fit a cigarette between his teeth. Then he did the same to Kade, carefully placing the cigarette between Kade's waiting lips.

Theo flicked the lighter. It spluttered to life on the first try, like always.

Kade leaned in, inhaling until his cigarette flared to life. His heart fluttered. He couldn't always look Theo in the eyes when they did this, but this time he risked it. He glanced up to see Theo's face, so intent and so close, his lips pink around his own cigarette. They were never pinker than after he fed. Flushed with Kade's own blood.

Kade averted his eyes, willing himself to stop blushing.

Theo leaned back, his own cigarette burning. "I have something for you."

"Oh?" Kade cleared his smoky throat. "More mushrooms?"

Theo shook his head. He reached into his pocket. He looked almost...nervous. Theo didn't look nervous often, even when he put himself in between Kade and a monster trying to kill them. It set Kade on edge.

Kade sucked in a deep lungful of smoke. "Hey, before that. I've been meaning to say something for a while now. To, um...apologize."

Theo paused, hand still in his pocket. "Apologize?"

Kade nodded, already hunching into his bony shoulders. "So...after we killed Hawthorn. There was a second where, uh."

He cringed just thinking about it. Both of them still in shock, covered in Theo's black blood. Kade dazed and shaking, staring at Theo's lips. Leaning in like an idiot. And Theo's awkward rejection. *Kade, we can't.* Kade still flinched every time he remembered Theo's pitying stare. Like he wanted to let Kade down gently.

"I got caught up in the moment," Kade said. "I don't want things to be weird between us. I know you wouldn't kiss me even if you could. So. Sorry."

He risked a glance up.

Theo was staring at him, mouth open.

Kade flushed, pinching his cigarette anxiously. "What? I said I'm sorry! Let's just forget about it and move on! Give me mushrooms or whatever it is you have in there."

Theo blinked rapidly. His hand twitched inside his pocket.

"I..." Theo started.

Then he froze. The wideness of his eyes, the pure panic in his face, made Kade's neck sweat. This wasn't a my-friend-awkwardly-brought-up-that-time-he-tried-to-kiss-me panic. This was mortal-danger panic.

Theo ripped the cigarette out of his mouth and shoved in front of Kade. Kade grunted, his back hitting the tree trunk.

"What?" he snapped, struggling to peer over Theo's shoulder. "What is it?"

Theo shushed him, still staring off into the trees. Kade followed his gaze and jerked, his cigarette falling out of his gaping mouth.

A monster stood in the trees. Tall and spindly and winged, joints almost poking out of its ghostly skin. Blood coated the lower half of its pointy face, viscera dripping down its chest. It was staring right at them, eyes liquid black.

For a horrifying moment Kade thought they screwed up, that Hawthorn was still alive and coming for them. Then he looked closer. No tree markings on its chest. And this one was even taller than Hawthorn, its skin even whiter, like an exposed bone.

"It's him," Theo whispered. "That's the one who sired me."

Kade blinked. It had been the middle of the night when Theo's sire attacked him, before Theo had night vision. Everything happened in a blur. Theo couldn't have gotten a good look.

"How can you tell?" Kade whispered back, clutching Theo's letterman jacket.

Theo shook his head. "I just know."

In my bones, Kade thought, and shivered. "What do we do?"

Theo didn't move. Neither did the monster. Blood dripped off its claws, a speck of torn flesh slid down its chin and splashed onto its still chest.

Theo crouched. "Get ready."

"Shit," Kade spat. He reached into his pocket, the one that had fire eye in it, and twined the vine around his fingers. Thorns poked into his palm. He was already shaking with adrenaline, tensing up for when that thing would charge.

"Come on," Theo whispered. "What are you waiting for?"

The monster blinked. The first time Kade had seen it move since it flew off after dropping Theo in the lake next to his house. Then it turned, dropped on all fours, and sprinted away. It was gone before Kade had time to say anything.

"What?" Theo said. He straightened, still standing in front of Kade like he was expecting a surprise attack. "Why didn't it attack?"

"Looked pretty busy." Kade wet his lips, trying to

stop shaking. "Think we caught it in the act."

Theo ran off into the trees. Kade cursed and followed him, tripping over his feet until he caught up. Theo bent down, touching the blood the creature had left on the forest floor. It was so dark red it was almost black.

Theo's nostrils flared.

Kade winced. "Any chance it's deer blood?"

Theo stood, brushing the blood on a nearby tree. "Let's go to Milly's."

MILLY'S DOOR flung open after one knock. Her long brown hair was frizzy in a way it only got when she got obsessed with something and forgot to shower, making her strange ozone scent stronger than ever.

"I got the translation wrong," she said before Theo could open his mouth. "Well, not wrong—I got all the words right, I misunderstood the context. *Rabbits* could just be what vampires call humans. It *might* still have something to do with a particular hunting family, but they might have just adopted the nickname as a..."

She trailed off. Her eyes were wide, the white one somehow wider than the gray one as she stared at them, taking them in: their stiff shoulders, the panic in their faces.

"Oh," she said. "Did something happen?"

Theo and Kade nodded in unison.

She held the door open. "Come in."

She led them into the living room. It was strewn with ripped out notebook paper, the black tome from her bookshop open in the middle of the room, full of water damage and old burns that made it mostly illegible.

"Sorry for the mess," Milly said as she brought water for her and Kade and set the glasses down on coasters. "I get a little scatterbrained when I get too deep into it."

"'S fine," Kade said. He stepped around the balls of discarded paper as he paced, worrying at his thumbnail.

Theo watched him from the couch and thought back to Kade's room, all that fabric and yarn cluttering up his shelves, designs pinned to the wall, fashion magazines piled so high they were falling over.

Milly sat on the couch opposite Theo, clutching her water.

"So," she said. "Tell me everything."

Theo did. Milly stayed quiet and stared intently into her glass. Kade kept pacing, thumbnail still in his mouth.

"It was him," Theo finished. "My sire. I could just *tell*."

"In your bones," Milly murmured, stroking her spiky wrist tattoo.

Kade twitched. His fingers were in his mouth. Any more gnawing and he'd bite to the blood.

"Cut it out," Theo told Kade, grabbing the sleeve of

his leather jacket and tugging him down onto the couch with him.

Kade grumbled. Their legs bumped together as he settled beside him, and Theo fought two instinctive urges: one, to move away in case he burned him. And two, to move closer. That second urge was getting harder to resist the longer he knew Kade.

Milly's finger squeaked against the wet rim of her glass, deep in thought. She was often deep in thought. The inside of her head seemed like an exhausting place to be.

After the Hawthorn incident, Theo and Kade had taken a risk: they'd gone over to Milly's and explained everything. Well, almost everything—they didn't mention killing Hawthorn. Not at first. Not until Milly had shared her own story, most of it revolving around the group of friends in most of the photographs around this room: all of them with some variation of the friendship bracelet that Milly wore, colorful thread with a small skull knotted in the middle.

We grew up somewhere full of rot and dark magic, Milly had told them, smiling down at her friendship bracelet and the spiky green tattoo under it. *It tried to eat us. So we killed it.*

Theo hoped that one day all of this could be summed up as quickly. *Someone turned me into a vampire and tried to use me to open a door so a monster could raze my town to the ground. We stopped them. Everything's fine now.*

"Well," Milly said. "It's still in town. That's good to

know. It means you still have a chance to turn human again."

"Wait," Theo said. "*What?*"

"Those are the rules. If a vampire kills their sire, they turn human again. That's how I knew it couldn't be Hawthorn. Did I not tell you that?"

"*No,*" said Kade and Theo in unison.

"Ah," Milly said, looking awkward. "Sorry about that. You said it was covered in blood, did it turn someone else?"

"It was a *lot* of blood."

"So, it killed them."

"Let's hope not," Kade said, drumming his fingers against his ripped jeans so fast Theo wanted to push his hand down to make them stop. He couldn't, of course. Not without searing Kade's hand.

Kade blew out a breath that smelled like smoke and meatloaf. "Why can these vampires turn into cool monsters and Theo can't? How do we trigger that?"

"Why would we *want* to trigger that?" asked Theo, appalled. He didn't want to turn into a seven-foot spindly monster with giant wings and claws, no matter how cool Kade thought it was.

Kade gave him an exasperated look. "So you don't get your ass kicked so hard in your next fight, mate. Remember Hawthorn? You looked like hamburger helper."

"I was fine," Theo said. He touched his shirt, trying not to remember the deep gouges in his torso. When he looked up Kade was watching him, his expression unreadable.

Milly placed her glass of water on the table—no coaster—and leaned over the black tome, leafing carefully through the scarred pages. "We know Hawthorn wasn't in charge. This sire of yours, he seems like the wisest bet for Cyth's lover and second in command."

Theo looked at Kade again. Kade looked equally lost.

"Second in command," Theo repeated.

"Hmm?" Milly barely glanced up from the tome. "Oh. Yes. That's the other thing I wanted to tell you. It's slow going, but I think I'm finally piecing together a narrative. Your counterparts—that is, the vampire and the human who were forced to become the key and the lock, the sacrifice and the sacrificer—"

"Lamb and the knife," Kade muttered.

Milly continued, undeterred. "They found a way to stop the ritual. It had something to do with Cyth's second in command. Her lover."

Kade made an excited noise in his throat. His fingers were drumming again, but this time with excitement. He always got like this when Milly made a breakthrough, treating it like it was some fun story and not a nightmare they were trapped in that could end up with both of them dead.

Theo sighed. "Milly. Next time, can you *lead* with that?"

"Of course," Milly said distractedly, still flipping

through the book's worn pages. She was almost at the end. Right before the pages went blank, she stopped, gingerly pressing the pages flat. "Okay. There is something here about the fire...failing? I can't read a lot of this yet. My point is, if they can stop it, then you can, too. I think."

"You think," Theo and Kade repeated in one.

Milly looked up at them. "Have you ever translated a dead language from centuries-old fragments written by someone with terrible handwriting?"

The boys looked down guiltily.

"No," Kade muttered.

"Thank you, Milly," said Theo, bringing out his extra-special polite voice he used with adults he needed approval from. "You've been such a great help."

You've been such a great help, Kade mouthed. He thought Theo's extra-special polite voice was hilarious.

Theo kicked him under the coffee table. Kade made a wounded noise, and Theo looked over in panic—he hadn't meant to kick that hard. He was met with Kade grinning, sticking his tongue between his teeth.

"One day I'm going to actually hurt you," Theo told him. "And you'll scream, and I'll think it's just a big joke and leave you abandoned in the forest or something."

"Can't wait." Kade batted his eyelashes, leaning in.

Theo shoved him. They were getting better at this whole no-skin-contact-but-still-touching thing, mainly because they both wore so many clothes. Pants down to the ankles, sleeves down to their wrists. Theo's parents had asked how he was surviving with all those layers, and Theo had said something about not feeling the warmth. Which was true. He didn't know how *Kade* did it, all those leather jackets and jeans in the July heat. He smelled like sweat the whole month, and yet he rarely took off that jacket.

"I do what I can," Milly said. Then she adopted that stiff semi-sweet tone that suggested that although she wasn't an open person, she would like to be one day. "Can I get you something to eat?"

Kade thought about it. "Do you have any of those strawberry bickies?"

Milly blinked.

"He means biscuits," Theo explained. "In British."

"Oh. Right. I do!" Milly got up and stepped cautiously around the paper as she made her way to the kitchen. The dark tome lay on the coffee table, filled with unintelligible scrawl Theo couldn't read even if he wasn't looking at it upside down.

He leaned across the table to flip the book closed. If he stretched a little further he could touch the golden sun embossed on the cover, flecked and decaying with age. They had until this spring before the ritual could be attempted again. The coming months felt impossibly long and full of terrors. Theo had tried to forget over the summer, busying himself playing effortless basketball with Aaron and choking down food at Fletcher dinners; gardening in secret with Russel when his parents were out; mushroom foraging; hanging out with

Kade and calling it research even if they spent five hours arguing over whether a TV show from the nineties was good or not; trying to goad Felicity into answering his damn *texts*—but something terrible was waiting for them, and it was getting closer.

Kade slung his feet up on the table. "What were you gonna give me, back in the woods?"

Theo paused mid-glare at Kade's dirty boots on Milly's clean coffee table.

"Uh," he said. He tilted his head, listening to Milly opening cupboards in the kitchen. It wouldn't take her that long to find the biscuits. "Uhhhh. Nothing."

Kade snorted, nudging Theo's knee with his boot. "Come on! You can't leave me hanging. You said it wasn't mushrooms, what was it? Edible moss?"

"No," Theo said. He dug his phone out of his pocket, hoping for a distraction.

Six missed calls from Carol.

"Oh," Theo said, stomach plummeting. He went over a mental list of everything he'd done wrong in the last week. Nothing that warranted six phone calls. Maybe his dad's speech this morning was a smokescreen and they had decided to follow through on a punishment after all.

Kade was still nudging him. Theo batted his boot away and scooted further down the couch.

"Cut it out! I need to focus." Something yanked behind his sternum. He jerked his head up. "Sparky's here."

Kade lowered his foot. "Huh?"

Something slammed against the front door with a yelp. Then the scratching started.

Theo leapt up. "Sparky! Bad girl! Don't hurt the door!"

He raced down the hall. Sometimes he got a second sense of where Sparky was, the same way he tuned into where Kade was when Hawthorn had him. Both were connected to Theo on some invisible wavelength, he just needed to tune into it.

Milly came out of the kitchen. "What's wrong?"

Theo jumped aside to avoid barreling into her. "Not sure yet! One second!"

He flung the front door open. Sparky jumped up at him and nipped at his jaw. Her eyes burned an even more intense orange than usual, too bright for Theo to pass them off as a birth defect like he'd been telling everyone.

Theo knelt, catching her head in his hands. "Hey! What's wrong? I told you to stay behind the fence!"

Sparky whined, licking his face anxiously and shivering. Her ears were plastered to her head, her tail between her legs.

"It's alright," Theo soothed. He twisted to check over his shoulder. Kade stood in the hallway with Milly, their faces grave.

Theo's stomach sank.

· · ·

"It's probably nothing," Kade insisted as they drove toward the cliffs where Theo lived. "We had a dog once, this weird little Pomeranian, she got spooked when she got tape stuck to her leg."

"This is a little more serious than tape," Theo snapped.

Kade fell silent. He scratched Sparky, who was curled up in his lap. Other than Theo, Kade was the only person she let pet her. Everyone else got a warning snarl.

Theo glanced over at his phone, which was sitting on the dashboard. "Anything?"

Kade checked it. "Nope."

Theo swore. He couldn't stop thinking about the blood dripping off the creature's bony chin, the flesh wedged between its fangs. The red splatters up his chest and arms. Whatever that thing had ripped apart, it had died painfully.

They turned the last corner before Theo's house. Theo pulled off the road, parking his Lexus near the tree line. It felt stupid, not wanting his parents to see him roll up with Kade. But even with all this panic in his stomach, even with something unnameable on the horizon—Theo didn't want to disappoint his parents.

"Stay in the car," he told Kade, who immediately opened his mouth to protest. "No, I mean it."

He turned to Sparky. Her tail thumped hopefully.

"You stay too," he said. "If anything comes after you, protect each other."

Kade sighed. "Theo—"

"Stay," Theo repeated, and slammed the Lexus door.

He ran as fast as he dared. He slowed as he turned the corner, the dread in his stomach flooding his system, making him lightheaded.

There was a cop car at the end of the driveway. An ambulance sat further up, the back doors firmly closed. The car's lights were off and a paramedic spoke in low tones to a cop who had taken his hat off, looking nauseous.

The front door was open.

Theo ignored anyone who tried to speak to him as he headed down the driveway, his ears full of static. He kept his gaze firmly on the open front door, which hadn't even been propped open with a shiny rock like it was on hot summer days. He could hear his mother's voice, thick and strange, from the living room.

Before he could reach the front door, Russel the gardener walked out of it. He was in his usual clothing, dirty jeans and rubber boots and a frayed T-shirt. He looked incredibly tired, and he only looked worse when he saw Theo.

"Oh," Russel said. "God. Theo. Hi."

"Hi," Theo said, too fast. He scratched his dry cheek. He couldn't cry. He *couldn't*, or everyone would see his black tears. And he didn't know what had happened yet. It could be nothing. It could be a misunderstanding. Maybe his parents had a crash and his mom was really upset about the new car. Maybe someone broke into the house and stole her family heir-looms. A thousand possibilities raced through his head, all of them hovering around the obvious one he didn't let himself think about.

Russel sucked in a bracing breath. "You should go talk to your mom. And I'm...I'm here. If you ever want to talk. If you want to call later, or...or get coffee. Or just work in the garden, I'm always here."

"Okay," Theo said, trying to force down the deep panic threatening to explode inside him. "Russel, what happened? Why are all those cars outside?"

Russel shook his head. His eyes were red-rimmed.

"You should go see your mom," he said hoarsely.

Theo shoved past him. Through the front hall, past the kitchen and into the living room, where his mom was talking to a cop in soft, stilted tones.

"Theo," she said faintly. "You're home."

That's when Theo knew. He didn't let himself believe it, but he knew. She looked the same as when he left her that morning: same pristine clothes, same blond hair she coiffed into curls that came so naturally to her husband and son. But her lipstick was gone, her eyeliner smudged. She only had one high heel on. The other was in her limp hands, like an injured bird.

"Mom," Theo asked, his mind full of that creature dripping with blood, staring at them with those endless black eyes. "Why are there cops outside? What happened?"

She blinked, dazed. A tear curved down her pale

cheek. "I'm sorry," she said to no one in particular. "This is so inappropriate."

The cop shifted uncomfortably. "That's perfectly fine, ma'am. Do you want me to tell him?"

"No, no. I'll...do it." She sniffed, and Theo wanted to run out the door, into the woods, hide in the car with Kade. But he stood there, rooted to the spot, as she said the words he was powerless to stop:

"Your father is dead."

KADE WAS CHAIN-SMOKING.

He'd already bit both of his thumbnails to the blood, and he didn't want to make Theo suffer any more when he came back. Especially not after Kade had already screwed up and let Sparky crawl out of the open window to chase after Theo. He'd tried to catch her, but she was a slippery little bastard.

At least he hadn't been spotted. A cop car had come up the road a few minutes ago, and Kade had ducked low into the backseat. He'd waited for the car to stop and see why the golden boy's Lexus was abandoned on the side of the road, but the cop kept going. Which was good. Kade really didn't want to get arrested tonight.

The sun was going down when Theo finally trudged back. Sparky lolloped at his side, butting her head into his hand. He patted her each time she did this, but always a second too late, like he had to remind himself to do it.

"I couldn't stop her," Kade blurted as Theo walked up. "I really tried, I just needed to smoke and she ran off."

Theo shook his head. Kade's jaw snapped shut, a hundred horrible scenarios running through his head.

"So," he said as Theo let Sparky into the backseat with Kade. "Is everything okay?"

Theo climbed into the driver's seat. His eyes were dull.

"No," he said. "Dad's dead."

Kade felt it like a punch. He never met the guy, but Theo worshipped him. Even if he didn't, losing a parent as a kid could screw you up. Foundations cruelly yanked out from under your feet. Kade knew *that* intimately.

"Bloody hell," Kade whispered. "Mate. I'm *so* sorry."

Sparky whined, pawing around the headrest to lick Theo's cheek.

Theo twitched away from her. "Can you take her?"

Kade pulled Sparky into his lap, holding her collar. She whined again, but settled against him.

Theo squeezed the steering wheel. A gentle squeeze, nothing cracking under his grip. He had gotten the covering replaced over the summer, and it was once again shiny plastic. No cracks or fissures from a vampire trying to contain his stress.

"Mom says he went for a walk in the woods," Theo

continued. "She heard him scream. Found him all torn up. Animal attack."

"Bloody hell," Kade whispered again. It didn't seem to have the right emphasis, so he continued: "*Fuck*."

His cigarette was burning close to his fingers. He threw it out the window, the fourth he'd smoked since Theo left him here.

The Lexus was silent. Sparky rubbed her nose into Kade's neck.

Theo sighed, watching them in the rearview mirror. "Sparky tried to bite a cop."

"Good girl," Kade said before he could stop himself.

Theo snorted. He'd never looked so tired before, even when he was starving on the basketball court, even when Kade helped him get home after fighting Hawthorn, all those rips in his torso.

"I'm gonna kill him," Theo said.

"Theo—"

"Mr. Hawthorn could look human. He could be anyone," Theo continued, like Kade hadn't spoken. "I'm gonna find out who he is, and I'm gonna kill him."

Sparky huffed into Kade's collarbone. Kade nodded silently, stroking her muzzle.

Theo twisted to look at him properly. "What?"

"Nothing," Kade said instantly. "Right on board the murder train with you."

"No, you have a face. What's the face?"

"Mate," Kade said softly. "I'm so sorry."

Theo stiffened. "Don't."

"My mum's dead," Kade blurted, as Theo started to turn away. It was enough to make Theo pause, so Kade grimaced and continued: "Car accident. I was ten. I know how—I don't know how *this* feels, your dad getting murdered by a monster who has diabolical plans for you. But I know how it feels to lose a parent."

Theo stared at the window near Kade's head. Then he turned back, sitting ramrod straight.

"Sorry," he said. "About your mom."

"It was ages ago." Kade wrestled Sparky off his lap, giving her a comforting pat when she whined. "What do you need? Do you need to punch something? You can punch me and heal me after, I'm game. Do you need blood?"

Theo laughed bitterly. "My dad's dead and you want to get high?"

"No!" Kade held Sparky back as she tried to climb into his lap again, trying to remember anything that Sundance had told him in the days after his mum died. She'd flown over to the UK to bring him back. It was all a blur of motel beds and microwave meals, a finicky funeral tie he forgot how to tie immediately after she taught him.

"I want to help," Kade tried. "I don't know what else to give you, man. We can sit here and talk? We can smoke and go look for mushrooms? I can hug you really carefully?"

Theo's shoulders got even higher. "I'm fine."

"Mate," Kade said helplessly. "Come on. We've both

got full sleeves, I'll hold my head away so I don't get burned—"

"I said I'm fine," Theo snapped.

Kade swallowed, stung. Theo hadn't snapped at him like that for months.

"We'll figure this out," Kade tried. "You and me, we're on the case."

Theo stared out at the road glowing orange in the sunset. Another cop car drove past. Kade ducked, not bothering to make Sparky follow suit.

The cop car passed without incident.

Kade blew out a breath against the leather seats. "Want to come around to mine?"

"No," Theo replied. "I should get back to my mom."

"Right. Of course. I'll get out."

"I'll drive you," Theo said before Kade could reach for the door handle.

"No, seriously, it's not that long—" Kade stopped. The Lexus was already moving, Theo pulling a too-fast U-turn to point them in the right direction. Kade rested his cheek against the leather seats, wondering what Theo was going to give him in the woods before Theo's life fell apart for the second time in a year.

Sundance was still on the couch with her cowboy book. She'd switched to lying down, the book aloft in her one good hand.

"It'll be a pretty late dinner," she said as he walked

in. She dropped the book on her chest with a sigh. "I almost gave in and started—whoa, hey, what's up?"

Kade gave her a tense smile. He must have looked awful, because she immediately sat up and scrutinized him.

"Why are you standing weird?" she asked, gaze roving over him like she was looking for bandages or bloodstains. "Are you hurt? Are you on something? If you're on acid again, you're grounded."

"That was *one* time," Kade complained. He dropped his backpack and slumped onto the couch next to her, lifting her feet into his lap. "Theo's dad died."

She stared at him. Once enough time had passed to let her know no, this *wasn't* a bit, she sighed. "God. Poor kid. What happened?"

"Animal attack," Kade said, pulling his knees up to his belly.

Sundance rubbed his arm. Kade made a mental note about how much skin she was showing, then remembered he didn't need to worry about Sundance burning him. It was becoming a habit. Not a lot of people touched Kade.

"How's he doing?"

"Pretty numbed out," Kade said cautiously. *Numb* was one of many words he would use to describe Theo's intense stare as he drove Kade back home. *Determined* was another. Whatever Theo's grieving process was, it wouldn't be pretty. Not that Kade could judge. *His* grieving had involved eighteen kinds of self-destruction, some of which he grew out of, others which stuck around.

Sundance patted his arm. "Glad he's got you."

"He doesn't *have* me," Kade replied automatically. "I was just...there."

"Well," Sundance said. "I'm glad you were there."

She'd taken a shine to Theo after seeing him around at the house so often this summer. She didn't like that Theo kept their friendship a secret, no matter how much Kade assured her it was a mutual agreement. But she couldn't help but be charmed by Theo and the free mushrooms he brought over.

Sundance lifted her feet out of his lap. "Don't worry about dinner. I got it."

"Come on," Kade said as she eased to her feet, bracing her good hand on the couch to push herself up. "I can bang something out."

"And I can put a frozen pizza in the oven," she replied. "Take a load off. You've had a hard day."

Kade rubbed his face. He wanted to tell her to sit back down, he'd go do a veggie stir-fry so they didn't get scurvy. But all he wanted to do was put on headphones, turn his music up as far as it would go, and try to forget the last hour ever happened. Preferably with the help of some illegally purchased alcohol.

"Give me a yell when it's ready," he told her, and headed to his room to find the half-drunk bottle of vodka he'd lost track of last week.

. . .

Kade woke the next morning sweaty and hungover, regretting every life decision that had brought him to this point. He groaned, fumbling blindly for his phone. It wasn't on the nightstand, which meant he had to actually open his eyes.

He did so, grudgingly. A quick scan revealed his phone sitting next to his pillow, the charger almost—but not quite—plugged in.

Kade sighed and plugged it in properly. He had two messages—one from Milly last night, replying to his text about Theo's dad getting murdered in the woods by an 'animal.'

Interesting, the text said. *We'll look into it. All my condolences to Theo.*

The next text was from the grieving golden boy himself, timestamped ten minutes ago.

Come over right now, it said. *I need you.*

Kade swore, surging out of bed so fast he immediately fell over yesterday's jeans, which were lying in a heap next to his bed. He staggered up, grabbing his nightstand for balance and spilling an open bottle of vodka down his arm.

"Jesus," he cried, throwing the now-empty bottle across the room. He ran to yank open his bedroom door, now clad in boxers, sweat, and at least five standard drinks of wasted vodka. "SUNDANCE, CAN I GET A LIFT TO THEO'S?"

"Gimme five minutes," Sundance called back from

her bedroom, voice thick with the groggy disposition of someone who had just been woken up against their will.

"THANKS," Kade screamed back, and ran for the shower.

The front door was open. Theo had texted him it would be, but Kade still felt like he was committing a crime as he slunk up to the door and knocked. They had a door knocker in the shape of a lion, shiny and golden. It was well maintained. Kade wondered if they had a guy for that, the same way they had a gardener. No maid, though. Theo had said something about Fairgoods not wanting anybody in their business.

Fair enough. Kade wouldn't want anybody rooting around his room, either.

He knocked with the gold hoop strung through the lion's mouth.

"Hello," he called when no one answered. "It's, uh. It's me."

He was profoundly glad he'd made Sundance leave after he got out. He'd driven them here, but since he was on a learner's permit, he needed a licensed driver in the car with him. She was driving back and hoping no cops spotted her driving one-handed with her arm in a sling.

His phone vibrated in his pocket. Kade dug it out wildly.

I said it's open. I'm up the left stairs, first door.

Kade opened the door. No dog came bounding up to greet him. He walked quickly through the house, shooting glances over his shoulder. He'd been here before, once to watch a movie, another time so Theo could show Kade his secret terrarium, which had been so adorable Kade chewed his cheek bloody trying not to coo at him. Theo had snuck him out fast and efficiently, so Kade hadn't had time to admire the first floor. He had no desire to do it now.

He climbed the left stairs and knocked quietly on the first door he found.

"It's open," Theo said, annoyed.

Kade entered an office with two desks at each side of the room. One desk was prim and tidy, holding only a laptop, a plastic fern, a family photo, and a copy of *Atlas Shrugged* that made Kade grimace. The other had a laptop, a snow globe of New York, moisturizer, a used makeup brush, and a jar full of pens, pencils and pristine erasers.

Theo sat in the middle of the carpet, folders open around him. He was wearing the same clothes from yesterday and he didn't look up as Kade entered, unlike Sparky, who had her head in Theo's lap and her tail wagging wildly as she gazed up at Kade.

"Hey," Kade said uncertainly. He swallowed, taking note of Theo's rolled-up sleeves: any bare skin was dangerous territory. "You okay, mate?"

"You're saying *mate* a lot," Theo said, turning to

another page. "Makes me feel like I'm in a Dickens book."

"Dickens books don't say *mate*," Kade said with the confidence of someone who had never read one. "What do you want me to say? *Wot wot guv'na, great day innit?*"

Theo didn't answer, staring down at the folders spread out around him. They looked legal and boring. Kade had no idea why Theo had called him over. Was something up with the will?

"Mom's at the funeral place," Theo said, and blinked. "Parlor. Funeral...thing. Anyway, she's gone all morning. We can still get to school on time."

Kade laughed. Theo didn't join in.

"Wait," Kade said. "What?"

Theo held up a piece of paper. Half of it was legalese, but there were scribbles at the bottom.

"Felicity broke into Cheech's house over the summer," he announced.

Kade flopped down hard on the carpet, careful not to touch any of the folders or Theo's exposed arms.

"I'm guessing she didn't tell you about this?"

"Nope," Theo said. "My parents didn't, either. Gag order. Also her mom sent them some really expensive watches."

"Okay," Kade said slowly. Sparky tapped a paw against his ankle. He patted it absentmindedly. "She... okay. Was this a dare or is she, like...*involved.*"

"Don't know," Theo said, sounding not even half as irritated as he should be about finding out his *other* best friend might be involved in eventually hunting him down. "But whatever it was, it led my dad to this."

Theo held the paper closer to Kade's face. Kade stared, not sure what he was looking at. Something about a gag order..

"The notes," Theo prompted.

Kade looked down at the notes scribbled at the bottom. They were bullet points, written messily but still mostly legible.

How often do they need blood?

Silver = Y/N?

Useful members of community or dangerous? Murders suggest danger.

SUNLIGHT??? If so, impossible to maintain normal lifestyle...Lemmings???

Theo—is he really eating?

Kade let out a half-shocked, half-horrified laugh. "You think he *knew* about you?"

"I don't know," Theo said defensively. Then, lower: "He'd been weird all summer."

"Do you think the Felicity case somehow led him to find out about...?" Kade waved at Theo noncommittally.

"I don't know," Theo repeated. "But look at this."

He flipped the paper over. In big black letters, drawn in a marker:

FOR MY FAMILY: IF I DIE SUSPICIOUSLY, DON'T LET THEM STEAL MY BODY.

Kade took the paper. The words were dark and rushed, as if written in a hurry.

"What are you gonna do?" Kade asked. "Lurk outside the funeral home until he goes in the ground?"

"No," Theo said, sounding like he thought that was actually not a bad idea. "We just...need to keep an ear out in case someone breaks in. And we need to check his body before the funeral, obviously."

"*Obviously*," Kade mocked.

"Well, it helped with Lemmings!" Theo checked his watch. "I need to get ready for school. I can't show up in yesterday's clothes."

"You're not going to *school*," Kade said. "What, are you crazy? Your dad *just* died. When my mum died I didn't go to school for a *month*, and only a bit of that was because I was moving to another country."

He went to shove Theo's arm, then remembered Theo's rolled-up sleeves and changed tactics, whacking their knees together. "Don't go to school, man. I'll pull a sickie with you. We can watch movies. Go for a nature walk. You can point out the slime molds you were so hyped about last time."

Theo looked at him. There were no bags under his eyes, not this soon after a feeding. But Kade had never seen him look so tired.

"Don't do that," Theo said.

"Do what?"

"Be all..." Theo waved at him, nonsensical. "I don't know. *God*. I want to sleep. I want to go to sleep so bad."

Kade itched to put a hand on his knee. Bare hand, clothed knee. He could do it.

But then Theo was standing up, placing the folders back into place with a speed no human could match.

"I'm going to shower," he told Kade. "Wait in my room. And keep her out of here, nobody's supposed to be in here."

Kade nodded, leading Sparky out. He paused in the doorway, watching Theo slot the important piece of paper back into his dad's tray with deep care. He almost asked why Theo wasn't taking it with them—then he thought better of it. He already knew: Theo didn't want to disappoint his dad, even when he was dead.

CHAPTER
FIVE

THE TEMPORARY COACH came up to Theo before he even got to first period.

"Hey, champ," said Mr. Wellerman, who up until late last year had only taught biology. "How are you feeling?"

Theo hated that question on a normal day. Today it was deeply insulting, to the point where he had to stop himself from snarling.

"I'm fine," he said curtly. "I have to get to homeroom."

"Right," said Mr. Wellerman nervously. He coughed into his sweaty fist, dodging a student who veered too close to him in the hallway.

As far as gym teachers went, he wasn't ideal. As far as basketball coaches went, he was even worse. He barely knew how to play basketball, and his one method of improving players was to tell them they were really, really great, even if they were coming to him with questions on how they could do better. Theo's teammates would ask how to improve a play and Wellerman would shoot them that anxious grin and say something like *you're killing it out there, fellas!*

Everyone consoled themselves with the fact that he was only taking over as coach until they found a proper replacement. Or until they found Coach Cheech alive and well, which was looking less and less likely as the months passed. The most popular theory was that he eloped with Mr. Hawthorn to Canada. Very few people believed it. But it was the one they whispered about the most. Better that rumor than the murder-suicide one.

"Listen," Mr. Wellerman continued. "Before you go. If you need to miss a few practices—or even a lot!—the team completely understands."

Theo stared at him. "Why would I need that?"

Mr. Wellerman shrank under his unrelenting gaze. "Just wanted to let you know. If you do need to skip a few weeks. Or months!"

Theo stared at him some more, vaguely aware he should probably blink soon. He didn't remember to do that enough since he died. It was just so tempting to stare at Mr. Wellerman until he scampered off like the weak idiot he was.

"Anyhoo," Mr. Wellerman squeaked. "Very sorry for your loss."

Theo didn't respond. He wasn't fully convinced his dad was gone. *Dead*, maybe, but not gone. He still hadn't seen the body. If the body was gone like his dad feared, then he could be a vampire, or some other undead thing Theo didn't know about. His 'death' could be a fake-out to throw the sire off his trail. It didn't sound unreasonable. Actually, it sounded sensible as hell. Theo could *fly*, why couldn't his undead dad be waiting for him somewhere?

Mr. Wellerman walked off, leaving Theo standing alone in the hall, his classmates doing a bad job of pretending not to watch him as they walked by. Theo resisted the urge to bare his fangs at them. He couldn't stop thinking about his last interaction with his dad. *I've been worried about things happening around town.* And the notes he'd found on Felicity's case file. *Theo—is he really eating?*

He must've known. He at least *suspected*. And he'd tried to...what? Talk to Theo about it? Tell him it was okay? *I'm proud of you, son. You're a Fairgood, through and through.* Those words hadn't made sense, not when Theo hadn't done anything to deserve them. But they made sense if Victor was trying to tell his son he knew he was a vampire.

Theo was so lost in thought he didn't pay attention while he was rounding a corner. He knocked straight into Skeeter Bass, sending her sprawling.

She hit the floor with a pained grunt, her braces flashing as she grimaced. The bandages from the crea-ture attack before the summer were long gone, her neck scarring pink underneath.

"Ow," she hissed. Then she looked up and blanched. "Oh. Hi. Um, sorry about that. And...everything."

Theo nodded. He felt like there was more he should say, but he couldn't think of it, head swimming with his last conversation with his dad. Only after he walked off did he realize what he'd missed: he didn't apologize for knocking her over.

Everyone looked surprised when he walked into homeroom with five minutes to spare.

Theo ignored them, sliding into his assigned seat next to Aaron—the happy accident of both having last names starting with *F*—and didn't breathe in. Once, the scent of Aaron's eucalyptus moisturizer and strong hair gel was comforting. Now it almost choked him. Reminded him of Aaron's cold sneer, his fist kissing Kade's cheek in a parking lot.

Aaron wasn't sneering now. He looked almost cowed, spinning a pencil in his thin fingers.

"Hey," he said quietly, eyes trained on the blank whiteboard in front of them. "Didn't expect to see you today, dude. Did you get my text?"

Theo had. Thinking up a reply to it had been so exhausting he'd closed the app without typing anything.

Felicity quickly shooed a classmate out of her assigned seat to sit across from Theo. She smelled like bruise cream and burned hair, like she'd messed up with her hair straightener. But when Theo looked at her blond hair, nothing looked out of place.

"Surprised you even showed up," she said, flipping her unsinged hair over one shoulder. "Remember when my grandma died? Stayed out for a whole week."

Theo remembered. It was back in grade school. She spent every afternoon at his house, watching cartoons and making homemade hummus. When Theo could still eat, hummus made him think of her.

Theo looked between Felicity and Aaron, waiting for them to snipe at each other. Or at least glare. He'd been caught in between their fights before, though never after a breakup. They'd never broken up before. He imagined it would be all jeering and power plays; that it would be impossible to be in a room with them both for weeks. And here they were, sitting one Theo-width away. They weren't looking at each other, but they also weren't glaring.

Aaron asked, "When's the funeral?"

"Friday," Theo answered. Then he realized: "Day before your birthday party."

Aaron grimaced. "Shit. Okay. We'll make do without you."

"Oh," Theo said. "I'll still come."

Aaron stared at him. His gaze flickered over to Felicity, uncertain and awkward, and Theo thought how nice it was not to have them fighting.

"Dude," Aaron said. "You don't need to come to my birthday party."

"It's fine," Theo assured him. "*I'm* fine."

"He's *fine*," Felicity told Aaron, only a little mocking. "*God*, Aaron."

Aaron ran a hand over his gelled hair, tweaking it at the front so it curled properly. Theo had seen him do that in public maybe three times since Aaron started gelling it in middle school. He usually saved fixing himself up for a bathroom mirror. *Never let them see you maintain the mask*, Aaron told him once, sounding like he was quoting from a movie Theo hadn't seen. Which was surprising. They had a very similar taste in movies, if you excluded Theo's documentaries and Aaron's war films.

"Do you..." Aaron twisted to check anyone was watching. No one was, although there were two girls whispering about them in the back.

Aaron winced. "Do you want a hug?"

"Do I look like I want a hug?" Theo asked dryly.

"I don't know," Aaron hissed. "If *my* dad—I don't know."

Theo stared straight at the whiteboard as Felicity and Aaron had a silent argument with their eyes. Then they leaned in. Theo barely felt the pressure. It was like he was outside of his body, watching them wrap their arms around him. His eyes stung. He told himself it was the eucalyptus-burned-hair combination of his friends so close.

They didn't look at each other after they pulled back. None of them were designed for comfort.

"Anything we can do, man," Aaron mumbled.

"Anything," Felicity repeated.

She blinked up at him with those deep blue eyes. She got more beautiful every year. His parents had been so annoyed when Aaron started dating her first. If they'd been around last night, Theo would've expected an excited talk about how Theo could swoop in and solidify the school's new power couple.

"Okay," Theo said slowly. "Why didn't you guys tell me Felicity broke into Cheech's house?"

Felicity blinked rapidly. Then she turned to glare at Aaron, who held up his hands.

"*I* didn't say anything," Aaron said.

Felicity's jaw flexed. She turned back to Theo, giving him a picture-perfect smile. "It was some stupid dare, alright? And it got me arrested. My mom said I couldn't tell anyone."

"You told Aaron."

"I thought I could trust him to keep it under wraps," Felicity said icily. "The less people know about a secret, the better. You know Lock."

"Who dared you?"

Felicity sighed, leaning in closer. "Delilah Emmerson. We got drunk, we were messing around, and everything got out of control. I barely even remember that night, his neighbors *totally* overreacted when they called the cops."

The bell rang. Mrs. Kettle strode in with a triumphant sigh.

"Still not late," she declared, heading to the front of the room and opening her desk to find the roll call sheet. "Alright, let's get this over with. Grejory with a J..."

She trailed off, staring at Theo in the middle row.

"Oh," she said, straightening. "Theo. Hi. I didn't think you'd be in today."

Theo thought very hard about smiling. He nodded instead, resigning himself to a very long day of avoiding people's eyes.

Their lunch periods didn't line up today, which meant Kade had to meet him in between classes.

"You said you called Milly," Theo said as Kade stumbled into the disabled bathroom. "What did she say?"

Kade gave him a bewildered look. Theo had been getting an annoying amount of those—people staring at him after he spoke. Like they expected him to be on the floor weeping and found it distasteful that he was walking around normally.

"I *texted* her," Kade corrected. "She said she was very sorry for your loss."

"Other than that," said Theo, already annoyed.

Kade shrugged, dropping down onto the closed toilet. "She's gonna keep translating. Says to come over anytime."

Theo hated it when people said that. *Come over anytime, call me anytime, whatever you need.* Lying to his face like he didn't know any better. People weren't available *all the time,* for *any* reason. He couldn't call someone at three a.m. just to complain about how boring it was, not being able to sleep. *Maybe* he would try that with Kade, but only because Kade kept weird hours and always wanted to talk about vampire stuff. He couldn't call Kade to talk about the deep hollow in his chest that had opened up when his mom told him his dad was dead.

Nobody *actually* wanted to hear Theo's stupid problems, and he hated when they pretended like they did.

"Sure," Theo said dismissively. "So what are we doing?"

"*I'm* going to class," Kade said, slipping a hand into his jacket pocket, where his cigarettes were. Theo could almost hear his inner dialogue: *should I actually go to class or should I skip and smoke in the woods?* Theo was tempted to join him, if Kade stopped looking at him all cautious like that.

"You know what I mean," Theo said. "I talked to Liss. She said Delilah Emmerson dared her to break into Cheech's house, but I don't know if I believe her. We should go ask Delilah about it. And we should go and check on my...on the..." Theo cleared his throat. "We should check the funeral home tonight."

Kade nodded, long fingers picking at the thick lines on his jeans where he'd sewn up the rips. *Preparing for winter,* he'd said when Theo asked him about it, like they weren't both on a mission to expose the least amount of skin possible when they hung out.

Kade sucked in a hesitant breath. Theo tensed up automatically, not wanting to hear whatever came out of his mouth next.

"Are you sure you want to see him?" Kade asked, almost timid, banging his foot against the toilet below him. "I didn't even look into the casket at my mum's funeral."

"Stop talking like that."

"Like what?"

"Like I'm gonna fall apart," Theo snapped. "I'm *fine*."

He was better than fine, while he was holding onto that small bit of hope that his dad wasn't gone. That they'd walk into the funeral home and find his dad chowing down on an unlucky employee. That Theo would slide the body rack open and find his dad pale and whole, shooting him a wink. *Took your time, kid. Let's get out of here.*

"Noooo," Kade said, the word forming a hooked question mark at the end. "You're not?"

Theo groaned. "Come on. I thought...you're the one person I hoped would talk to me normally. Just be *normal*."

Kade grinned. "Never been good at that, sunshine."

"Then *try*," Theo snapped. "Just—go back to making fun of me and rolling your eyes at everything I say."

Kade shrank back. But only for a moment. His lip

twitched, like it was going to peel back in a snarl. Then it, too, relaxed.

"Whatever the golden boy says," he said, reserved but not half as bitter Theo would have liked. No acid, no bite. It sounded...sad.

A knot of guilt tightened in Theo's stomach as he watched Kade stand up and fish cigarettes out of his jacket. No next class for him. Which was unfortunate, since Theo had finally talked him into doing homework for it.

Kade saluted him with his cigarette pack. "See you tonight."

Theo nodded, still hoping for something he could push against. A dickhead comment or a mean new nickname. But Kade just stepped carefully around him and left the bathroom, leaving Theo alone with a thick throat and burning eyes, wondering why he was suddenly forcing back tears.

CHAPTER SIX

KADE LEANED against the wall of the science building, their go-to spot for these Felicity deals. One hand pinched a cigarette, the other typed out a text to his aunt: *hey i was a total dick to u after mum died right?*

He hit send right as Felicity came careening around the corner, wobbling in her high heels. Her hair was messy, her mascara smudged. She'd been showing up like this more often this year. At least the bruises were getting smaller. Kade could see a tiny one poking out from under her skirt, bright yellow and ugly.

"Price has gone up," she announced before he could say anything. "My stash is dwindling. You'll have to steal shit from house parties until my mom restocks."

"Great," Kade said dryly, almost meaning it. "I've been meaning to cut back."

He really had. Getting blind drunk got less appealing the more his life improved. Not that it improved a *lot*—but he had a friend now. Sort of. And he had a purpose: helping Theo figure out how to get them both out of this ritual before spring. His schoolwork was improving, thanks to Theo's incessant whining that they should study together. He was learning how to drive. The more his life filled, the less he had to drown everything out with overpriced booze and loud music and stupid fights.

Then Theo had snapped at him in a way he hadn't in weeks, possibly months, and what did Kade do? Text Felicity for an after-school appointment. Old habits.

Kade continued, "What's the damage?"

Felicity twisted her backpack straps against her shoulders, pretending to think. "Sixty."

Kade blew out a plume of smoke and cackled. "Go to hell. I'll steal from house parties."

"I'll tell everybody not to let you in."

"Like you could keep me out," Kade whispered, shoving an arm in front of his face like he had a cape. The move was a lot weaker without one.

Felicity still laughed. It had none of the usual bitchy delight as usual.

Kade sighed. "It's not fun if only one of us is putting the effort in, Sloan. What happened to *the show must go on?*"

"That's for actors," Felicity said, a beat too late. "I'm a model."

There was something in her eyes now, determined and reluctant. Kade had never seen her reluctant before. Not openly, anyway. Felicity gave the constant impression that everything she did was with her whole chest: no doubts, just action.

"I..." she started. Then she stopped, her lips tightening. "I've been meaning to talk to you."

She was being strangely polite. Kade hadn't heard her talk that way to anyone, not even adults. It put him instantly on edge, glancing around to check Aaron or a teacher or a camera crew were going to jump out and bust him for buying booze illegally.

"What the hell would you want to talk to Monster about?" he asked. "Want some tips on how to self-destruct? Because it sounds like you're doing great on your own."

He blew a line of smoke in her face.

Felicity barely blinked. "About Theo. About you two hooking up."

Kade choked on his next mouthful of smoke. He coughed, slapping his chest, eyes watering.

Felicity cocked her hip, waiting.

Kade stared up at her, still coughing. He opened his mouth to deny it—then snapped it shut. What the hell else could he say? *No, those people who have seen me in Theo's Lexus were wrong. See, he needs blood to live, and I go into withdrawal if I go a few days without his venom...*

"Oh shit," Kade managed. "You figured it out."

She rolled her eyes, flipping her hair over one shoulder. "I've been shutting down any rumors about you two. You're *welcome*."

"I doubt that's for my benefit."

"Well, it's the last thing he needs. People knowing about you two. His parents..." Felicity pressed her lips together again. The middle of the lipstick was fading, leaving the center of her mouth pale pink while the edges remained dark.

"Is it serious?" she asked.

Kade laughed shrilly, glad Theo wasn't around, for a hundred reasons, but mainly because he would have been able to hear Kade's heart thundering.

"*God* no."

Felicity made an annoyed humming noise, like someone swatting a bee. "Ugh. I was hoping you could, like. *Be there* for him."

"Why can't *you* be there for him?" Kade croaked. He threw his cigarette down and crushed it under his boot. "You know, his oldest friend? I know you guys have drifted apart, but like. *Still.*"

"I'm not good for anybody right now," Felicity said, oddly sing-song. Then she dropped back to her normal tone to continue, "I just—he *needs* someone. *I* can't do it. And Aaron's...not a good idea, either."

She smiled at him with a ferocity that made Kade sway back. It wasn't the smug poison he was used to. This smile stung, sure. But it was all directed inwards. Kade knew that smile intimately. He'd seen it in the mirror.

Part of him wanted to jeer in her face. Hold it over her head. But another part of him—smaller and softer and too damn stubborn, still gasping no matter how hard he tried to smother it—wanted to comfort her. Just a little.

"Sounds like you want to step up," Kade said slowly. "You know. Not be a selfish asshole for five seconds."

Felicity giggled. If she aimed half a pitch up, it would almost hit her party-girl laugh. This laugh teetered straight off a cliff.

"Have you *tried* that? Hard than it looks. Fighting our nature." She took a step closer and grabbed his jacket collar, the leather creasing under her tight grip.

"If we try to hold someone, we just cut them on all our sharp edges," she whispered. "Right, Monster?"

"Right," he muttered. He pulled against her hand. Her toned arms flexed, keeping him close. Kade laughed nervously. "Gonna let go, Sloan?"

"Or what? You'll break my nose?" She grinned harder. Then she let go, rocking back on her high heels. "Sixty."

It took Kade a moment to remember what she was talking about. He fumbled in his back jeans pocket for his wallet, shelling out all his cash. "I have fifty-seven."

She pulled her backpack off and produced a decent-sized bottle of whiskey.

"I'm having a party tomorrow night," she announced. "A Thank-God-I'm-Single party. You should come. See if you can talk Theo into it."

He took the whiskey gingerly. "Aren't you scared I'll steal your booze?"

"I think we both have bigger things to worry about."

"Uh-huh." Kade eyed the bruise yellowing on her thigh. "Is this your weird way of being there for him? Giving him an excuse to go apeshit?"

"Everybody needs to go apeshit sometimes." She shot him a wan smile. "Right, Monster?"

He watched her walk off, trying to suppress the roiling in his stomach. He wasn't surprised that Felicity Sloan had hidden depths. He was just surprised and appalled by how much they looked like his.

He slipped the whiskey bottle into his bag. It was glass, so he'd have to walk carefully. Last year Sundance had caught him red-handed because a bottle of vodka clinked against his pencil case. That was the main reason he stopped bringing his pencil case.

He eyed the woods longingly. He wanted to walk deep in there and open his whiskey. But in a few hours he had a break-in. Theo was relying on him. So he started off toward his house, checking his phone as he went.

There was a reply from Sundance. *I don't know if I'd call a 10 yr old a dick. U were very sad and angry. It spilled out on me.*

Kade bit his tongue hard enough to bleed.

yeah, he sent back. *thought so.*

Theo ripped the doorknob off the back door of Hersay's funeral home.

Somewhere in the building, an alarm sounded. Theo tore open the door and blurred in.

Kade stood outside, frozen in shock. He'd been making jokes about lockpicking when Theo went full Hulk on the door.

There was a low *crunch* from inside the building. A moment later Theo appeared at the back door, looking expectant.

"Yeah," Kade said. "They're gonna notice that."

"Hurry up," Theo said.

Kade couldn't tell if that was part of the plan or if he just walked up to a funeral home after hours and decided to cash in on his vampire strength for once. He barely got to use his vampire powers in real life, which was bullshit. The most he'd gotten to use his powers out of a life-or-death situation was the one time Kade talked him into throwing uprooted trees around in the woods, which led to one of the biggest smiles Kade had ever seen on him. It took Kade's breath away to watch him with bark in his hair, throwing around tree trunks and laughing like a little kid.

Theo frowned. "What?"

"Nothing," Kade said, putting the memory of Theo's grinning face out of his mind. "Let's get this over with. That alarm might go to the cops automatically."

Theo held the door open. Kade stepped into the back of the funeral home. It looked the same as last time: same vase of plastic flowers, same painting on the wall of dogs playing poker, same magnet on a storage fridge door: CRACK OPEN A COLD ONE.

"Still want to put that on a shirt," Kade muttered.

Theo ignored him. His gaze ticked over the storage drawers.

Kade swallowed. "Smell anything?"

Theo nodded. "He's in there."

He pointed at the storage drawer furthest away from them.

Kade thought back to Lemmings's cut-off eyelids and resisted the urge to vomit.

Theo surged forward. Kade leapt in front of him, hands up.

"Wait," he said. "You shouldn't—I can look! You've done the heavy lifting, you can go wait outside."

Theo scowled. He looked offended, like Kade had insulted him by saying he probably shouldn't look at his dad's mauled corpse. But mostly he looked *raw*. His chin kept twitching like he was near tears. And there was something else in his face, something horrible and *hopeful*, like he wasn't entirely sure it was really his dad in there. Like he was expecting his dad to sit up, healed and fanged, and tell Theo to fill him in on what the hell was going on.

Kade got smacked with a memory from his mum's funeral—ten years old and staring down at his rented shoes. Not looking into the casket no matter what his aunt told him about *closure*. If he didn't look at her, she wasn't really dead.

Kade swallowed. "Theo."

Theo stepped past him and yanked the storage drawer open, revealing the man from his head to his belly button.

Or, where his belly button should have been...

Kade gagged.

The man's stomach was a gaping hole, the organs cleaned out by the creature or, more likely, the funeral workers. One of his nipples was missing. Several fingers hung on by a thread.

"God," Kade said. He covered his mouth. "Jesus."

Theo didn't reply. He was staring down at the man's face, which was almost gone. They'd cleaned it up, but they couldn't grow new skin, couldn't insert more flesh. Half the man's jaw had been torn away, exposing a set of dentist-perfect teeth. The eyes were gone, gouge marks in their place. His scalp had been hacked off, only a few blond curls left.

If not for the blond curls, so similar to Theo's own hair, Kade would have doubts. But there he was on the slab: Victor Fairgood, ripped to shreds.

Kade shuddered. He wanted to puke. He wanted a drink. He wanted to run out of this place and never come back. Mostly, he wanted to get Theo out of here.

He pulled at Theo's hoodie-clad shoulder. "Come on, mate. Cops might be on their way."

Theo didn't move. Kade would have better luck yanking on a stone.

He stopped pulling. Got beside him, trying to get

into his eyeline. "Theo. No clues. And the body's still here, you made sure no one's taken it. You did good. Time to go."

Nothing. Theo stared down at the ravaged face, those few bloody curls. His chin had stopped twitching, his expression totally numb.

Kade wanted to cry, watching him. He took Theo's jacket sleeves, shaking him gently.

"*Hey*," he said. "We might get arrested. Time to *go!*"

Theo didn't answer. Kade sucked in a breath and wrapped his hand around Theo's wrist, skin to skin.

Pain sparked down his fingers, instant and agonizing. Kade flinched hard, jerking back as the stench of burned flesh filled the room.

Theo jerked. He looked down at Kade's burned hand like he'd never seen it before. His face twisted in shock. "Are you *crazy?*"

Kade motioned at the back door, still ajar. "Move!"

Theo blinked at him, black tears collecting at the edges of his eyes. For a moment Kade thought he was going to tell him to get out. Then he launched into motion, slamming the body drawer shut and stepping back.

"Let's go," he snapped.

CHAPTER
SEVEN

THEO DROVE them into the woods, pulled over, and punched a tree until splinters rained over his jeans. For the first time since he died, he wished he could feel the pain. But his hands were as pale and smooth as ever as he pulled back, bark sticking to his dead skin.

"Better the tree than the car, I guess," Kade said from where he was standing a sensible distance away. He rubbed his newly healed hand and glanced over his shoulder. "Could've done this further from the road, y'know."

Theo shrugged. It was a dark, moonless night. Nobody would see them.

Kade shuffled forward. Theo wondered how much he could see, or if he was just relying on Theo's useless panting in the darkness. He still breathed on instinct when he got too into his head. Like his body was remembering an echo.

"Look," Kade said. "This...self-destruction thing. You don't have the *flair* for it."

Theo groaned, stalking deeper into the woods. "Go away."

"No, come on," Kade said, following him. "You're not alone in this. We're trapped together, right? So you're not alone."

Theo slowed. Everything in him wanted to run as fast as he could into the trees. But there was something else inside him, the part that had to force back tears when Aaron and Felicity had hugged him earlier. *You're not alone.*

"Let's go to your place," Kade continued. "We can watch that tree documentary."

"You didn't want to watch it *before* my dad died," Theo called back.

"Yeah, well, I have a sudden passion for trees," Kade argued, branches cracking under his boots. "Wait, shit. Let's watch something you only kinda want to see."

Theo stopped. "Why?"

"Because—" Kade bumped into a low branch and swore. "Shit. Stay still, will you? Not all of us have darkvision."

He stumbled up, gait stiff, hands in his pockets. He'd followed Theo half-blind into the dark forest to ask him to come back. He'd burned his hand to get Theo out of the funeral home.

Theo stopped.

"My aunt let me watch stuff I liked," Kade said. "After my mum died. And now every time I see it I remember that time. So I always told myself *next* time something absolutely wrecks my life, I'd watch shit I didn't really care about."

He turned a rock over with his boot, shoulders hunched. Theo watched a beetle crawl out from under the rock Kade had turned over. He didn't know the species. He could get Kade to look it up later. The guy had a creepy fascination with bugs.

"That's smart," Theo admitted.

"I'm a smart guy," Kade said, and grinned thinly.

Shaky guy, Theo remembered. *Loud heart.*

He breathed in, tasting dirt and pine and faraway rabbit fur. And bigger than all of it, Kade Renfield. Smoky and soft. Sometimes he smelled like yarn, dye, pencil shavings. Other times like old whiskey, sweat, the nicotine gum he pretended not to chew in the evenings.

Kade turned. "You coming?"

Theo nodded.

"I hope that was a yes," Kade said. "Because I can't see shit. Lead me to the car, dead boy."

Theo was pretty sure Kade could see the car from here. But he fell into step in front of him anyway, leading Kade out of the dark.

Approaching his front door, Theo focused all his attention on the soothing sound of Kade's heartbeat.

He barely noticed Sparky jumping to lick his face, let alone that anything was amiss.

"Mom will be in bed," he told Kade, pushing Sparky off. "So be quiet."

Kade zipped his lips.

"Seriously," Theo whispered, pushing Sparky off yet again. "She has bad blood pressure, so she gets faint sometimes and has to lie down, and if anyone makes *any* noise or turns on a light—"

He pushed the front door open. Kade went rigid. Theo frowned, turning back toward the house.

Carol stood at the end of the hall, eyes puffy, a silk dressing gown tied tight around her waist. Her hair was up in curlers, her smile strained. She was holding a tray wrapped in foil, something warm and fishy.

The Fletchers stood behind her, all three of them dressed in muted colors, like they were going to a funeral. Aaron was even wearing a tie.

Sparky barked, pawing at Theo's waist.

"Not right now," he told her. He waved at the Fletchers. "Uh, hey."

"Hi," they chorused back, staring past Theo to look at Kade, who was doing his best to blend into the background.

Carol's smile grew even more strained. "Boys! You're just in time for casserole."

"Oh, I was just..." Kade sent Theo a panicked look. *Get me out of this!*

"There's too much for Theo and me," Carol replied, heading down the hall and into the kitchen. "We need help eating. Come on, I'll grab plates."

Kade shrank under the Fletchers' gaze. "I should really..."

"Stay," Mr. Fletcher said, his booming voice making everybody jump.

Mrs. Fletcher smiled. "Any friend of Theo's is a friend of ours. You're Sundance Renfield's nephew, yes?"

"Right," Kade muttered. "Kade. Nice to meet you."

"And you too." Mr. Fletcher looked Kade up and down—sewed-up jeans, wallet chain, black shirt with a skull in the middle—and Theo had a bizarre urge to bare his teeth. Aaron was the only one openly glaring, but his parents weren't kidding anybody with their faux politeness. Renfields were dirt on the Fletchers' boots, and everybody knew it.

"Think of it like a reconnaissance mission," Theo whispered to Kade as they slunk down the hall after the others. "We can *use* this. This is an *opportunity*. Quit looking so nervous or they'll rat you out."

"They've already ratted me out," Kade hissed back. "They know about you, right? The parents? Who knows how much Cheech told them?"

Theo nudged him to shut up as they followed the others into the kitchen.

Carol slid the casserole onto the counter, then paused, staring at it like she'd forgotten what came next.

"I'll get plates," Theo offered. He'd had a few moments like that since the night before, complete blankness where he forgot basic tasks: he'd forgotten his backpack and had to go back to the house to get it. Then he'd used the wrong key to get in the house, getting increasingly frustrated until he figured out what he was doing wrong; *then* when he forgot the locker combination he'd been using for years. Nobody had told him that would happen after somebody died.

Aaron pulled out forks from the cutlery drawer. They usually hung out at Aaron's house, but Aaron had been around here enough to know the kitchen layout.

"Thanks," Theo said as Aaron laid the forks out next to the casserole.

Aaron shrugged. He was still shooting dubious looks at Kade skulking in the corner, but he was almost contrite as he sidled up to Theo.

"Missed you at practice," he said quietly. "Like, it's good you weren't there. But still. You're the champ."

He thumped Theo affectionately on the shoulder. Theo pulled out plates from the cupboard and nodded, realizing he *did* take the coach up on his offer, but only by accident. He'd forgotten they had practice today.

Mr. Fletcher turned to Kade. "So, you play any sports?"

Kade choked on a laugh. "I'm not much of a sports guy."

"Huh. How'd you and Theo start hanging out?"

"School," said Theo and Kade in unison, so fast that all the Fletchers turned to blink at them.

Carol peeled the foil off the casserole with an appreciative noise. "Oh, wow. That smells amazing! Thank you so much!"

"It's the least we could do," Mrs. Fletcher replied, looking equal parts pleased and solemn. She could never take a compliment without smiling.

Carol started slicing the casserole into pieces. "So how was your day?"

"Oh, you know," said Mrs. Fletcher. "Your robe is lovely."

"Oh, thank you. It was a Christmas present from—" Carol faltered, a slab of casserole falling off her knife and splattering onto the floor. She stood there and stared at it, dazed.

"Oh," she said, a second too late. "Damn."

"I can get that," Aaron said hastily, bending down to scoop it up with his bare hands, face twisting in disgust as fish got on his fingers.

Sparky whined, tail thumping against Theo's legs.

"He's already got it," Theo told her.

Sparky whined louder. In the corner Kade kept trying to make eye contact with Theo, inching slowly toward the door like he wanted to make a run for it.

So much for reconnaissance missions, Theo thought. He gritted his teeth and turned to Mr. and Mrs. Fletcher. "Can I talk to you guys? Alone?"

All eyes turned to him again as the room processed

the strangeness of this request. Sparky licked fish bits off the floor, growling at Aaron when he stepped too close.

"Wait," Aaron said, eyeing Sparky warily. "Why?"

"That's private."

"What?" Aaron wiped his fishy fingers on a dish-towel and looked at his parents expectantly. "Mom? Dad?"

They didn't look at him. They were too busy holding hands and staring into each other's eyes, a conversation held in complete silence. Mrs. Fletcher's head inclined in the smallest nod.

Mr. Fletcher turned to Theo with a sunny laugh. "Lead the way."

Theo led them into the first-floor bathroom. Sparky licked up the last blob of fish casserole and followed, sitting down on the bathmat and watching Mr. and Mrs. Fletcher file in. Her ears kept twitching, like she was waiting to know when to start growling.

"Easy," Theo told her.

Mr. Fletcher closed the door behind him. "Well, Theo. What did you need to talk to us about so badly that you pulled us away from my wife's wonderful casserole?"

He had his back to the door. But Theo heard the lock sliding into place, hidden by Mr. Fletcher's bulk.

Theo's fangs thickened in his mouth. He forced them back.

"Look," he said when his teeth were blunt once

more. "We've been pussyfooting around this all summer. You want to try and kill me while Aaron and my mom are right down the hall? Go ahead. We'll both have a lot of explaining to do. But you'd be attacking an innocent guy. I don't hurt people. I eat animals and *one* willing human. Okay? I'm not a threat."

Mrs. Fletcher looked at her husband. She looked almost pitying—but not quite. Her hand kept twitching toward her pocket, like there was something in there.

Mr. Fletcher's smile softened into something wry and knowing. For a moment Theo thought he'd deny it, keep playing the game Theo had grown so tired of this summer.

"Theo," he said instead. "We can't talk about this."

Sparky growled.

"Easy," Theo told her warily.

"We have to be careful," Mrs. Fletcher said. "You understand."

"Do I? Nobody's told me shit. Getting any information out of Cheech was like pulling teeth!" Theo stopped, watching the Fletchers trade a look. "I didn't kill him! Jesus! *Hawthorn* killed him."

Mr. Fletcher made a considering noise. Both looked confused.

"He was a vampire! Come *on!*" Theo groaned, digging the heels of his palms into his eyes. "Why did you come around? Force me to eat so I'll have to throw it up later? You guys already know I'm a vampire, now you're just being assholes."

"Language," Mrs. Fletcher said reflexively.

Mr. Fletcher nudged her, but it was too late. Sparky growled at Theo's feet, lips peeling back to expose her teeth.

"My dad is dead," Theo hissed. "Someone *killed* him. I don't care if you hear me *swear*."

Mr. Fletcher wrapped an arm around his wife's waist. "Theo. We're *truly* sorry about Victor. He was a good man. He..."

He paused. Gave his wife a sidelong look, another silent question. They looked deeply worried.

Mrs. Fletcher nodded.

"Last week," Mr. Fletcher continued, speaking strangely slowly. "He showed up at the house. He seemed...stressed. He asked me to promise that if anything were to happen to him, we'd take care of you."

"Big ask," Theo said, horrified to find there was a lump in his throat. He swallowed hard. "Asking a vampire hunter to take care of a vampire. Did he know about you?"

Mr. Fletcher squeezed his wife's waist. "Theo, we *can't* talk about this."

"Dad was weird all summer." Theo ran a hand through his hair, remembering his dad ruffling it for the last time. "I think Felicity's case might've led him to something. He left these notes..."

He swallowed again, the lump still there. He wasn't a detective. He wasn't like Kade, eager for anything that would unfold another corner of the story. He was a sixteen-year-old kid who wanted everybody to sit him down and explain what the hell was going on.

He slumped. "Why me? Why did they choose me?"

"Theo," Mr. Fletcher said desperately. "When I say we can't talk about this, I *mean* it."

A commotion echoed down the hall: Kade and Aaron were arguing. The bathroom door handle rattled, the Fletchers stepping back to watch it vibrate.

"He said it's a private conversation," Kade said behind the door. "Let it *go*, man."

"They're *my* parents," Aaron replied angrily. "And *my* best friend. What the hell are *you* doing here, Monster?"

Sparky growled again, deeper and more guttural.

"Easy," Theo whispered, but there was something rearing inside him too. The argument was turning into a scuffle, grunts and angry noises leaking through the door.

Mr. Fletcher frowned, reaching for the door handle and unclicking the lock. "Aaron! We're *guests*!"

"Let it *go*," Kade said. Then: "Ow, shit!"

Sparky barked. Theo reached for her collar, but it was too late: she was launching toward the door, teeth bared.

The door flew open. Sparky barreled into the hall, where Aaron had Kade in a headlock. She jumped up and closed her jaw around the soft meat of Aaron's palm.

Aaron shrieked. His grip on Kade loosened, yanking desperately at the death grip Sparky had on his hand. Kade fell to the floor, head slamming into the wall.

"WHAT THE HELL," Aaron screamed. "HOLY SHIT! THEO!"

The Fletchers piled into the hall. Theo knew he should join them, but he couldn't stop staring. Aaron's blood dripped down Sparky's muzzle, wetting her fur. Kade sprawled on the floor behind them, his face twisted in horror.

Theo's gaze locked on Aaron's bleeding hand. He could feel his teeth starting to thicken again, his eyes flickering black. He blinked hard, forcing his teeth to dull.

Mr. Fletcher raised his leg like he was going to kick the dog off, then paused, looking over Sparky's violent orange eyes. His foot thumped back to the ground.

"Theo," Mrs. Fletcher cried. "Call him off!"

"Her," Theo corrected automatically. He stepped up, locking a hand around Sparky's collar. "Hey. *Hey*. You can stop now. Kade's not hurt. See? Everyone's safe."

Sparky's growls quietened.

Carol came sprinting into the hall, carrying a full pitcher of lemonade. Her mouth fell open, a terrified gasp spilling out as she took in the scene. Lemonade sloshed out of the pitcher and onto the floor, splashing onto her slippers.

"It's fine," Theo assured her. "Right, Sparky?"

Sparky growled uncertainty, tugging on Aaron's hand.

Theo stroked her head. "We're okay," he repeated as Aaron sucked in a pained gasp. "Go see Kade. Alright? Go see Kade."

Sparky whined, the noise muffled around Aaron's hand. Her jaw relaxed.

Aaron ripped his hand out of her mouth, whimpering. Tears streamed down his face as he stumbled back.

Sparky grunted and crept toward Kade, who was still lying against the wall, and curled up in his lap. After a moment's hesitation, Kade stroked her head. His hand was shaking, his eyes glazed.

"I need to go to the hospital," Aaron sobbed, clutching the wrist below his bleeding hand. "Holy shit, I need to go to the hospital."

"No," Mr. Fletcher blurted.

Everybody turned to stare at him. Mr. Fletcher was watching Sparky, her eyes fiery, blood on her teeth.

Aaron let out a wet laugh. "N-no? What are you talking about? That dog ruined my hand!"

"No hospital," Mr. Fletcher said, making pointed eye contact with his wife.

Mrs. Fletcher straightened. "We'll get that cleaned up at home, honey."

Aaron stared at his parents, eyes still streaming. Blood dripped down his wrist and onto his shirt.

"I need stitches!"

"Guys," Kade muttered, trying and failing to push Sparky off him.

Theo whistled. Sparky crawled off Kade and slunk over to Theo, ears plastered to her head.

"Bites don't get stitches," Mr. Fletcher said impatiently. "They don't want to risk sealing the bacteria in. There's nothing the hospital can do but clean and bandage it, and we can do that at home. Let's go."

Aaron made a wet noise. "But—"

"Aaron," Mr. Fletcher said, whirling on him so fast Aaron flinched. "Quit being such a fag and *get in the car*."

The hallway fell into shocked silence. Aaron stared at the floor, shaky and pale, his hand cradled to his chest. He looked so much younger like this, and Theo's chest twisted in unwanted pity. He might not like Aaron very much lately, but he didn't deserve this.

Mr. Fletcher patted down his tie, flashing Carol a tight smile. "Apologies for my language, Carol. It's been a stressful night."

"That's fine," Carol replied faintly. Her hands spasmed around the dripping lemonade pitcher, staring down at the blood spots in the hallway. "I'll clean the, uh...the, uh..."

"Guys," Kade said, louder, wobbling to his feet. He put a hand to the back of his head, where it had connected with the wall. Theo wanted to go over and check him out, but that would only make things worse for everybody. Even if they were alone, Theo wasn't even wearing gloves. He would sear Kade's scalp through that fine fuzz of hair.

"I need a rabies shot," Aaron whispered.

"We'll get that sorted," Mr. Fletcher told him. He patted Aaron's arm, looking almost apologetic. "Come on, son."

Kade made a noise deep in his throat. His eyelids shuddered. He stunk of sweat. Theo hadn't noticed it with the intoxicating scent of Aaron's blood and all the yelling.

"Theo," Kade said, high and strangled.

Then he crumpled to the floor.

CHAPTER
EIGHT

ONE YEAR *and three days before the boy dies, he crouches in the bushes to listen.*

A twig pokes at his newly stubbled cheek. He ignores it. He is unkept and underfed. He was making his daily slog home through the woods when he heard angry voices and—on instinct—dropped to his belly in the dirt to listen.

The group has been in town for two years. They are moneyed and educated, but most of them have laborers' hands. They are a strange and brutal bunch, and they have been meeting in the woods to whisper things they won't tell the town about.

The leader of the group is whispering, but he's getting angrier and louder with each sentence. His wife stands before him, not cowering like the boy is used to seeing, but meeting her husband's eyes steadily.

"How dare you consider such a thing," the leader hisses, clenching the sun necklace dangling around his neck. "She is our

pride and joy, and you would have her fighting these vile things? She must be protected!"

"She must be ready," *his wife replies evenly. "Who are you to decide who gets to fight?"*

A voice speaks up softly behind the boy. "What are you doing on this side of town?"

He barely manages to hold in a shriek. He turns to see a blond girl crawl under the bush with him, settling her sharp chin on his shoulder.

He hisses, shaking her off. "What are you *doing? You're getting your expensive dress dirty. Your high and mighty father will have your head."*

The girl smiles, whip-sharp. She is sixteen, only a few weeks older than him. She got a cake from the baker and that pretty dress her mother ordered all the way from England. The boy heard stories about it while he dug in the baker's trash the next day, looking for burned bread. She invited him, to his surprise. He was too busy looking after his ailing mother to attend.

"Then hush and he won't hear you," the girl tells him, eyes brighter than he's ever seen them in school. "Mother told me the truth of their demented whispers. She showed me the most terrifying photographs."

The boy looks up at the group leader—the girl's high and mighty father—who has turned from his wife, wiping spittle from his beard. He looks angry and ashamed.

The group moves away from the bush, toward the woods. The leader of the group grows hushed as they walk away.

The boy sighs, turning in the dirt to face the girl. "And?"

"And they aren't as demented as we thought. The scourge they whisper about when they think we cannot hear—it isn't demons or spirits. It's vampires. They're going to banish them from the town, and I'm going to help."

The boy laughs as loud as he dares.

The girl doesn't join in.

The boy's smile dims. "You aren't serious. Vampires are just fairy stories from back home."

She cocks her blond head, which becomes more dirt-smeared with each tiny movement.

"And the murders?" she asks, keeping her voice low as her parents and their group move out of earshot. "Those tears in their neck, they're the work of a beast, I suppose? Do you believe everything the preacher tells you?"

The boy scoffs. He hasn't listened to a word the preacher says since he arrived in this godforsaken town.

The girl grips his hand. Her skin is newly blistered. You would have her fighting these vile things, *her father had hissed.*

"I've seen them," she says. "They're real. I've been training in secret."

"You're too wild," the boy whispers, unable to hold back a disbelieving smile.

"Says you," she replies, flashing her white teeth. "I'm going to help rid the town of this scourge."

A voice pipes up from beyond the bushes: "Do we have a new scourge in town? I was hoping with the illness, the poverty and the strange murders, we were all full up."

The boy groans and crawls out of the bush.

"You'd know all about poverty, sir," he says as he pushes himself to his feet, brushing dirt off his thin breeches.

The vampire smiles at him. He has not been dead long. There's a flower in his hand.

The boy notices none of this. The vampire was in the boy's class at school, before the boy left to find work. They arrived in this fledgling town around the same time, but their paths never crossed. Not until three months ago.

At first the boy thought he was being attacked. A mysterious figure followed him through the dark. When the boy tried to run, he slipped on the mud near the lake. As he lay there, ears ringing, blood dripping into his eyes, he watched the vampire loom over him and thought of those dark creatures his mother whispered bedtime stories about.

The boy closed his eyes, waiting to be eaten up.

Then the vampire spoke. "Are you planning on sleeping there or will you let me help you up?"

The boy opened his eyes. The vampire had a hand extended, smiling so beautifully that the boy's heart spasmed in his chest.

The vampire has called on the boy twice a week since then. Always after dark, always in secret. The boy understands. It wouldn't do for a nobleman's boy to be seen with a peasant like him.

The girl stands up from the bush, brushing twigs from her dress.

"Poverty indeed," the girl says, giving the vampire a short curtsey. She glances back at the boy curiously before following her father's odd group into the woods.

The boy nervously adjusts his dirty shirt. "What happened to not being seen in public together?"

"She'll keep it quiet. It's not like there's anyone else around." The vampire's gaze lingers on the group retreating into the woods, the girl's parents among them. "Ah. Another secret meeting. What do they discuss, I wonder?"

The boy shakes his head. He notices the flower in the vampire's hand, and his heart jumps in his chest.

"What's this?"

The vampire sees him staring and grins. "Come and see me tonight. Where we first met."

He gives the boy the flower. It's a forget-me-not, its petals fresh and white.

The boy takes it. It's the most beautiful thing he's ever been given. He thinks about saying so, then says instead: "Sounds dangerous. Haven't you heard? There are monsters about."

"I'll protect you." The vampire smiles, and the boy's heart flutters.

"You make me feel like I'm in a dream," the boy says, and then grimaces. "Bloody hell. Pretend you didn't hear that."

"No," the vampire says, surprised by how much he wants to hear the boy say it again. Mostly, he is surprised by how desperately he doesn't want the boy to die.

He reaches out, taking the boy's hand.

"A dream," he echoes. "I hope we never—

—wake up."

Kade wrenched his eyes open.

Theo loomed over him, expression set in such beautiful worry that Kade forgot how to breathe. Blond curls fell wildly over his forehead. A splinter nestled in the biggest curl, a memento from punching a tree. Kade had wanted to point it out when he noticed it in the light of the kitchen, but he hadn't had a chance.

For a second Theo was the only thing that existed, and Kade relaxed.

Then he blinked. His vision cleared. Sparky was lying beside him, his head on Kade's chest. The Fletchers stood behind Theo, parents crowding around their bleeding son in the hallway. Carol Fairgood was next to them, hands trembling around a dripping pitcher of lemonade that made Kade suddenly aware of how thirsty he was.

"Can I have some lemonade?" Kade croaked.

Theo's grip loosened. He was holding Kade's jacket, the leather creaking in his grip. Some of the worry flooded out of his face, replaced by an exasperation Kade was much more familiar with. Then Mrs. Fletcher took a step forward, and Theo whipped around.

"He needs air," he said.

Mrs. Fletcher stumbled back. "Right."

Carol spoke up. "Should I call someone?"

"Does *he* get to go to the hospital?" Aaron asked, voice thin with disbelief. He cradled his punctured hand to his chest. Blood dripped into the sleeve of his nice shirt, soaking it up to the elbow.

"No," Theo answered. "He's fine. I'll take him home."

He turned back to Kade, motioning for Sparky to get up. She did, but not without giving Kade's cheek a meaty lick. Kade shivered and wiped his face. His hand came away streaked with spit and sweat and Aaron's blood.

"Come on," Theo whispered. "Can you walk?"

"You have wood in your hair," Kade muttered.

Theo frowned. "What?"

Kade shook his head and pushed himself up, leaving smears of sweat on the shiny floor. He wobbled, and Theo's grip tightened once more around his jacket. Just for a moment. Then he stepped back, posture becoming cool and unaffected like it did at school, hands dropping from Kade's jacket like they had never wrinkled the leather.

Sparky sat on Kade's lap on the way home. Neither of them wanted to leave her in that house where she'd just bitten someone.

"They just said something about my dad," Theo said distractedly, picking the wood splinters out of his hair. "I'll tell you later. What was *that*? Did you see something?"

Kade nodded. He slapped himself in the face— ignoring Sparky's concerned whine and Theo's muttered *what the hell*—trying to make himself feel less asleep.

Theo pulled into the street.

"Lights," Kade reminded him.

Theo swore and flicked them on.

Kade sighed into his hands. "Okay. Theory time. The visions I've been having are the memories from the last guy who got chosen for my spot in the ritual."

"Okay," Theo replied, significantly slower than Kade. He kept glancing at Kade in the backseat as they drove, like he expected Kade to pass out under Sparky's furry bulk. "Why do you think that all of a sudden?"

"It just..." Kade wiped his sweaty forehead. "It *felt* like memories. It was clearer than the time at the tree. I think the memories are what I've been having bad dreams about. The ones I can't remember."

"What did you see?"

Kade squeezed his eyes shut. Something about a bush. Something about a flower.

"There was a boy," he started. "About our age. He hasn't been bound to the ritual yet, but it's...it's gonna happen. And there's a vampire, I think he's got your role. *Will* have it."

Theo nodded. The woods blurred around them, too fast. Kade sunk his hands into Sparky's fur, trying to make his heart stop racing. Sometimes he didn't have a problem with speeding cars. Other times it made his throat close up. Which was stupid, since his mom had been driving at a perfectly reasonable speed when she smashed into another car. He wasn't even with her. She'd forgotten to pick him up from school.

"What did they look like?" Theo asked. "What were their names? We'll look them up, find out what happened. If we're lucky someone will have written down how they stopped the ritual."

Kade closed his eyes, focusing on the vision. Trying to make any of the faces come into his mind. As soon as they started to form, a dark cloud blotted them out.

"It's..." Kade sighed. "I can't see. I can't even remember what they *sounded* like. It's like somebody doesn't want me to know."

Houses and buildings blurred past, almost as fast as the trees. Theo had slowed down once he hit civilization.

Kade's eyelids sagged, head drooping to rest against the window. Sparky was a warm weight in his lap and Theo's Lexus was so smooth as it glided through town toward Kade's house.

"They're not always bad," he muttered as sleep tugged at him. "The dreams. Sometimes I wake up and I'm so happy and I don't know why."

Theo didn't respond. Kade lifted his heavy head and saw Theo staring out beyond the headlights, into the dark. He looked numb again, steering wheel flexing dangerously under his hands. It had barely been twenty-four hours since his world fell apart.

Kade sat up with a sigh, shifting Sparky in his lap. "Stay home from school tomorrow. Help me see more visions. We'll call Milly, she keeps talking about that... cat...thing?"

"She said it wouldn't work for you," Theo replied. His grip loosened on the steering wheel.

"Worth a shot," Kade said. But there was still that faraway look in Theo's eyes, so he continued: "You should stay over. Go back, then sneak out once your mom's asleep."

That shook some of the numb out of Theo's expression. He snorted, giving Kade a sideways look.

"And what," he asked. "Watch you sleep?"

"Ha ha," Kade said, too loud. "*No.* Explore a different patch of woods. Watch movies on my laptop or something."

Theo's hands tightened on the steering wheel. He didn't squirm, like Kade. You had to really watch him to see all the small, hidden movements that Theo let slip past his cool, confident demeanor.

"Do it for Sparky," Kade tried. "She's worried about me. Don't separate us."

He lifted her furry face, tilting it toward Theo as he took on a deliberately stupid falsetto. "*Don't separate us, Theo! I love him! He sneaks me food when you're not looking!*"

"I knew it," Theo said. But he was almost smiling, the most genuine smile Kade had gotten out of him all day.

Kade slumped back, fighting the urge to fall asleep right there in the backseat. "Is that a yes?"

Theo didn't respond. Then he reached into the backseat, scruffing Sparky around the ears. "I can't say no to that face."

Kade's cheeks heated. He looked out the window at the town blurring past. But he could still see Theo's hand from the corner of his eye, bare and gentle on Sparky's soft head.

For once, Kade woke up before his alarm. He was wearing a shirt and boxers. He usually slept just in boxers, but it had felt weird to do that knowing Theo would be around, so he kept the shirt on. He was shockingly warm for this time of the year, and not because of the shirt. Sparky had curled up against him in the night, her muzzle resting on his stomach.

He scratched her neck. "Hey, girl. Sleep well?"

Sparky huffed sleepily, her leg twitching. Still in a dream.

Kade smiled down at her fondly. Then he stretched, yawning. The yawn turned into a scream mid-yawn, producing one of the strangest noises Kade had ever made.

Theo was standing in the doorway, watching them with a bemused expression. He almost looked like the jokey guy from a few days ago who had teased Kade for calling him *sunshine*.

Kade slouched over a newly awakened Sparky, panting. "Jesus. I was *joking* about you watching me sleep."

"I'm not watching," Theo said hastily. He scratched his head. He didn't have bedhead, since he never went to bed nowadays. His curls were as perfect as ever. But he'd changed his clothes while Kade slept: he'd picked the *U STAY SOFT / U GET EATEN* shirt, plus his baggiest pair of sweatpants. The shirt strained around Theo's chest and arms, which wasn't a surprise. What was a surprise were the sweatpants, which weren't baggy at all on him. His thighs filled out the worn gray material, the hemline stretching over his waist. Kade had always assumed their waists were the same size. Was Kade really that skinny?

Theo coughed. "Breakfast is ready."

Kade ripped his gaze away from Theo's not-so-small waist, turning to search for his phone so Theo wouldn't see him blush. Smell him, sure. But Kade had *some* dignity.

"What?" he said, trying to sound distracted and unfazed, like he hadn't been perving on his grieving friend. "Sundance has one arm, I told her to take it easy."

"I made it. And Sundance is calling in sick for you today," Theo continued. "Remember any dreams?"

"Sure. I had to give a history presentation on shrimp in my aunt's factory. Also I was naked and no one would give me clothes."

Sparky licked his cheek. Kade kissed her soft forehead, then asked: "I fell asleep before you got back, did your mom say anything about Sparky?"

"She wants to talk about that after the funeral." Theo crossed his arms over his chest, so the shirt just read *STAY SOFT*. "So I have until then to talk her out of putting her down, I guess."

"She can come live with me," Kade offered, folding her into his arms. It was a stretch—she just kept growing. "Or, I don't know. In the woods near your place. I don't think she'd deal well with being away from you."

"She could stay with you," Theo said thoughtfully. "If she has to."

Sparky looked up at Kade, touching her nose to his chin. Her tail thumped against his thin mattress.

"She's bound to me," Kade said. "Right? A little bit? Because of the ritual. She was made *because* of you, she's *attuned* to you, but you're, like...connected to me with weird, burny vampire magic. So in a way, she's bound to me, too."

Theo rubbed a bare foot against the worn carpet. "Uh. I don't know."

"It's the only thing that makes sense," Kade said. "She hates everyone but us. It's gotta be magic."

"Gotta be," Theo said faintly. There was a strange, scrutinizing look on his face as he watched Kade pet Sparky, one that made Kade deeply glad he wore a shirt to bed last night.

He was relieved and disappointed when Theo looked away.

"Anyway," Theo said hastily. "Breakfast. Hurry up before it gets cold."

"You can't even—" Kade stopped before he could

say eat it, all too aware of the thin walls in this house. "Sure. Be there in a jiff."

Theo's eyes widened. Kade grew suddenly, mortifyingly aware that he'd just said something far too British in front of him.

"*In a jiff,*" Theo repeated, tone that special kind of flat that meant he was going to make fun of Kade for this mercilessly until the end of time.

Kade threw a pillow at him. Theo pulled the door shut with a speed and strength that made it tremble, pillow whacking harmlessly into the wood.

Kade fell back against the bed. He'd get up in a second. For now, he needed to lie here and feel heavy and bittersweet, thinking about his mum and Theo's mom and wondering how he could get Theo to look like that again: no numbness, no weight on his shoulders. Just tired and smug and maybe a little shy, forgetting for a moment all the horrible things yet to come.

It was the best breakfast the Renfield house had seen in a long time: poached eggs, fried sausage and bacon, sautéed spinach. Even fancy bakery bread, sliced and toasted and smothered in butter.

Sundance offered to pay Theo back for the food he'd brought. But Theo waved her down, insisting it was thanks for being so good to him this summer. Then he fed Sparky his portion under the table while Kade distracted her with a fashion show displaying his latest creations. Kade got the feeling that Sundance had talked to Theo before he woke up, and that was the main reason why Theo had seemed so normal when he invited Kade to breakfast. That, or making food really calmed him down. But based on how Sundance and Theo talked to each other—quiet, jovial, weirdly tender—he was betting on the first option.

Kade's phone vibrated on the kitchen table. Kade leapt to grab it before Sundance or Theo could see who it was.

It was Milly. *If you want Theo to take a day off,* the text said, *I don't think we'll need to deliberately botch it. This probably won't work.*

Bad news for their continued efforts to figure out a way to stop the ritual. Good news for Kade, who was trying to find a way to make Theo chill the hell out with his vengeance quest and take a second to grieve.

"We should go for a walk," he told Theo.

Theo stood. Sparky stood with him, growling at Sundance when she stretched too close to grab her coffee.

"Easy," Theo told her. Then, to Kade: "I'll go get my shoes."

WHEN MILLY first suggested using a cat to induce visions, Theo had felt a second of queasy horror thinking Milly wanted to cut up a cat and consult its innards. Then he remembered this was *Milly* he was talking about, who once went on an impassioned rant about how she would love to have a pet, but she wasn't sure she could give it the life it deserved since the house was empty half the time. Not to mention her habit of getting obsessed with things for weeks on end, leading her to neglect her own hygiene and feeding. She didn't want to see if that carried over to a pet.

The cat plan, it turned out, involved Kade staring deeply into a cat's eyes, and...that was it. Kade spent a lot of time crouching in front of Milly while she struggled to hold the cat still.

Theo leaned against a tree, waiting. Milly had lured a stray into a cat carrier and lugged it to the woods. So far, the biggest obstacle was making the cat look Kade in the eyes.

"It's easier if you're freshly resurrected," Milly told them, readjusting her grip on the squirming cat. "Or if the cat is closer to death. This one's far too new."

Kade glanced away from the cat long enough to shoot Theo a look, half excited, half incredulous. He often did this when Milly came out with insane crap about her life before Lock, which got more terrifying and ridiculous every time she brought it up. Resurrections, dreamscapes, visions. An evil town that Milly and her friends defeated sometime in the early 2000s.

Vanquished with the power of friendship, gay love, and incredible violence, she'd said once. They had to go home immediately after that so Kade could stitch it into a shirt.

The cat meowed unhappily, wriggling in Milly's grip.

"Good kitty," Kade coaxed, following its disgruntled gaze. "Gooood kitty. Stay still so I can stare into your eyes and see unspeakable horrors."

Something rustled in the bushes behind Theo.

"No," Theo said automatically.

Sparky whined. Her nose poked into the back of Theo's knee.

"You'll freak the cat out," Theo reminded her. "You don't need to be near me every second of every—"

Before he could finish, the cat writhed out of Milly's hands and sprinted off into the woods. Sparky darted forward, only stopping when Theo grabbed her collar.

Kade sighed, climbing to his feet with a wince he was far too young for. Theo would have to talk him into stretching.

"Oh no," he said, tugging at the hem of his home-made DIE YOUNG crop top. "The cat was a bust. Sorry, Milly. Theo, want to go watch some semi-entertaining movies?"

Theo narrowed his eyes. "We can find another cat. Or we can try Sparky, she's magic, right? Or...something. Stare into her eyes."

"I've stared into her eyes a hundred times," Kade reminded him. "Have you seen those beauties? Like a sunset."

He clapped until Sparky jogged over, rubbing her furry cheeks and cooing. Usually it would make Theo smile. Today it only pissed him off. He couldn't go back to Kade's place and watch movies. He needed to *do something*.

"We skipped school to get more visions out of you," Theo pointed out. "Milly, is there anything else?"

Milly turned. She'd been watching the trees where the cat had run into the woods.

"Nothing I would recommend," she said.

Kade shrugged, patting down Sparky's flank. "Movies might help with visions! Or listening to music. Or going on a walk in the woods—"

"We tried the tree a few days ago," Theo said, but he already knew that wasn't what Kade meant. Kade meant one of *Theo's* walks in the woods, which involved a lot of

Theo pointing and explaining to Kade what a particular plant was, and Kade repeating his words in a high voice until Theo threatened to throw something at him.

Theo checked his watch. "First period isn't over yet. I can get there in time for second."

Kade laughed loud enough to startle birds from trees. "What is with you and *school*? I thought jocks got to take it easy."

Theo spun to face him. "Some jocks, sure! But not Fairgoods. Fairgoods have to be the *best*. Best in the class, best in the school, best on the court, best in *everything*. So *yeah*, I work my ass off. Maybe I don't have to do that for basketball anymore, but I do have to do it for classes, so *yes*, Kade, I'm going to school."

Kade shifted, chastised. Next to him, Milly was pretending to examine the leaves above them. Theo almost felt bad. But the dark feeling in his stomach was still there, coiling, demanding. He couldn't *rest*.

"Besides," Theo continued. "Felicity and Aaron are at school. Maybe I can get some information out of them."

Kade groaned. It was much less enthusiastic than his laugh, like he was forcing himself into it. "Come *on*, mate. Let's just hang out! I'm *so* tired from my vision last night."

"You slept for nine hours," Theo pointed out.

Kade ignored him. "I *passed out*, Theo. I'm *traumatized*. You need to take care of me. Sparky, are you traumatized?"

Sparky's tail thumped against the forest floor.

"Yeah you are," Kade crooned, cupping her furry face and turning it so their cheeks were next to each other. "Take care of us, Theo."

Something small and warm unfurled in Theo's chest, not unlike when he watched Sundance and Kade eat the breakfast he'd made them. It sounded lovely—taking Kade back to the house, turning on some crappy TV show. Maybe getting him a blanket, jokingly tucking him into the couch. Sparky sprawled over both their laps. Sundance in the corner of the couch, providing dry running commentary. She'd sat with him as Theo made breakfast this morning, telling him a story about her and Kade's mother going to a Dairy Queen after their own mom died—both mid-twenties, hungover, and cry-laughing over a fudge sundae at six a.m.—and by the end of it, the dark knot in Theo's chest had uncoiled. For a second he even thought everything might eventually be okay.

But only for a second.

Theo shook his head. "No, I need…I need to do something. Okay? I need to do SOMETHING."

Kade scratched his mouth, mumbling, "Okay, don't know why I thought that would work." Then, louder: "You don't need to do something *right this second.*"

"Yes, I do!" Theo yelled. "My dad got *murdered!* We only have until spring to stop some weird plan where I burn you to death and let Cyth free to destroy the town! If you're not going to try anything else to get visions,

I'm going to...I don't know. Raid my parents' office again, see if my dad left any more notes I couldn't find last time."

Theo charged off. Kade called his name, but Theo didn't turn back. He could hear Sparky running to catch up, falling into step easily beside him, ears pricked and anxious. She whined, and Theo couldn't help thinking she would enjoy a day of TV-surfing on Kade's couch more than whatever crap Theo was about to drag her into.

"You can stay with him today," Theo offered as he strode through the woods.

She cocked her head. Then she swayed closer, her front paws almost tangling with his legs.

Tears gathered behind Theo's eyes. He blinked them back furiously. He could see his Lexus from here, parked down the street from Kade's house.

Russel was stepping off the front porch when Theo got in the gate. His gardening bag hung at his side and his forehead was smeared with dirt.

"Hello again," he called as Theo came up the path. He had that face on, that stupid pity face that everyone kept wearing around him yesterday. "I was just, uh..." He pointed back at the house. "Free of charge this week. Any way I can help, you know? Been with you guys a long time."

Theo nodded. He had hoped Russel would say

something about the hedge out back, which Theo had violently over-trimmed several nights ago in a haze of grief and rage. Or about the dahlias, which were blooming wonderfully. Or the trees around town, which were vibrant orange in a way that reminded Theo of Sparky's eyes when she was happy.

Russel clapped a hand on Theo's shoulder. "I'm so sorry, bud."

Theo nodded again, even tighter than last time. His dad hadn't even been dead for two days and Theo was already sick of condolences. The funeral was going to *suck*.

Russel hesitated. His hand flexed on Theo's shoulder, brown from the sun and covered with tiny scars from a lifetime of working with sharp objects.

"I'll see you Friday," he said.

"See you," Theo said dully, and headed into the house.

Carol was cooking up a storm. Theo heard her before he even got up to the porch, banging pots around and cursing under her breath. Which was strange, because she was never much of a cook. Anything more basic than a roast, Theo had learned from cooking blogs.

He pulled off his shoes and set them near the door. A loud bang echoed from the kitchen, followed by another round of cursing that she would never say around him. Her voice was watery.

Theo thought about creeping past her, up to the offices. Leaving her to it, like his parents so often left him when he was upset. They were a family who liked to deal with their emotions privately. The idea of taking on an angry, maybe-crying mom sounded like something he wanted to avoid. He needed to check his parents' office, anyway.

Theo started for the stairs, completely intent on ignoring her. But then he passed the kitchen doorway and saw her hunched over the stove with a twisted expression, and Theo's dead heart lurched in his chest.

"Mom," he said, poking his head in timidly. "What're you making?"

She jolted in surprise. "Theo! Oh my gosh. Make some noise when you walk."

"Sorry." Theo squeaked his feet against the polished wood, hoping to make her laugh. It didn't work.

"That smells nice," he offered. "Can I help?"

She sniffed, turning away to wipe her face. She wasn't crying yet, but it was a close thing. She had her robe on again, something red and slick smudging the silk. It smelled like tomatoes and wine.

One pan was filled with garlic and oil, heating slowly. The other was a boiling pot of pasta. Food lined the bench behind her: salami and pesto, capsicum, green onion, Himalayan rock salt, three types of oil.

"I know we have so much food in the fridge," Carol said, twisting her hands together. "But I just—I had a craving for this dish your father and I ate together in

Rome once. I looked up a recipe, it's probably going to be nothing like I imagined it. Especially with me at the wheel..."

She trailed off, gaze traveling down his body.

Theo tensed. He was still wearing Kade's clothes. He tugged at the hem of his *U STAY SOFT / U GET EATEN* shirt, trying not to look self-conscious.

Carol laughed, wet and airy. "What are you *wearing*?"

"Nothing," Theo said. "It's laundry day. I'm sorry, I'll go get changed."

"You do that," she said faintly. She pursed her lips. She looked at his clothes like they genuinely disturbed her, and Theo got the feeling it wasn't just because she thought they weren't his style.

Theo petted Sparky as he headed into the hall. She licked his hand. She knew what he was feeling. She always did.

"Wait," Carol called.

Theo turned around. Carol was standing in the kitchen doorway, holding a spatula.

"It's a school day," she said waspishly. "What are you doing here?"

Theo winced. It had totally slipped his mind that she would notice. A lot of things had slipped his mind lately. Why had no one told him that grief turned your brain to mush?

"I just..." Theo wet his lips. "I couldn't do it today. I'm really sorry."

Carol's stern expression wilted. "No, I know. I mean,

I'm not at work. I probably should be, the case we wrapped up isn't as…Anyway, I need to call the school."

"Someone already did that," Theo said.

She gave him a suspicious look. Then she seemed to decide she was too exhausted to follow it up, and turned back toward the kitchen.

Theo lingered in the hallway. "The case you wrapped up isn't as what?"

"It's not as wrapped up as we thought," she replied. She rubbed her forehead, frowning when she accidentally hit herself with the spatula. "Your father—it doesn't matter. I can't understand it. Something for another day."

"No," Theo said desperately. "What is it?'"

Sparky nipped Theo's thumb. He ignored her.

Carol sighed. "I'm not allowed to talk about specifics, honey."

"Right," Theo said hastily. "Sure. Sorry."

She gave him another look. Then she readjusted her robe, the red stain gleaming in the light.

"That is terrible grammar," she told him, pointing at his shirt.

"Right," Theo repeated, tugging at it protectively. He liked this shirt. It was one of his favorites out of Kade's whole wardrobe.

Water spat and bubbled in the kitchen. The pasta pot had boiled over.

"Dammit," Carol hissed, ducking out of the hallway.

Theo breathed in: tomato, oil, wine. Then he

headed upstairs to change into something acceptable and break into his parents' office for a second time.

Forty-five minutes later, Theo sat on his bed in a sensible pair of jeans and a polo, waiting for Kade to pick up his phone.

"Hello?"

"Hey," he said before Kade had even finished his greeting. "Can't find anything else in the office. I think I was hoping for a secret compartment, since we've had pretty good luck with secret rooms, but no dice. Want to break into Felicity's house before everybody gets home?"

Silence.

"I phrased that wrong," Theo said. "I'm breaking into Felicity's house as soon as I hang up. Are you coming?"

Kade sighed. Theo heard something clacking down the line, like Kade was putting down a pair of knitting needles.

"If you can wait until tonight," Kade said reluctantly. "You won't need to."

Theo waited for Kade to explain what the hell he was talking about.

"What the hell are you talking about?" Theo said finally.

"The Sloan house will be home to an 'absolutely killer party,'" Kade recited.

Theo frowned. "It's a Thursday."

"Uh-huh."

"Felicity's hosting? She didn't invite me."

"I got the feeling it was pretty last minute," Kade said. "Like, she planned it yesterday. The day after your dad died. So no, she wouldn't have invited you to a party."

This was weird. Felicity had always struggled with impulsivity, but a last-minute party usually required an *event*. Like when she got her first modeling contract. Or she thought it would be fun to sleep with Aaron at a party and there were none coming up in the next month.

Theo frowned. "Is this an I'm-Single-Again party? Because I should go anyway. Make sure she doesn't do anything stupid."

"I don't know Felicity very well," Kade said dryly. "But the little I do know suggests she's going to do whatever the hell she wants. You being there won't stop shit."

Theo lay back on his bed, full of fidgety energy. He'd been planning to go break into a house. Now he had hours before he had to go anywhere. He'd go for a sprint in the woods. Study. Drink some woodland animals. Find some new moss for his terrarium. He could go and see Kade, but he was still annoyed at Kade for trying to get him to relax today.

"Alright," Theo said. "We'll go crash a party."

"*You're* crashing," Kade corrected. "I'm *invited*."

Theo laughed. "She invited *you*?"

"Hey," Kade said. "I'm a *hoot*." Then he coughed, more clacking coming down the line. Like he'd never actually put down the knitting needles. "She invited me...when she was telling me to take care of you?"

Theo swallowed. How much did Felicity know? She'd heard that someone saw them together in a car, but that was it, right? How much did Aaron tell her?

"So," Kade said. "We're going?"

Theo nodded. Then he remembered Kade couldn't see that and said, "Yeah."

"Great," Kade said, sounding very tired. "Let me go pick an outfit."

THEO PULLED up right in front of his house.

Progress, Kade thought. He decided to test his luck and open the passenger door. Theo gave him a hard look.

"I think it's time to let me in the front," Kade announced into the car. "Your mom knows. Aaron found out ages ago. Felicity knows and she's been shutting down rumors left and right. But even the fact that she's gotta do that means the secret's out, baby! We're *friends*."

"That's not the secret," Theo said. His voice sounded strange. "That's what you're wearing?"

Kade looked down. He'd paired a fun, trashy skirt with fishnet tights, a crop top that said DEVOUR in blood red, and knee-high boots. They were all different shades of black, and very tight.

"These are my party clothes." Kade wiggled his

brows—darkened even further with eyebrow pencil—then jingled his silver skull earrings, the only part of his outfit that wasn't dark.

"I've seen you at parties," Theo mumbled, eyes on the dark road ahead. "Those are *not* your party clothes."

Kade waved at Theo's jeans and button-down shirt. "What are YOU wearing?"

Theo glared. "I look great! *You* look like you're going to a Halloween party."

Kade ran a tongue over his lipsticky lips. "Thank you. Do I have front seat privileges or not?"

Theo jerked his head at the backseat.

Kade groaned and climbed in, pressing his face down into his stockings. They were much more fun when he was hyping himself up in his room. Now he felt stupid. Especially with Theo avoiding looking at him like that.

Theo pulled into the street.

"Lights," Kade reminded him.

"Goddammit," Theo said distractedly, and slammed them on. "Sorry. Shit. That's so dangerous, I gotta stop doing that."

Kade glanced at him, trying to gauge how he was doing. No visible numbness, but he was obviously agitated. *Much* more agitated than he would've been if he'd spent the day shooting the shit with Kade.

"What did you do today?" Kade asked, making sure to keep his voice cool and casual, like he didn't care at all. The way his aunt did when she was worried about him. When Kade was younger he tended to blow up in her face if she dared let it show that she was concerned about her kid doing a series of *very* concerning things.

"Hunted," Theo replied. "Scoped out the funeral home."

"Anyone steal your dad's corpse?"

"Not today."

Kade clicked his tongue. "Another successful day for The Lamb And The Knife!"

Theo was turning a corner, so he couldn't stare at him. But he gave it his best shot. "*What?*"

"Oh." Kade examined his nails, squinting through the dim light at the wonky polish. He'd done a rush job, the black polish drying over his cuticles and overlapping onto the skin.

"The ritual wants you to sacrifice me, right," he continued, muffled as he chewed a shard of nail polish off his finger. "It's like our band name. If we had a band. Do you not like it?"

"*No,*" Theo burst out. "God, Kade."

"Fine, I won't give you the matching shirt."

"Don't make us shirts about the ritual that wants me to kill you!"

"Yours says *knife,*" Kade said, and grinned at the angry look Theo shot him. "You're such a party pooper. Onwards!"

"*Onwards,*" Theo muttered mockingly, turning the steering wheel with more force than necessary, sending Kade sliding into the window. Kade giggled, smile fading even as he did so. If he couldn't be a comfort, he at least wanted to be a distraction. Theo seemed like the kind of guy who would take anger over grief. Most days, so did Kade. He just wished he could make Theo understand how much that anger calcified over time, turning hard and unyielding over all the actual problems you were using the anger to distract yourself from.

As if Theo would listen to that. Kade sure hadn't when his aunt tried to tell him. He had to learn it the hard way, and so did Theo. No matter how much Kade wished he could save him from it.

Theo dropped him a block away from the party.

"See you there," he said, and peeled off.

It took Kade five minutes to get to Felicity's house. She lived near the woods in one of the oldest houses in town. Or, she used to. Then her mom remodeled the entire place when she was in grade school. It was a whole ship-of-Theseus situation: was it still the same house if every plank had been replaced? Kade made a mental note to ask Theo about it.

The front hall was dark and crowded and even more minimalist than Theo's house. Why were rich people so *boring*, Kade wondered as he pushed through his drunk classmates. If he had this kind of money, he'd have all kinds of crazy shit. Not gray ceilings and polished white tiles and washed-out beachscapes on the walls.

He scanned the crowd. Half for Theo, half for the drinks table. He'd go for whichever he found first.

"Hey," Theo said behind him.

Kade swore and turned. Of course Theo would find him instantly. Kade imagined his heartbeat slamming louder than the music, louder than the chatter, drawing Theo toward him.

"Hey," Kade said. "What's up?"

Theo shook his head. He was standing a weird distance away, turned so Kade couldn't see his face.

Kade rolled his eyes. "Right. Sorry. Can't be seen with Monster."

Then he turned, pretending he was examining his bitten nails and not talking to the guy behind him.

"Looks like half the school showed up," Kade reported, peering into the sea of familiar faces. "Except Aaron, of course. I assume Felicity's single-again party explicitly excludes her ex?"

Theo was quiet. Kade was about to turn around and ask what was going on when Theo said, "Incoming."

Before Kade could ask what he meant, Felicity barreled into him. She spun him to face Theo and hooked an arm around each of their shoulders.

"You *made* it," she crowed. She gave Theo a shake. "Answer my texts next time, bitch."

"I've been distracted," Theo said, hunching so Felicity could reach him easier. Kade followed suit. He hadn't realized how short Felicity was until now, teetering on her tiptoes to reach them. Her outfits,

Kade was amused to realize, looked like a ghostly mirror of his own: a short white skirt and a pink crop top paired with dangly champagne glass earrings. Even her boots were similar, pale and cutting off right below her thigh. She stunk of schnapps and a specific brand of bruise cream that sent Kade right back to childhood, standing on a chair to examine his back in the bathroom mirror.

"I bet," Felicity said in a stage whisper. She seemed torn whether she should be fun or sympathetic. She gave Kade a shake. "So glad you made it! I've been wanting to get to know you better."

Theo snorted. "Not too well, I hope."

"Ooooh," she crooned, flicking Theo's ear. "Don't be jealous! You know I was always going for girls after things ended with Aaron. Kade's safe from me. Probably. Are you even into girls?"

"A little. But mostly guys," Kade said, feeling strangely squirmy as he admitted it. Nobody asked him this kind of thing. Especially not since he came into school wearing that glittery shirt with a word on it that got him suspended for a week.

"Same. Opposite with Theo, he's more girls than guys." Felicity did a little jig, hugely impeded by the tall boys she was hanging onto. "This is fun, we're such a fun group! Let's dance."

"We'll come find you later," Theo told her.

Kade couldn't help but be relieved when Theo plucked her arm off his shoulders. He was curious about

Felicity, and he did want to get to know her better. He just didn't know if that was a good idea. He always got the feeling that if he got too close, she'd pull him into a sickening orbit doomed to crash and burn.

Felicity groaned. "Come onnnn—"

"Later," Theo told her.

Felicity's eyelashes fluttered. She'd painted them white, pale glitter dusting over her cheeks and her stark hair. For a moment she really did look like a ghost.

"Oh. Okay," she said, surprisingly small. Then she grinned, some of that dangerous light coming back. "Hope you had fun ditching today! Don't get too drunk, you can't be hungover tomorrow morning for the...you know."

She swooped in and hugged him with a strange tenderness, her grin faltering. For a moment Kade got a glimpse of a messed-up girl doing her best to comfort her grieving friend.

Then she leaned into Kade, white eyelashes brushing his cheek.

"Don't steal anything from the drinks table," she whispered.

"No promises," Kade replied.

She vanished into the crowd. Kade wiped Felicity's eye makeup from his cheek and turned to Theo.

"So," he said.

That was as far as he got before someone bumped into Kade's side, splashing beer over his boots. Kade turned around to glare.

Delilah Emmerson—student body president two years in a row who had promised better water fountains and never delivered—leered at him, her badly dyed hair flopping in her face.

"Oooh, Monster's gonna *eat* me," she said. Then she looked at Theo, mouth dropping open in shock, to find him also glaring.

"Oh. Sorry." She peered at Theo's jeans. "Did I get you?"

"Nope," Theo cleared his throat and took a step away from Kade, trying to look casual.

Kade told the disappointment churning in his stomach to quit it.

"Hey Delilah," Theo said as Delilah turned to leave. "You party with Felicity, right?"

Delilah gestured at the house party around them. "I mean...yeah?"

"A few months ago," Theo said. "Liss says you dared her to break into Coach Cheech's house."

Delilah looked startled. She brought her cup up to her mouth, mumbling into it. "Not Coach Cheech's anymore." She glanced over at Kade, frowning when she saw him still standing there.

Theo stepped forward. "Did you do it? Did you dare her?"

"What? Sure I did. Totally." Delilah's head bobbed wildly. She took another gulp of beer. "I think I see my friend over there, I should—"

"You're lying," Theo said flatly.

Delilah shrank under his glare. "She said...she just needed a cover, in case...she said nobody would..."

She trailed off. Gave Kade another look. Then she stumbled back into the crowd, shouting for a friend that may or may not exist.

"Well," Kade said to Theo, who was still standing away from him. "That's not suspicious at all. Should we go find Felicity again?"

"No," Theo said. His jaw flexed, glancing up at a nearby staircase.

Kade waited for Theo to tell him to split up and search for clues, Scooby-gang style. They'd get fewer weird looks that way.

"Follow me," Theo said instead.

Theo led him up one of the multiple staircases in this boring minimalist house. Felicity's room was on the third floor, which was empty except for a couple making out sloppily against the wall.

"I'm guessing this is it," Kade said, pointing at the door with a swoopy metal *F* on it, so big it nearly cut into the doorknob.

Theo nodded. He glanced over at the couple—so entwined in each other that they would not have broken apart if a fire alarm went off—and then snuck in.

Kade followed.

Felicity's room was luxurious, but only if you didn't look too closely. The carpet was plush white but stained. The mirror was lined with lightbulbs like in the backstage of a theater, but several of them were dead. An old, grimy teddy bear sat in the tangled bedsheets of her giant bed. A heap of dirty sports clothes sat in the corner, expensive leggings and sports bras and bright pink knuckle wraps.

The biggest thing in the room was a poster, one of her latest gigs: Felicity posing in front of an electric car. She had a spray tan, which wasn't really her style, and her shrewd eyes had been photoshopped to look bigger. But her expression was what Kade was used to seeing in the halls, smug and knowing.

Kade turned around. Theo was still in the doorway, staring with a surprised expression.

"Just realized I haven't been in here for…" Theo frowned. "Over a year now. Huh."

"Has it changed much?"

Theo shook his head.

Kade scanned the bookshelf. Most of the books looked like she'd bought them in middle school, all Baby-Sitters Club and horse books. Old-school DVDs, old coffee mugs, a half-popped sleeve of aspirin, a massive jar of mints, a bottle of vodka hidden behind a book.

Kade tucked the vodka into his jacket.

"Nothing that looks like Milly's book in here," Kade said. He pulled halfheartedly at the book that had been hiding the vodka. It was a frayed book of children's poems. Nothing slid out to reveal a hidden room.

Kade sighed, starting to put the book back. Then he noticed something strange about the pages—they were irregular and jagged, like this was a scrapbook and not a poetry collection. He flipped it open. No children's poems—it *was* a scrapbook. Felicity had torn the pages out and sewn new ones in covered with pasted-in magazine images. Cars, beaches, diamonds, lip gloss, a hundred girls in bikinis or trendy belts or long flowing dresses. Neat scribbles around the pictures: *live fast die young leave a beautiful corpse*, with hearts above the *i*'s.

"You should dance with Felicity," Kade said, flipping through the scrapbook. "If you want. Could be good to let loose."

Theo didn't respond, leafing through Felicity's drawers so fast his hands blurred. Drawers snapped open and closed, Theo staring into them with increasing frustration.

"Hey," Kade said. "Hello? Dancing?"

He wiggled his hips as he flipped another page. Then he stopped. The scrapbook pages were getting... dark. Less beaches and more blood, knives, loose teeth, a girl with her eyes cut out. Angry song lyrics scribbled so deep the paper ripped.

"You think I want to dance," Theo said.

"I think it might be good to take a break in the vengeance quest," Kade replied, flipping faster. The lyrics turned into nonsense, until it was just Felicity's neat handwriting turned huge and feral: *SHIT SHIT SHIT SHIT SHIT.*

"I've never seen you dance," Theo said, heading over to the makeup table. "Bet you step on everyone's toes."

"Nope," Kade said distractedly. "Can't step on people's toes if you've never danced with anyone."

He turned another page. Something heavy and golden fell out of the scrapbook. Kade stooped to pick it up, heart plummeting. He held a necklace: a golden sun, old and dull. The same sun embossed on the cover of the book Milly was translating. The same sun Cheech had been wearing. The symbol of the hunters.

Theo started, "You've never—?"

Then he cut off.

Kade turned to find him staring out the window, head cocked. Listening.

Kade wet his lips. "Theo?"

"I hear trouble," Theo said. Then he ran out of the room, leaving Kade standing there holding the proof that not one, but *both* of Theo's childhood friends were against him.

THE HOUSE WAS EMPTIER when Theo ran through it a second time. Everybody had followed Felicity out to the woods, toward the rising smoke.

"Careful," joked Finn Harley—a fellow Nightfowl who excelled at jump shots and absolutely nothing else—as he toyed with Delilah Emmerson's hair. "You know they keep finding deer drained of blood, right? You know what *that* means. Everybody says golden boy's dad got attacked by a bear, but *I* bet—"

Finn stammered to a stop when he caught sight of Theo stalking past him and glowering.

"Never mind," Finn squeaked.

Theo ignored him. Finn wasn't his only classmate joking about what was lurking in the woods. Theo could smell the fear on them. Teenagers clutching their cheap beers and sticking close to their friends. Like the thing they feared wasn't walking among them right now, following the stench of smoke from the fire Felicity had set.

The bonfire was deeper into the woods. A dead tree trunk burned, helped along by orange leaves and generous splashes of spirits. Theo's classmates huddled around it, laughing and joking and pretending like they weren't glancing out into the dark, worrying what was out there.

Somewhere behind him, Kade called Theo's name.

Theo kept walking. Kade could catch up.

Felicity stood behind the flames with her hand twisted in a girl's hair. They were kissing, the slick sounds of their mouths almost as loud as the fire.

"Hey," Theo barked as he stormed up. "Liss! What the hell?"

The girl she was kissing jumped back. It was Skeeter Bass. Felicity's lipstick was smeared all the way down her scarred neck.

"Um, sorry," Skeeter said, flushing tomato-red.

"I'm not pissed at *you*," Theo snapped. "Liss, it's fall. There are dead leaves *everywhere*. Are you crazy?"

Felicity leaned back lazily, hands still in Skeeter's mousy hair. Her eyes were glazed, her breath stunk of beer and spirits. She'd somehow managed to jump up several levels of wasted since Theo left her.

"Town pride," she drawled. "Lock started with fire."

"So you'll burn down the whole forest?" Theo stepped in closer. Skeeter Bass wisely untangled herself from Felicity's grip, slinking into the trees with hunched shoulders.

"Liss," Theo hissed. "You're in enough trouble already. If your mom finds out—"

"Like I'm afraid of her!" Felicity laughed and spun, her eyes bright with firelight. "There are worse things out there in the dark. Right, guys?"

She yelled the last words out at the teenagers gathered around the bonfire. A cheer went up, tempered slightly by some of them noticing who was standing with Felicity and how mad he looked.

Theo glanced back at the fire. The dead stump was far enough away from the rest of the trees that nothing was catching, but that didn't mean a flaming leaf couldn't drift off and start a wildfire.

Kade's heartbeat was getting closer. Theo could hear it the whole time he was charging out of the house, could hear Kade swearing as Theo got further and further away.

He grabbed Felicity's arm, stilling her spin. "Has anyone called you about your case?"

Felicity's smile died. Then it started up again, a pale imitation of itself. "Why would they? We won. No juvie for me! Not even a fine!"

"So nothing's been reopened? There's no new evidence?"

"No," Felicity said slowly. "Evidence, what do you mean?"

Kade's heartbeat thudded louder. He yelled Theo's

name through the trees, and Theo watched a few people turn toward it.

"It wasn't a big deal," Felicity said slowly, staring off into the woods. "It was...it was just a stupid *dare*."

"Was it?" Theo asked. "Because we asked Delilah. She said you told her to cover for you. What's going on?"

Felicity laughed. "I don't know."

"Liss."

"I don't *know*," she repeated. She reached up and squeezed his cheeks. "I don't know anything that's going on in this batshit little town, Theo. Do you? Can you tell me?"

Theo frowned. Felicity looked desperate. Like she really wanted him to sit her down and tell her everything.

"Liss," he started. "Did someone...did your *mom*—?"

A familiar voice drifted in from the tree line. "HEY!"

Theo turned, Felicity still squishing his cheeks.

Kade was limping. He was almost *hopping*, holding his left foot like he couldn't put much weight on it.

He spotted Theo and sighed. "Asshole! Hey! I found something!"

Then he stopped. His eyes were locked on something behind Theo's shoulder.

Theo whirled.

There, in the distance, standing predator-still in the trees: the creature. Deathly pale and spindly, even taller than Hawthorn's towering bulk. Its wings were pulled tight against its back. Its black eyes drilled into Theo, and something resonated deep in Theo's bones. Knowledge. Belonging. *I am his.*

The creature blinked. Then, before anyone else could register where Kade and Theo were looking, it took off, blurring into the trees.

Rage bloomed in Theo like someone had dropped a match in a pot of gasoline. Theo took off after it—not blurring, but still too fast. Scarily fast, judging by the shocked gasps he heard as he ripped past his classmates, Felicity among them.

Further behind them, Kade swore again. His limping shuffle resumed.

Theo could still hear Kade's unsteady heartbeat. He blocked it out, forcing himself faster as he got further into the trees. Nobody could see him now. He could run as fast as he wanted. The creature wasn't too far ahead. Theo caught glimpses between the trees, bone-white in a sea of bark and dying leaves.

Then, suddenly, it was gone. Theo couldn't tell where it went.

He stumbled to a stop, growling.

"COME ON," he screamed. He didn't know if they'd traveled far enough to hear him back at the bonfire, and he didn't care. He bared his teeth, yelling louder. "COME AND GET ME! THAT'S WHAT YOU WANT, RIGHT? WANT TO USE ME FOR

YOUR CREEPY RITUAL SHIT? GET CYTH BACK? COME ON, I'M RIGHT HERE!"

A flash of white off to his left. Theo took off. They were heading to the cliffs near his house. Theo could smell the lake water, tepid and still.

They sped past the tree line. Finally, the creature came to a stop and turned to face him. They were at the edge of the cliffs. Behind them sat the lake he'd died in, and just next to them, his house. It was dark and silent.

Theo braced himself, waiting for the inevitable attack.

It didn't come. The creature stood there, staring at him. Its eyes were so shiny Theo could see himself in them, crouched and snarling.

Theo growled again. "Why won't you attack?"

The creature cocked its head again. Not listening this time, just...curious. Its mouth opened, huge and filled with long teeth that had ripped Victor's face off.

"I wanted to see what you would do," it said. Its voice was just like Theo remembered: thick and distorted, sending shivers down his spine.

Theo screamed. "I'm gonna KILL you!"

The creature didn't respond. Its wings cracked open, huge and horrifying, blocking out the moon.

Theo surged forward, but it was too late: the creature leapt off the cliff, wings flaring. He flew into the night. Theo stumbled to a stop at the cliff's edge.

He howled. He picked up a rock and threw it with all the strength it could muster. It sailed harmlessly over the lake and hit a faraway tree on the other side, snapping off a branch under the impact.

A light turned on inside his house. Theo froze. If he focused hard, he could hear his mother coming down the stairs.

Theo thought about going to her. About collapsing into her arms, finally crying the tears he'd been pushing back for days. Asking her how that meal went.

Then he turned around and ran back into the forest.

It didn't take him long to find Kade. Theo had barely been running for thirty seconds when his heartbeat came back into range.

"Oh good," Kade panted when Theo emerged through the trees. "You're not dead. Or any more dead than usual. What happened?"

"Nothing," Theo said, the word coming out more brutal than he'd like. "It just—it wanted to see what I would do."

He sucked in a breath, tasting dirt and dead leaves and Kade's blood rushing hard underneath his skin. Kade's heartbeat was racing too fast for it to be a comfort right now.

He ground his teeth together. "Dammit. *Goddammit!*"

"We're fine," Kade croaked. "Hey. We're good. No fighting is good."

Kade leaned against a tree, taking the weight off his

left leg. He'd definitely injured it. Theo could smell the ankle swelling under his boot, fluid rushing to the injury. He had scratches on his arms, too, bright red where the branches caught him.

Theo looked around. They weren't that close to Felicity's bonfire. Theo had expected Kade to turn around after some aimless chasing, but Kade had kept following him into the dark.

"Now that you *finally* stopped," Kade said, and paused to wheeze. He held out his hand. A necklace rested there, small and golden.

Theo's stomach sunk in recognition. "Was this in Liss's room?"

"Yeeeeep." Kade straightened up against the tree, then groaned when the movement jarred his ankle. "Shit."

Theo pressed his teeth together hard enough to hurt. He needed to learn how to sprout wings so he could track that murderous bastard down and rip his head off. He wanted to check the funeral home to see if his dad had been stolen yet. He needed to stop feeling like a failure, disappointing his parents no matter what he did. He needed to charge back to Felicity and shove the necklace in her face and finally demand some answers, even if she really was as confused as she claimed. He needed—

Kade made a soft noise through his teeth.

Theo sighed. "Sit down. Jesus. What did you do?"

Kade slid down the tree and landed on his butt, wincing.

"Tripped on the stairs. Think I sprained it." He unzipped his knee-high boot and eased it off carefully. They both grimaced at his ankle. It was tender and an angry red, already twice the size it should've been.

"You definitely did *something*," Theo scolded. He reached out, then realized his hands were shaking. When did that happen? He clenched them into fists, willing himself to calm down. He wasn't chasing anything, wasn't gearing up for a fight. He was just sitting here in the dark with Kade, trying to heal his ankle.

Kade groaned through his teeth. His head was tipped back, eyes squeezed shut in pain.

"Easy," Theo told him. His hand hovered over Kade's foot. "Ready?"

Kade nodded.

Theo pressed down.

Kade yelped as his flesh sizzled.

"I know," Theo said, already concentrating. The burn faded. Something cracked into place inside Kade's leg, and Kade hollered again.

"I know," Theo repeated. He pressed harder, the burn creeping back and then fading away again. The swelling shrank until it was Kade's ankle once more, thin and pale and whole.

Theo let go, suddenly exhausted. He wanted to go home, but home would just remind him of all the shit he was going through. Mostly, he wanted to sleep. *Really* sleep, check out of the world for a while.

"Alright," Kade wheezed. He wiped sweat off his forehead, wiping it onto his peach-fuzz scalp. "Back to the party? You gonna grill Liss, or do you want me to do it? She does wanna *get to know me better.*'"

The idea of going back to the party made Theo want to scream and punch something. Or cry. Probably both. He blinked back an infuriating swell of heat gathering behind his eyes.

"Fine," he said, and stood. He offered a hand before he remembered they couldn't do that. He took Kade's shirt instead, hauling him up until they were face to face.

Kade stared at him, eyes wide. His cheeks were pink.

Theo's mouth watered.

He let go of Kade's shirt.

CHAPTER
TWELVE

THE FIRE WAS SMOLDERING when they got back to the clearing. People were drifting back toward the house, shooting nervous glances into the trees and at the few who were drunk enough to stay out there.

Felicity was passed out against a tree. A puddle of vomit lay next to her.

Kade sighed. "Classic Felicity party."

Theo nodded, stomping out the last of the embers from the fire. He was usually gone by this point in the night but would hear the stories. Aaron always tried to keep them to a minimum, viciously tearing down anyone he caught spreading gossip, but they leaked through anyway.

Kade reached out with his boot, dragging Felicity's skirt down where it was riding up. "What next? You take the legs, I take her arms?"

Theo bent down and hoisted her over his shoulder,

gratified when he heard her let out a queasy grumble. He was pissed off and more than a little betrayed that she hadn't told him about the hunter shit, but he wasn't about to leave her unconscious in the woods.

"Or we can do that," Kade said, falling into step beside him.

Theo gave his classmates a cautious look. There were only a few of them, and far enough away none of them had noticed Theo yet.

He gestured for Kade to leave. "Meet me at the car."

Kade snorted. He pulled a cigarette carton out of his pocket and lit up.

"Right," he said sourly. "Still pretending like we don't know each other. Even though a *lot* of people just saw me chase you through the woods, which nobody will think is suspicious at *all*."

"Just..." Theo turned, wincing when he almost slung Felicity's legs into Kade's face. "Sorry. Look, I parked down the street. Go stand by the Lexus and smoke."

Kade groaned loudly enough that Theo glanced worriedly at their classmates, who were busy trying and failing to climb trees.

"Got it," Kade said flatly. He turned and headed toward the edge of the forest. Theo watched him go, keeping his eyes on Kade until he reached the path that led out onto the street. Right at the last second, he spotted Kade dig a bottle out of his jacket and take a sip.

. . .

Theo had to fight the urge to speed up the stairs to Felicity's room. Everyone who noticed Theo gave him a sympathetic nod or quickly pretended not to see him, all the while whispering to their friends about how Theo was at Felicity's party the week his dad died, wasn't that *weird?*

Theo placed Felicity face down on her bed. Theo had read about rock stars drowning in their own vomit from sleeping on their back while drunk. He didn't know if Felicity was drunk enough for that, but he wasn't taking any chances.

Felicity nuzzled into her pillow, smearing makeup into the material. She mumbled something unintelligible, then she started snoring.

Theo took out the sun necklace Kade had given him. He pressed his thumb into one of its sharp points, wondering about all the secrets she'd kept from him. She'd always been so squirrely about personal stuff, even when they were growing up.

"You're going to be so hungover tomorrow," Theo whispered.

He dropped the necklace on her nightstand with the other discarded jewelry she hadn't gotten around to putting away: a dangly pair of earrings, a beaded bracelet, and—surprisingly—a mood ring. It was one of three matching rings that she, Aaron, and Theo got during a school trip. Felicity was the only one who could pull off wearing it in public, but Theo hadn't seen her wear it in years. He'd assumed she'd lost it.

He touched it. The ring stayed default green. He imagined Kade telling him to put it on so they could see if it would react to his cold, dead skin. Kade could probably wear a mood ring, Theo considered as he stroked it. He could make it work.

A throat cleared behind him.

Theo whirled around to find Mrs. Beverly Sloan standing in the doorway in a pair of silk pajamas. She looked shockingly old, and Theo realized he hadn't seen her without makeup in years. He hadn't had a sleepover here since middle school.

"Another stunning end to a Sloan house party," Beverly said, tucking her black hair behind her ears. She had none of her daughter's fair features, but all of her sharpness: razor chin and blade cheekbones, her dark brown eyes just as sharp and keen as her daughter's blue ones.

"I'll take care of her," she continued. "You can go."

Theo stepped in front of the nightstand, all too conscious of the hunter necklace mixed in with the others. If she thought he'd seen it...

"I'm surprised you gave her the night off," Theo said, keeping his voice casual as she strode up to the bed. "She says you've been pretty intense about practice."

"Yes," Beverly said, rearranging her daughter's head gently on the pillow. "Well. It's been...a strange week. I thought she deserved a break."

Then she smiled, strained. She had a very perfunctory smile, one that let you know she'd stop doing it the second you looked away.

"Are you having a good night? Not stressful, I mean. Obviously it isn't a good night. For you."

Theo blinked. This was the most flustered he'd ever seen her. He waited for some hint of threat, a thinly veiled accusation like Aaron's parents had been getting bolder with over the summer. She had to *know*. Right? The Fletchers knew, they'd tell her.

But Beverly just looked...awkward. Like she wanted to get her daughter a bucket and go to bed with the industrial-strength ear plugs she always wore when her daughter hosted a house party. Maybe she, like Cheech, wasn't all in on the Let's Put Theo Down Before He Brings About The Destruction Of The Town train.

"Right," Beverly said as the silence stretched. "Of course. Well, I'll see you tomorrow."

"Right," Theo echoed, heart growing heavy even thinking of it.

He gave Felicity one last look. Then he left, ignoring the bitter betrayal swelling in his chest, ignoring his classmates' averted eyes and barbed whispers, ignoring everything except the soft metallic scent of Kade growing ever closer.

Kade was still drinking when Theo got to the Lexus.

"Liss said not to take anything from the drinks table," Theo reminded him as he pulled into the street.

"Not from the drinks table," Kade replied, taking a swig. "It was from her room."

"Great," Theo muttered. "Much better."

Kade shifted lower in the backseat. He was lying in the footwell this time. It would be pretty impossible to drink while he was hunched over like he usually was.

Kade asked, "How was Liss?"

"Fine," Theo said curtly. "Her mom's taking care of her."

"Is she safe?"

Theo frowned. "What do you mean?"

Kade waved the bottle at him. "In general."

"Sure. Why wouldn't she be?"

"I don't know. Her mom sounds like a bitch." For a moment it sounded like Kade was going to say something else. Then he took another swig.

Theo cruised down the road, waiting for Kade to put the bottle back in his jacket. But Kade kept drinking: large, grimacing sips, mouth twisting in disgust after every pull.

By the time they pulled into Sundance's driveway, half the contents of the plastic bottle had vanished down Kade's throat. Theo didn't know how significant that was—he'd stayed away from spirits even when he could drink them—but he knew it wasn't good.

"Slow down," Theo said as he followed Kade down the driveway. "What are you trying to do, make yourself puke? You're going to bed soon, there's no point anyway."

"I've had a very stressful night," Kade replied.

They reached the front door, the automatic porch light flickering to life above their heads. Kade fumbled for his keys, then swore as he upended the bottle. Vodka spilled down his crop top, soaking into his tight skirt.

"Shit," he whispered, pawing at his skirt one-handed. "Hold this."

He handed the bottle over. Theo was so distracted by the suffocating stench of liquor he didn't hear the footsteps until it was too late.

"Kade..."

The door opened. Sundance squinted out at them. Her arm was out of its sling but still wrapped in the cast, held gingerly against her rumpled sleep shirt.

Kade waved with his vodka-soaked hand. "Hiiii, Auntie."

She sniffed him and wrinkled her nose. "You stink. What did you do, roll in it?"

"Pretty much." Kade burped. "Excuse *moi*."

Sundance stared at him, face firm. She had that look that adults sometimes got when they were deeply disappointed but didn't want it to show. Even a hint of it made Theo's stomach clench in panic.

Then she turned the look on him, and Theo had to fight a flinch.

Sundance's eyes softened. "Sorry about this. Last thing you need right now."

"It's fine," Theo said hastily, praying she wouldn't say

she was sorry about his dad. She hadn't this morning, and he'd been so grateful for it.

"I didn't get in a fight," Kade declared.

"Great job," Sundance said dryly.

She stepped aside. Kade lurched in, unsteady on his feet. Theo wondered how much he'd eaten today. He ate like a bird, even on good days. He watched Kade wander to the sink and turn on the faucet, then dip his head to drink directly from it.

Sundance sighed. "I'll get him to bed. You go home, get some sleep."

Theo ached with how much he wanted to go to sleep.

"I got him," he said instead.

Sundance paused. She'd been about to close the door. "What?"

"I'll do it," Theo said. He took a step inside, pulling his shoulders in to make himself smaller. "You go back to bed. I'll take care of him. It's kind of my thing tonight."

Kade pulled back from the faucet and stared, water dripping down his chin. His eyes were wide again, and so very dark.

Theo swallowed. Sundance was still eyeing him, like she was turning something over in her head. Did she think Theo would crawl into bed after Kade? Did she know he hadn't slept on the couch last night, like he'd told her? She'd caught him creeping out of Kade's room at three a.m. When he'd frozen guiltily, Sundance had just given him a nod and walked past him to the bath-room. Theo didn't know what to say. *I was watching your nephew as he slept, like a creep. I like listening to his heartbeat. I'm a great big vampire cliché, and now I'm going to go eat fluffy animals in the woods behind your house.*

Sundance yawned. "Make sure he drinks enough water."

"What does it look like I'm doing?" Kade said, a beat too late. The faucet was still running. He ducked down toward it, taking long, deep pulls.

While Kade got changed, Theo waited in the hall, digging his fingers into his palms and remembering the sharp points of Felicity's hidden necklace.

So, the Sloans were hunters. Was Felicity in the dark, like Aaron? Or did she know even more than Theo did? He needed to confront her. Tomorrow, at the funeral.

Kade's bedroom door swung open. His eyeliner was gone, as was his lipstick. He'd changed into boxers and his favorite wear-around-the-house shirt, which had a sentient lasagna eating Garfield. Theo had to stop himself from staring at Kade's skinny legs. He saw them so rarely, especially now they'd taken up the habit of wearing clothes that hid the most amount of skin when-ever they were around each other.

"I'm clean, dry and watered," Kade said, leaning hard into the British side of his accent. "I even ate that bread you gave me. You can leave me to my own devices now."

Theo stepped into his room, sniffing surreptitiously. The vodka was tucked behind his nightstand. The liquid had gone down since he last saw it. Kade had drunk even more while he was getting changed. What was the point? Did he need it to sleep? He didn't need it last night. At least there were fresh crumbs on Kade's shirt, so he wasn't lying about the bread.

"Theo," Kade said, back to his normal amount of British. "Seriously, man. I don't need a babysitter, I'm not Liss levels of trashed. You can go."

Theo thought about going back to that dark, silent house. He shook his head. "You said I needed to do something that wasn't my vengeance quest, right? Here I am. Doing something else."

He gestured toward the bed.

Kade's heartbeat sped up. It took Theo an exhausted second to realize the implications of what he just said.

"Making sure you get to bed okay," Theo said in a rush. "Obviously."

Kade nodded. He was blushing again, bright red spots on his cheeks that Theo wanted to press his mouth against.

Theo waited for Kade to make some smart comment, or argue to stay up longer. But he just walked straight to bed and climbed in, no theatrics required.

"You look like shit," he told Theo as he settled under the sheets.

"I'm fine," Theo said quietly.

Kade sighed. "Bone's a lot harder to heal than skin, huh?"

Theo didn't reply. Kade scooted to the side, patting the empty space he'd left on the mattress.

"Come on," he said. "Feeding time. We're coming up to it anyway."

He sat up and shuffled his sleep shirt down his shoulder, exposing his pale neck.

Theo swayed toward him automatically, catching himself before he could sit down on the bed.

"You're drunk."

"Yeah, it's really hitting." Kade tapped the base of his neck, right next to the mole that Theo often pressed his tongue into while he bit. "Think you'll get a buzz?"

Theo glared at him halfheartedly. He was so, so tired. And he couldn't sleep. Not ever again. He could get energy, sure. He could drink Kade and be up again, keep moving forward. But Theo didn't want to move forward right now. He wanted to lie down and hit pause. Be dead to the world for eight hours, no cares, no worries, no deadlines counting down to his inevitable doom. Just...go away for a while.

Biting Kade was the closest thing he had to that now.

"Come on. I'll drink so much water." Kade's voice softened. "Seriously. You have to be okay for the funeral. It'll suck way more if you're already feeling like shit. Trust me."

Theo thought about asking Kade what his mum's funeral was like. But Kade was wasted, and he didn't want him to say anything he would regret the next day.

Theo hesitated. "You should come."

Kade blinked. Theo watched his brain catch up.

"You sure?"

"I want you there," Theo admitted.

Kade put his thumbnail in his mouth, gnawing worriedly. The nail beds were red and raw, and Theo tensed, waiting for blood.

It didn't come. Kade dropped his hand into his lap.

"Okay," he said, very quietly.

Theo nodded, surprised by the intensity of relief that rushed through him.

Kade yawned, reaching up to scratch his forehead. He missed, palm skating over his forehead before fumbling back down to his eyebrow.

Theo snorted. "Are you even going to remember this conversation tomorrow?"

"I'll set an alarm," Kade said. He grabbed his phone off the nightstand and started typing. He turned it toward Theo, showing him an alarm set for 8.30 a.m.: PUT THE FUN IN FUNERAL.

Kade put the phone down. "Bite me, blood boy."

I like it better when you call me sunshine, Theo thought.

Then he leaned in and sunk his teeth into Kade's neck.

Blood flooded his mouth. It tasted different than usual. But the sour, metallic note from the vodka wasn't nearly enough to drown out the addictive taste Theo had grown to crave so badly.

He sucked hard, pulling Kade closer by his Garfield shirt. Sometimes he wrapped an arm around Kade's back, but he couldn't do that with both of Kade's arms exposed. Too risky.

Kade relaxed against him with a happy sigh. Theo heard it like it was coming from the other end of a long tunnel. It was hard to hear anything over the pleased thump of Kade's heartbeat, the blood rushing from Kade's veins into his waiting mouth.

He pressed his tongue to the mole on Kade's neck. It blistered under his touch.

Theo pulled back, smoothing his thumb over the burns and the puncture wounds until they sunk back into Kade's skin. Then he lowered Kade back against the bedframe by his shirt.

Kade smiled up at him as the endorphin high faded. "Are you buzzed?"

Theo shook his head. He wasn't any more buzzed than he usually was after biting Kade, and the sour taste of secondhand vodka was already gone.

"Tragic," Kade muttered. His eyelids fluttered.

Theo stood.

Kade caught his sleeve.

"I'm just going to get you some water," Theo said. "Then I'll go."

Kade didn't respond. His fingers were tight in Theo's sleeve, rubbing the material with a strange expression. Theo couldn't tell if he was mentally cataloging it for one of his projects or something else entirely.

"After my mum died," Kade said, "I dove into whatever distraction I could find. You know? Video games, crafts, music, books. Then drinking. Fighting. You run as fast as you can, but the pain always catches up. Better to have someone with you when it does."

He dropped Theo's sleeve. He suddenly looked very small in the blankets, eyes on his own lap as he talked.

"Look," Kade continued, worrying at his hands. "I'm not a good example of moving past shit. But I'm a great example of what not to do. I'm the ghost of Christmas future. *Don't ignore your feelings, Theo! Or you'll end up sad and alone!*"

Theo thought back to Kade in middle school, sitting alone in the cafeteria. About Kade last week, still alone in the cafeteria. That shirt he'd uncovered in Kade's drawers, that wonky red stitching spelling out *I AM SO FUCKING LONELY*. Sundance admitting they didn't have a lot of visitors, making sure not to look at Kade as she said it.

Theo asked, "Are you sad?"

"Not as much as I used to be," Kade said, sounding surprised. But there was still that terrible vulnerability in his eyes, like he hated himself for admitting any of this. Like he was waiting for Theo to sneer at him.

"You're not alone," Theo tried. "Like you said. I'm...
I'm with you. I know I've been...I'm kind of a dick right
now—"

Kade laughed loud enough to startle them both.

"You're *fine*," Kade said. "Jesus, mate. It hasn't even
been a *week*. You're smack dab in the deep. Can't even
see the surface where you are."

Theo was struck with an image of himself in an
ocean so dark he couldn't even see where it ended. The
idea made him so tired he wanted to cry, again, which
made him angry, again. Mostly at himself.

"See you at the funeral," he said, and stood.

Kade was asleep when he came back with a glass of
water. Theo set it on his nightstand, plugged his phone
into the charger. Then he rolled Kade gently over onto
his stomach, in case of sleep vomit.

He stood there for a minute longer, watching Kade
breathe. He didn't know why his parents always made it
sound like such a chore, taking care of Theo when he
was a kid. Always rolling their eyes when he wanted to
be tucked in or telling him to make his own soup when
he got sick. Even when Theo was angry and tired and
wanted to cry, it was nice to take care of someone.

Kade shifted in his sleep. The sheet fell down his
shoulders.

Theo pulled it back up. Careful, as always, not to
touch Kade's skin.

CHAPTER
THIRTEEN

KADE WOKE UP FORGETTING SOMETHING.

The dream was already gone. He barely registered the emotions attached to the dream before they slipped away, violent stabs of grief and anger draining from him as he woke.

Must've been a bad memory, Kade thought. *RIP, my dude.*

Then the headache hit. No dreams or memories required, just Kade's pounding skull and dry mouth and stupid decisions. There was a moment of reprieve—his hangover wasn't too bad—then dread as he realized that was because he was still drunk. It made the hangover easier now, but there would be hell to pay later.

He groaned, reaching for his nightstand to check his phone...

And immediately knocked over a glass of water.

Kade sat up, watching it seep into the carpet. Who set out a glass of water for him? When Kade took water into his room, he made sure it was in a bottle to avoid mistakes just like this. *Especially* if it was hangover water, which this seemed like.

What happened last night? Kade rubbed his muzzy eyes. He'd gone to Felicity's party with Theo. Stolen a bottle of vodka from her bookshelf. Found the hunter necklace confirming that the Sloans were going to be a problem. Snapped his ankle on Felicity's stairs. Limp-chased Theo into the woods. Saw Theo's sire. Limp-chased Theo through the woods some more, completely wrecking his ankle. Found Theo. Theo healed his ankle...

After that, things got fuzzy. He remembered drinking in the car, Theo telling him to cool it every time Kade took a swig. He sort of remembered drinking straight from the sink. Then...what? He'd gone to bed? He had the vaguest flash of Theo sitting on his bed, talking about something Kade couldn't remember. Oh god, had Theo babysat him while he was drunk?

He stared down at the empty glass. The water was sinking in, and he didn't need yet another stain in his carpet.

He pulled himself out of bed, then stopped. What day was it? Was it a school day? He checked his phone. Friday. Shit. He had to be at school in an hour.

Something niggled at the back of his mind. He was forgetting something important.

He tugged on a pair of sweatpants and stumbled to the kitchen. First, he'd clean up his latest mess. Then he'd shower. *Then* he'd figure out what he was forgetting. Maybe text Theo asking if they'd come up with a new plan last night. That sounded like something Theo would do—except his head hadn't exactly been in the revenge game after he'd come back from chasing his sire. Kade had expected him to be frothing at the mouth, but instead he'd just been...sad. Angry, sure, and very lost. But not all-engines-go like he'd been the past couple of days, charging ahead without stopping. Which was good. Right? It meant Theo finally took a break. For a few hours, anyway. Kade hoped he'd helped. He doubted it—babysitting a drunk idiot didn't sound like much of a break. But he hoped he'd said something useful, or made Theo laugh, or found some way to make Theo's shoulders unclench while he was blackout wasted.

He bent down to open the rag drawer in the kitchen and immediately regretted it. His vision tunneled, his stomach rolling into his throat.

"Oh *shit*," he gasped, lurching back up.

"Having a nice morning?"

Kade turned. Sundance was peering into the fridge, her back toward him. She was wearing real-people clothes, which was a good sign. She'd been bumming around in PJs since she hurt her arm. She was even wearing her best belt, the one studded with tiny whales that Kade had got for her birthday a few years ago.

Kade forced a thin smile. "Having a *great* morning, Auntie. How's yours going?"

"Great," she said, desert-dry. She still didn't look at him.

Kade's heart sank. He didn't remember seeing her when he came home last night, but he had significant gaps in his memory. Maybe she gave him a whole lecture and he forgot. Probably not, though. She saved big talks for when he was hungover.

Sundance eased the fridge door shut and turned to him, holding a bottle of cream in her good hand. She liked to drink it straight out of the bottle.

"Theo practically had to carry you in last night," she said flatly. She took a sip of cream.

Kade thought about telling her she had a cream mustache. She didn't, but sometimes that made her laugh.

"Better him than the cops," he said, trying to sound like he wasn't still drunk. His voice was hoarse, he smelled like sweat and vodka and, for some reason, smoke. He didn't remember smoking last night, but— wait, no. The bonfire. The deeply irresponsible bonfire in the middle of a forest during fall. Theo had gotten adorably indignant about it on the way home.

Kade gave her his best 'aw shucks' smile. She stared back with a weariness that he would always hate himself for putting there. She was tired before she got stuck with him, sure. But that was job tiredness, life tiredness, the tiredness of being an adult. Not the bone-deep exhaustion of taking care of a kid who seemed deter-mined to screw over all your efforts to turn him into a decent human being.

"Sure," Sundance said with a sigh. "Always glad I don't have to shell out another eight hundred bucks for property damage to those neighbors who *still* don't wave back at us when we put the bins out. Jackasses."

She slurped her cream. They were running low. Maybe Kade could grab some on the way home from school today as an apology. One of the endless apologies he owed her for putting up with his shit for all these years.

"I really..." She paused, looking down. That was how Kade knew this talk was going to be brutal. She always looked him in the eyes when she spoke to him.

"I really thought you were getting better lately," she admitted.

Kade's stomach rolled. "I am! I *am* getting better. My grades are up. I know it's only the start of the year, but no one's threatened to expel me in weeks! Teachers are pulling me aside after class to ask if I'm cheating, *that's* how good I'm doing!"

"What are those?" She pointed at his arms. "You said you didn't get into a fight!"

Kade tugged his sleeve down, like his Garfield T-shirt could even *start* to cover all the scabbing cuts.

Her jaw flexed. "Did you—?"

"I didn't hurt myself," Kade said, rushed. "*God*, Sundance. I don't...I don't do that anymore. I promise. I ran through the woods and got torn up. You can ask Theo."

Sundance looked him up and down. Trying to tell if he was lying. Kade hated that. More than that, he hated that she was right to do it. Kade couldn't be trusted with most things, especially not with his own wellbeing.

Whatever she saw, it made her sigh. She slugged the rest of the cream and tucked her thumbs through her belt loops, rubbing the leather distractedly. It was an anxious tic, but with the whale belt it made it look like she was petting a whale. It was one of the reasons Kade brought it in the first place.

"You said I wouldn't have to see you like that again," Sundance said, voice low and serious.

Kade nodded, the movement making his head swim. "I know. I'm sorry."

"Your dad was sorry too."

The kitchen fell silent. Nobody moved.

Kade thought, bizarrely, of the water soaking into his carpet right now. A water stain on a pile of water stains from all the glasses he'd knocked off his night-stand over the years. Stains on top of stains on top of stains, just like his entire family tree, which Sundance had always said—always *promised*—he could free himself from. That he wasn't doomed.

"Wait," Sundance said. "I didn't mean that."

But Kade was already moving. Not toward his room, to clean up what he could from the carpet. But toward the door.

"Kade," Sundance tried.

He shook his head. "I'm going for a walk."

She started to move like she was going to put herself in front of him. Like he was so bad he couldn't even go on a walk without needing supervision.

"I'm fine," he whispered. "I promise. I'm just going on a walk."

Then he barreled out the door, feet still bare, no phone, not even his headphones. Just him and his sentient-lasagna-eating-Garfield-shirt, his sweatpants, and his spinning head. He considered sneaking in his bedroom window to grab the rest of his vodka—he was still drunk, why not keep it going—then thought about Sundance catching him and kept walking until he reached the woods.

His mind reeled. She'd finally said it. She'd sworn she never would, but she'd basically told him he was doomed to the same swirling-drain life his family had been living for generations: addiction, divorce, assault charges, prison, an early death from something stupid and preventable. Sundance had promised him otherwise, but he'd known, deep down, that she knew. She knew the same way *he* knew that he was never getting a happy ending.

He walked deeper into the woods, eyes burning, hands shaking. Dead leaves crunched under his feet. A twig cut into his toe. He swore, shaking the blood off.

He should've brought shoes. Music. The goddamn *vodka*. Some days you woke up and everything went to shit before you even had time to brush your teeth, and on those days he wanted to do something really destructive. Get into a fight. Day-drink and trash the sewing machine he spent months saving for. Screw school. Everybody expected him to ditch anyway, what was one more day? Kade was destined to spend his life alone in his room, working on his dumb little projects nobody cared about and destroying everything around him until he got annihilated in the crossfire. He knew it, his aunt knew it, most of Lock knew it by now.

Even Theo knew it. He told Kade he wasn't doomed, but that was only because Theo didn't want to be the one to doom him.

Kade arrived back at the house twenty minutes later. Sundance was gone and his alarm was going off.

Kade sighed and slumped toward his room. He'd turn the alarm off, then find his vodka. Text Theo he was going off the grid and to not antagonize any sires until he got back.

Something niggled again at the back of his mind as he pushed his bedroom door open. He tried to focus on it, but the alarm was making his head throb.

He reached for his phone to tap the alarm off.

Then he stopped. This wasn't his school alarm.

"*Put the fun back in funeral,*" he read. "What the hell?"

He stood there in drunk silence. Then it hit him, and he yelled.

Friday. The funeral. Had Theo invited him? He must've, if there was an alarm in Kade's phone he didn't remember putting there.

He strained, sifting through the previous night's memories. Theo on his bed. Theo biting him. Theo asking Kade if he was sad. Why the hell would he ask that? What did they talk about last night?

Kade ran through every room in the house, yelling. "Sundance! Aunt Sundance, I screwed up! I need the car!"

No answer. Kade called her. Her phone vibrated on the couch. She never took it with her on walks.

Kade screamed at the ceiling. He wasn't allowed to drive without a licensed driver in the car. He *definitely* wasn't allowed to drive drunk.

He ran to the bathroom mirror and sucked in a breath.

"Okay," he told his reflection. "How to deal with this like a non-idiot-screwup."

He could wait for Sundance to come home, then get her to drive him. He sighed and shook his head. He'd be waiting ages if it was one of her long walks. If he ran to the graveyard it would take an hour.

"Let's be real," he eyed his reflection. "Two hours. You can't run for shit."

He grabbed his phone and hovered his thumb over the Uber app. Maybe their shitty town's one Uber driver wouldn't be busy or asleep right now.

"Wait, shit," He realized. "That guy moved. *Shit*!"

His reflection stared back at him, haggard and sweaty. All his options ended the same way: Kade jogging up after the wake was finished, full of useless apologies.

Except one.

"Option three. Steal Sundance's car."

A memory flooded back: Theo sitting on his bed, his face soft and miserable in the dark.

I want you there, he'd said.

Kade ran for his keys.

FOURTEEN

IT WAS a beautiful morning in the graveyard.

Gentle sun on Theo's suit-clad back, cool autumn breeze ruffling his artfully tousled hair. He'd forgotten to brush it before he left. His mom'd had to fix it in the car.

"Sorry," he kept saying as she brushed.

She just shook her head, eyes on his curls. Her own curls were perfect as always. She'd stayed up late undoing and redoing her curlers. Theo had heard her cursing when he'd snuck home after Kade's house.

And here they were. Burial first, then the wake. Theo and his mom stood at the mouth of the grave, the coffin held in place by a pulley, waiting to be lowered.

There was a joke in this somewhere about dead boys and coffins, Theo thought as he stared at the polished wood. He just couldn't think of it. If Kade were here—

He squeezed his nails into his palms. If Kade were

here, he would be standing awkwardly at the back of the crowd while everybody came up to him and his mom and told him how *sorry* they were. Maybe Kade would mutter things under his breath, knowing Theo would hear it. He would try to make Theo laugh, and everybody would stare at Theo giggling at his own father's funeral. Theo could imagine Aaron's parents trading a concerned look, Felicity and Aaron glancing at each other automatically before remembering they didn't do that anymore.

But Kade wasn't here. So that didn't matter. Theo wondered if he was too hungover to move or if he was just silencing his alarm. Maybe he really had choked on his own vomit in his sleep, but Theo doubted it. He would feel it if Kade died. He was certain. Just like he was certain that he would be really, *really* mad about this later. He could already feel it now, the rage bubbling just under the surface of the suffocating numbness. He was going to give Kade the lighter, finally. He'd been putting it off too long. And Kade couldn't be bothered to show up.

Carol nudged him, bringing him back to the moment. "Have you eaten?"

Theo thought about it. Then he remembered he didn't eat human food. How out of it did he have to be to forget that?

"I'll eat at the wake," he told her.

She nodded. "The catering company is very good."

"Good," he echoed. "That's good."

The funeral director came up behind them. "Well, folks, it's nine. How are you feeling?"

"Fine," said Theo and Carol as one. Theo was gratified to see his mother look just as disgusted at the question as him. Why did everyone keep *asking* that?

"Okeydokey," said the funeral director, whose name Theo had immediately forgotten the second he told it. He had a bad combover and an ill-fitting suit, which enraged Theo for reasons he didn't understand.

"Well," said the funeral director, adjusting his crappy tie. "We're ready whenever you want to start."

"Just a few more minutes," Theo said.

They both looked at him. Theo pretended not to notice, looking toward the street for Sundance's car. Maybe he should've told her to get him here. But then she'd want to come, too, and she might look at him all pityingly. She'd been on the verge of it so many times.

Theo turned. The crowd behind him had grown. All his parents' lawyer friends were here, along with a bunch of teachers and what looked like a third of the population of Lock High, most of them pale and hungover.

Aaron's family clumped together, dressed in their finest suits. Aaron's mom had a hand on her son's shoulder. He was stiff and silent under her touch, staring down at his injured hand. He wore gloves, but Theo could see the tell-tale white of a bandage peeking over his wrist.

Felicity stood several feet away from them in a modest dress and giant sunglasses,

sweating through her makeup and wincing as her mom leaned over to whisper something in her ear. Felicity nodded, looking annoyed, and Beverly set off toward the parking lot.

Theo swallowed. He needed to stop this numbness. He needed to get mad. Anger was productive. *Be vicious* —the Fairgood motto. It was time to deliver. He just needed something to jolt him out of it.

He turned back to the coffin.

"I want to see him," he said.

The funeral director stared at him. "Excuse me?"

"I have to see him," Theo said.

The funeral director looked between Theo and Carol, twisting his sweaty hands together.

"It might be a good idea to stick with the memory of him," he said. Then, when Theo didn't look deterred: "Just...he's...well. He's quite torn up, buddy."

Theo wanted to shove him. Wanted to punch every adult who had called him a nickname in the past few days, like that would make everything better. Like they knew what he was *feeling*.

There we go, he thought as the anger started pushing past the numbness. *That's what I need.*

He turned to his mom. "I'm sorry. I'm...I need to. Just for a second. Don't look."

She stared at him, her lips parted. She wasn't wearing lipstick. In all her preparation this morning—

pulling the curlers out, doing her lashes, moisturizer, foundation, concealer—somehow she'd forgotten. Theo had thought there was something off, but he hadn't been able to figure out what until now.

"Just for a second," he repeated, and stepped forward. The coffin was closed, but it was easy enough to find the latches and pop them open. The lid followed—just a crack, since Theo could already hear the murmurs starting up from the crowd behind them.

His dad's hands sat folded on his chest. Even though it was a closed-casket funeral, they'd still put him in a suit. The fingers which had been hanging off by a thread had been stitched back on. His face was still the brutal-ized pink mess that Theo remembered: exposed teeth, empty eye sockets, the skin even stiffer and paler than last time. Theo stared at the remaining tufts of blond hair on his dad's ravaged skull and felt it: rage, blinding and pure.

Be vicious, he imagined his dad saying.

He slammed the lid shut and stormed into the crowd. His mom said something behind him, but Theo didn't hear it over the thrum of heartbeats getting faster. He approached Felicity, who was still watching her mom jog toward the parking lot.

"Hey," Theo barked.

Felicity turned and gave him a strained smile.

"Hey," she said, her voice so syrupy and sympathetic Theo could choke on it. She stunk of mint and flowers and burned hair.

He grabbed her arm and hauled her away, out of earshot of the others.

"Uhhh," Aaron said behind them. "You guys all good?"

"I'll get to you," Theo called over his shoulder. He turned to Felicity, whose smile had gotten wide and panicked when he grabbed her. "You want me to tell you what's going on? You first."

Felicity blinked rapidly behind her sunglasses. From shock, sure. But also because the sun was hitting her right in the eyes, and sunglasses only did so much when you had a hangover as violent as hers.

"Could you move an inch to the left?" she asked Theo as he dragged her. "You're big, you can block the light."

Theo whirled to face her. "I said *cut the shit*. People are dying."

Felicity stared, lips pressed together. Then she twisted to look at the parking lot, where her mom was rummaging in the car.

"We need to do this fast," she said. "She'll freak if she thinks I'm talking to you about whatever the hell is going on. So what is it? Is it a doomsday cult? Are we culting? Mom keeps having whisper fights with the Fletchers and they all *freak* when I try to listen in, and she's been upping my training."

"Training," Theo repeated. Finally, it clicked. "Wait. The gymnastics—it's not actually gymnastics, is it? Not all of it. It's *hunting* training."

A desperate grin bloomed over her face. She grabbed his elbows, squeezing hard.

"I *knew* it. We're hunting vampires, aren't we? *That's* what she's training me for. That shit about the founders of Lock, it's true. Right?"

Theo stared at her, the death grip she had on his elbows, her eyes bright and wild. She didn't look like she was baiting him into saying something incriminating. She looked like a deeply stressed teenager who had been keeping secrets for a long time and wanted an explanation.

Felicity smacked his arms excitedly. "*God.* Shit, it's so good finally talking to you about this. I don't care if she takes away my college fund, this is worth it."

"You really don't know?"

"No," she hissed. She shot another furtive look over her shoulder at the parking lot, where her mom was still going through the backseat. "Thank god she left her water in the car. Quick, keep talking."

Theo opened his mouth. Closed it. The Fletchers were watching them, Aaron trying to talk to his parents while they pretended not to stare daggers in Theo's direction.

"Vampires *are* real," Theo said. He hesitated. Looked into her blue eyes, his first ever friend in the world, first kiss when they were in middle school, first foray into sex when they were tipsy and bored a few months before she and Aaron started dating. The first person who ever kept a secret for him in first grade after he broke a vase in his parents' house. They still made him clean it up, pricking his tiny fingers on the shards—but only after Felicity insisted with deep sincerity that it wasn't Theo, it was a giant bird that immediately vanished out the open window.

Theo sucked in a breath. "I'm a vampire."

"Oh shit." Felicity's smile dimmed. She looked past him, toward the coffin. "Did your dad—?"

"*I didn't kill my dad*," Theo snapped.

Felicity scoffed. "No shit, I mean did some *other* vampire do it? How many vampires are there? Something's gearing up, right? Something bad?"

"The vampire who sired me did it. He wants me to open up a hole in the ground and free his murderous vampire wife."

Felicity stared at him, eyes tracking. "Holy shit. Holy *shit*. That's what we're trying to stop? This is *insane*. Cheech was in on it, right? That's why Mom made me steal shit from his house?"

"Your mom made you?"

In the parking lot, a car door slammed. Theo looked over and saw Beverly Sloan straighten, then stop dead when she saw who her daughter was talking to.

"Yes," Felicity said. "She said it was stealth training, which I totally failed. She said it was important, but surprise surprise, she didn't tell me why, because she never tells me why we do *anything*. She didn't even let me look inside the box I stole! And oh my *god*—"

"Talk faster," Theo urged. Beverly Sloan was striding

across the grass toward them, her dark eyes steely. A few paces ahead, the Fletchers were sending a confused Aaron in their direction.

Felicity glanced round and cursed. "Shit. Okay, they were all telling me to tell them everything about you, what you've been doing, what you're saying, and *then* Mom was like, don't tell the Fletchers anything! Only me! We don't trust them anymore!"

"Why?"

"I don't know, I think she said they're too extreme? I didn't hear. They get really angry when I try to eavesdrop, and they speak so quietly. Last thing I heard was about your dad. He found something out. They said he was going to tell them who it was."

Theo swallowed hard. Beverly Sloan was getting closer, Aaron ducking out of the way just in time to avoid her charge.

"Said he needed to 'make sure,'" Felicity continued. "Something about small jar—I think. Or tar? Small car? I was behind the door, I couldn't hear much—"

Theo shushed her. Felicity fell silent as her mom charged up and grabbed Felicity's newly muscled arm. There was the woman Theo had been expecting last night, intense and intimidating, dark eyes drilling straight into his.

"I'm so sorry for your loss," said Beverly Sloan with a tight smile. "Felicity, can I talk to you?"

"I would *love* to talk to you, Mom," Felicity said icily.

"We really should talk more. I love it when you tell me things."

Aaron cleared his throat behind them. "Every-thing...okay?"

He flexed his injured hand warily, the leather glove creaking. Theo had never asked if he was okay, he suddenly realized. Hadn't even texted. This was the first time they'd seen each other since the bite.

"We're okay," Theo replied. "Are *you* okay?"

Aaron slipped his bandaged hand into his pocket. There was a strange smell emanating from it: wet mulch. Decaying tree trunks. A fruit going bad.

Rot, Theo realized. It smelled like rot.

"I'm fine," Aaron replied, guarded. He shifted on the spot, like he wasn't entirely sure he was welcome. Theo wondered what it was like, every single person in your life suddenly acting weird and no one telling you why. Peeling off to whisper in corners and then insist every-thing was fine, you were imagining things. Why weren't these hunter parents telling their kids what was going on?

Felicity sighed. "Look," she started, and Theo was consumed by a momentary panic that she would dump everything on Aaron right now, as her mom's hand tightened around her wrist and everyone was waiting for his dad to be lowered into the ground.

"Your dad loved you," Felicity continued.

Theo felt his face tighten back to that neutral

receiver of well-wishes, which was not as polite as he wanted it to be.

"Maybe he wasn't good," Felicity said. "But he did love you. A lot."

"Felicity," Beverly said sharply.

"Liss," Aaron said, voice low. "*Now?*"

Theo blinked. This wasn't where he thought the conversation would go. Behind him, he could hear the funeral director whispering with his mom about schedules.

"He was good," Theo said faintly. "What are you talking about?"

Felicity ripped her arm out of her mom's grip. She glared, then turned to Theo.

"Theo," she said. "Come *on*. The way your parents *push* you. Keeping you awake all night if you get a bad grade. Making you sit in that ice bath until you needed to go to the hospital? *And* they argued about taking you to the hospital. Your lips were *blue*."

"*Felicity*," Beverly repeated, appalled. She stared at Theo in shock. That was good. It meant Felicity had kept her promise. She hadn't told.

"That's not—" Theo shook his head, stomach churning. "That was ages ago. And I deserved it."

He looked back at his mom, standing over his dad's grave. Russel stood next to her, fiddling with the collar of his cheap suit, telling her how sorry he was. Carol nodded along blankly, patting her curls like she was worried they had unfurled since she took them out that morning.

The funeral director was walking over to them, toying with his badly fitting suit. He waved timidly when he saw Theo looking and tapped his watch.

Theo thought very hard about biting him.

"Liss," Aaron whispered. "Come on. It's his *funeral*."

"I *know*," Felicity snapped, whirling on him. "I just wanted—oh, shit."

Her mouth dropped open. Her gaze was trained over Aaron's shoulder, eyebrows raised high over her sunglasses. Her mouth twitched into a small, awful smile that only occurred when something bad was about to happen, and she was going to find a way to laugh at it or die trying.

Theo turned.

Sundance's battered Honda Civic sped down the road toward the cemetery. The car backfired, making everybody turn to see who was making all the commotion right next to a graveyard.

Theo watched, chest filling with a confusing mix of relief and panic. Kade had made it. Late and with a dramatic entrance, but still.

Panic quickly swallowed the relief as Theo realized the car wasn't slowing down. Nor was it on a straight trajectory for the parking lot entrance. It was careening toward the trees that lined the lot. What was Sundance *doing*?

Theo squinted. It wasn't Sundance in the driver's

seat. It was Kade, alone, breaking the rules of his learner license. He was slumped over the steering wheel, sliding sideways, causing the car to veer dangerously to the left.

Theo ran as fast as he dared. He barely made it two steps.

The car slammed into a tree, shuddering to a violent stop. Gasps rang through the crowd. Somebody shrieked.

"Holy SHIT," Felicity said. A terrified laugh escaped her throat, high and razor-sharp. "Who the hell is that?"

Theo knew he should fake ignorance. Keep up the fiction. There were so many people here, and his mom had looked at him with such shock and disappointment when he'd walked into the house with Kade. *Fairgoods don't make friends with trash like that*, she'd told him later that night. *Don't see him again. Okay?*

Carol had her hands over her mouth, Russel clutching her shoulder. She looked around wildly, gaze settling on Theo. She took a step toward him.

Theo hesitated.

Then he turned and ran for Kade.

CHAPTER
FIFTEEN

ONE YEAR BEFORE HE DIES, *the boy finds a note shoved under his front door.*

Don't come tonight, *it says.*

The boy has roughly three seconds to feel hurt.

Then the wailing starts. The boy rushes out into the town square to find the girl who had invited him to her birthday party limp and bloodless in the dirt, her father cradling her blond head.

"Who told?," he snarls at the gaping townsfolk. "Which one of you told? She tried to fight. This is why we keep our secrets! Who TOLD?"

He says more things, harsh and hissed as his group tries to keep him quiet. Vows of revenge. Plans being moved forward. Something about underground, something about burning.

Kade slips away and stumbles into the woods.

Trees loom behind him. The lake lies ahead, cliffs casting strange shadows over the still water.

"Hello," the boy croaks. "Is anyone here?"

There is no rustle in the trees. No sound of footsteps. But the boy turns, and the vampire is standing in the trees, stricken.

"What are you doing?" the vampire asks in a strange, thick voice. "I sent a note. You weren't to come."

The boy shakes his head. "I needed to see you. Something terrible is about to happen."

"Something terrible," the vampire echoes. He stares at this boy—drinking in the sight of him for what he hopes and dreads is the last time—and steps back toward the forest. "You need to run. Go to your mother. You two can leave town. Forget about all of this."

"Why?" the boy asks, trying to ignore the sick realization creeping through his veins, all the way up to his heart. "Do you know something?"

The vampire laughs bitterly. Everything he's been taught instructs him to get it over with. Drop the charade and bring out his fangs. But there is another part of him, small and stubborn, that tells him to protect this strange boy who has captured his cold heart.

"Please," the vampire says. "You have to go."

A woman's voice echoes from the trees, rough and deep. "Boy. What are you doing out here?"

"Nothing," the vampire says, too hasty.

The woman steps out from the trees.

The boy gasps. She is taller than any woman he's ever seen. Her eyes are liquid black. Her red plait is draped around her head in a makeshift crown.

"Ah," says Cyth. "The one you were supposed to kill months ago. Better late than never, I suppose. Bring him to the—"

"—hospital," said a voice above him, worried and loud.

Kade cracked his eyes open, spots dancing in the corners of his vision.

He was lying on his back in the grass. Theo hovered above him, his jaw tight. Sundance's car sat next to them, the hood crushed by the tree Kade had swerved into while the vision took hold.

"Shit," Kade mumbled. His tongue was thick. His mouth tasted like blood.

His stomach was rolling. He tried to sit up.

Theo pushed him back down and whispered near his ear. "I burned you while I was pulling you out. I'll heal it later. Was that a vision?"

Kade nodded. His head was pounding and he was pretty sure he'd bitten his cheek. But the sharpest pain was a throb at the back of his neck, pulsing in time with his heartbeat. The burn had gone deep.

"Saw Cyth," he mumbled, the vision already blurring, fading away. "Saw the boy and the vampire again."

"We can talk about it later," Theo said. He leaned back, calling to someone behind them. "He's alright, everyone! Put your phones away! And stay back, give him some air!"

Kade lifted his head groggily. Half of Lock was watching from the graveyard, far enough away that

Kade didn't start immediately hyperventilating. Aaron and Felicity stood in the street just behind him, both watching Kade with an intensity that made him want to snarl, or, failing that, curl into a tiny ball. Aaron's gaze was more baffled than anything else, but had an undercurrent of disgust. Felicity was smiling that same smile she'd gotten when she ripped her knee open on a stone in middle school: delighted shock, waiting for the horror to set in.

Their parents stood behind them, caught in the depths of a whisper-argument that Kade would be curious about if he wasn't fighting the urge to pass out.

He looked up at Theo. He was wearing a tie. Charcoal, like the rest of his outfit. It suited him.

Kade tugged the end of it, twice, like a bell. "Did I miss the funeral?"

Theo stared down at him. He had a strand of grass hanging off his biggest hair curl, right at the front. Kade reached up and plucked it out. Theo flinched, and Kade thought about reminding him that *hair* was fine, it was only skin that would get them in trouble.

"I think I am concussed," he told Theo instead. Then he turned over and vomited in the grass.

"Oh god," Aaron said, dry heaving.

"Sure *looks* like he needs a hospital," Felicity said beside him, and giggled nervously. She put a hand over her forehead, shielding herself from the sun. By the looks of her and the dozen or so of their classmates donning sunglasses behind her, Kade was not the only one hungover this morning.

"He's fine," Theo insisted.

"I'm fine," Kade slurred, gripping the end of Theo's tie. It was narrow and sleek, none of those ugly bulky ties Kade hated so much. "Theo's got me."

Theo shushed him.

"Is he *drunk?*" Aaron asked. "We should call the cops."

"*Do not call the cops,*" Theo snapped, fierce enough that all of them jumped. He squeezed the bridge of his nose and sighed. "He just needs to walk it off. Can you go find him some water?"

Aaron looked insulted at being asked. But he took a few hesitant steps back, like he had reminded himself this was Theo's dad's funeral, and friend duties included going along with weird shit.

Felicity grabbed Aaron's elbow hard. "Come on."

Theo watched them go. Everybody else was hovering anxiously back by the grave, too far away to hear them.

Kade squinted. If he concentrated, he could kind of see the coffin between the crowd, ready to be lowered into the ground. Theo's mom was standing next to it, speaking to a stressed man in a terrible suit and tugging at her perfect curls.

Theo leaned down again. "I gotta heal you a little bit. Just so you can...get up. Okay? Don't react."

Kade gave him a thumbs-up. Theo reached around his neck again, pressing his fingers into the burn.

A noise slipped between his teeth. The pain was excruciating without the venom to sweeten the pot. But the cotton balls in his head were clearing, the spots at the edges of his vision fading. His stomach settled. By the time Theo let him go, his skin was unburned and the ache in his head had reduced to a dull throb. Theo's healing touch couldn't cure dehydration.

Theo leaned back, looking him deep in the eyes.

Kade squirmed.

"Okay," Theo said. "Your pupils are normal. Get up, act normal."

"Never been good at that," Kade muttered, cheeks burning. He'd just realized he was still wearing his lasagna-eating-Garfield shirt and sweatpants. At least he'd put on sneakers before he'd left.

"Just stay here. I'll—" Theo stopped. He was staring at his mom, who watched him with such wary disappointment that Kade's stomach shriveled in sympathy.

Theo swallowed. He blinked hard, a scowl hardening his features.

"I gotta take care of this," he said. "Then we'll... we'll, uh."

Kade touched his sleeve. The lightest touch, the kind you couldn't see unless you were standing close. Which nobody was, even Felicity and Aaron, who were jogging over with a water bottle.

"It's over quick," Kade said.

Theo nodded jerkily. He was still watching his mom.

"Right," he said hoarsely. "Yeah."

Kade hesitated. Rumors were already flying. They had come to the party together last night, and now everyone had seen Theo tending to Kade after a car crash.

Kade asked, "Do you still want me to be at the funeral?"

"Not *now*," Theo said. He looked at the car, crushed and smoking against the tree. "Go home. I'll see you there after the wake."

Kade shrunk back. "Sure. Yeah."

Felicity and Aaron ran up, Felicity lugging a pink water bottle. Kade barely had time to take it from her before Theo walked off, gesturing for Aaron and Felicity to follow.

Kade sat at the edge of the grass and waited. He couldn't hear much of the funeral from here, but some of the funeral director's words drifted over: "Do his family wish to say any parting words?"

Kade caught snatches of Carol Fairgood talking. Then nothing. He swallowed, picturing Theo standing next to the hole in the ground, his dad's mangled body just a thin layer of wood away.

Kade took the long way home, through the woods. He sucked on the water bottle—it was one of those sports ones festooned with encouraging messages like YOU CAN DO IT—and tried not to think about how badly he'd screwed up. Sundance was already pissed at him, and he'd gone and made it a hundred times worse. *Everybody* saw him puke, most of them would know he was driving drunk. The only reason he wasn't in a holding cell right now was because Theo had talked them into not calling the cops.

After twenty minutes of walking, his phone rang.

"Where's my car?" Sundance asked flatly.

Kade rested his head against a tree, water bottle dangling from his hand.

"I crashed it," he admitted.

There was a silence big enough for Kade to go through all five stages of grief.

"You crashed it," she said finally.

"In front of the cemetery. Theo invited me to the funeral last night. I forgot until I saw the alarm. I called you, but you'd left your phone. I…" Kade pressed his forehead against the tree until the bark bit into his skin. "It's pretty bad."

Another long silence.

Sundance sighed. "Where are you?"

"Not in jail."

"Kade."

"I'm walking home." Kade's voice wobbled. He slapped his narrow chest until it steadied. "I'm really, really sorry. I'll pay to fix it. I'll get a job."

"Are you hurt?"

"No." His voice broke. "*Shit*. I swear I'm not hurt, I'm just feeling really stupid. I'm so sorry."

"It's okay," she said tightly. "It's...as long as you're not hurt. How was the funeral?"

Kade sniffed. "I didn't go. He told me to go home. Everyone was staring. He asked me to do this *one* thing, Sundance—"

"Kade—"

"And I screwed it up!" Kade was crying now, fat ugly tears sliding down his cheeks. He banged his head against the tree. Dry leaves and dirt rained down on his head. It was all catching up with him: the humiliation of everyone watching him puke; the crumpled hood of Sundance's car. Theo looking at him like he was a problem. He hadn't looked at Kade like that in *months*.

"I can't do one thing right," he sobbed. "*One* thing! Shit!"

He slapped the bark, deeply glad he'd decided to go through the woods and not through town. He couldn't take it if one more person saw him making an idiot of himself today.

"Okay," Sundance kept saying. "Okay. You're alright. Everything's gonna be fine."

Kade gulped a breath. He wanted to tell her about the visions. He wanted to tell her everything. *Auntie, I've been locked into a ritual that's gonna kill me. The last person like me must have found a way to stop it, but I don't think he got out. I got kidnapped last year, I wasn't passed out somewhere like I said. I watched my history teacher murder my gym teacher. My only friend is a vampire and I think I love him and you're right, Aunt Sundance,* everyone *was right: I* am *doomed. More than you know.*

"I'll get a job," he croaked when he could finally speak.

"Is the car still there?"

"Yeah. I can call someone."

"Nope, I got it." Sundance sighed again and something rustled on her end of the line. Kade wiped bark off his forehead and imagined her going through insurance paperwork that had been stacked on the couch for weeks.

"Honestly," Sundance said. "Car's probably not worth fixing. Might as well get a new one. Been meaning to for a couple years. Now you get home, alright? No detours. I'll...I'll make some soup."

"Okay," Kade whispered. He sniffed. "I'm really sorry."

"I know. We'll sort this out. I'll call the school, tell them you're sick again."

"Right," Kade croaked. "Shit. I didn't even—thanks."

"See you soon."

"See you." Kade hung up, wiping his cheeks. The forest was silent except for a birdcall in the distance. Once, he came out here to escape. Now everything was the ridge of a strange ear, the nub of a wing, a pair of black eyes watching him from the branches.

Kade blew out a breath. No one was watching him. He was alone in the forest, for better or worse.

Theo found him an hour later sitting on his back porch steps. Sparky trailed behind. He must've found Theo after the funeral.

Kade waved with his soup spoon. Split pea from a bag, plus white bread from the supermarket that Kade had finished off before he got even halfway through the bowl.

"Hi," he said.

"Hey," Theo replied. His voice was dull and scratchy. Kade wondered if he'd cried at the funeral, then remembered Theo's black tears. If Theo cried in front of people, they would have bigger things to worry about than Theo being embarrassed.

Theo sat on the bottom step, as far away from Kade as he could get without sitting on the ground. He trailed an absentminded hand over the wisteria hanging off the porch. Mid-morning sun shone through his hair, making him look like a painting: *Boy In Suit Sitting On Wisteria Porch, Dog In Lap.*

Kade scraped his spoon around the bowl and tried to think of something appropriate to say. *Sorry for ruining your dad's funeral and making everyone witness you dragging me out of a car.*

"What's with your forehead?" Theo asked, plucking a bulb of wisteria off the stem.

Kade rubbed his skin. It was still irritated from grinding it against the tree bark.

"Nothing worth healing," he said. He picked up a pebble from the porch step and threw it into the woods. "Look, I'm really sorry—"

"*Don't*," Theo snapped.

Sparky startled. She leaned up, licking Theo's chin.

Theo sighed, flicking the wisteria bulb away and scratching Sparky's head. "It's...fine. You had a vision. It wasn't like you passed out at the wheel because you were wasted."

Kade decided not to mention he was still drunk from last night. At least, he had been until Theo laid his healing hands on him. Now he was painfully sober.

"Still," Kade tried. "I kind of ruined the funeral."

Theo stared into the woods. His tie was still askew, like he'd never fixed it after Kade tweaked it back at the car.

"It gave people something to talk about," he said. "Everyone was so busy whispering about you that no one came up to say they were sorry for my loss. It was... nice."

"Oh," Kade said faintly. "Well, in that case..."

He trailed off. He'd been about to bow, but he figured now wasn't the time.

"I talked to Felicity. She said...she said a *lot*."

"Like?"

"She said to keep an eye on Aaron's parents. That the Fletchers were too intense."

"Intense," Kade repeated.

Theo got a look on his face like he just realized how much explaining was in front of him and how incapable he was of stringing all those words together. He slid off his tie, threading it neatly between his fingers.

"I'll tell you later," he said, rubbing Sparky between the ears. "What was your vision about? You saw Cyth?"

"Yeah," Kade said dryly. He swallowed, trying to remember. Everything was foggy. "They were in the woods. The boy and the vampire."

Kade scratched his head, like he could dig through to where the dead boy's memories were stored. "The lead hunter's daughter got killed trying to hunt the vampires. I *think* he's the one who seals them under the tree."

Theo drummed his fingers against Sparky's head. He hadn't always done that, Kade was almost sure of it. He'd only started doing it over the summer. Like he'd absorbed Kade's anxious fidgeting along with his blood.

"Okay," Theo said, looking into the woods with a thousand-yard stare, trying to keep racing forward like he'd been doing every day since his dad died. "Okay. Alright. We can...we need—"

Kade cut him off. "Mate. I'm *so* tired. *You're* tired."

"I'm fine."

"You haven't taken a day, man."

"I took a day."

"You did *not*." Kade put his bowl down, licking brine off his teeth. Packet soup was always saltier than he liked. "You need to turn your brain off. Watch some mindless TV, wrap yourself in a blanket and eat some crappy food. Speaking of—"

Kade pulled his shirt down his shoulder, exposing his neck. "You look like shit," he said as Theo started to protest.

"Then quit getting injured," Theo retorted. There was nothing bitter behind his words, but there wasn't much fondness in there either. Just weariness.

He stood with a sigh. "I'm gonna go. Sparky, stay."

Sparky obediently marched over and put her head in Kade's lap. Kade barely had time to move the soup out of the way.

"Where are you going?"

"I'll be back soon," Theo said. "Don't get into any trouble."

"Who, me?" Kade lowered the soup bowl gently onto Sparky's head. Her tail wagged gently.

"Both of you," Theo said, and vanished into the trees.

THEO RAN through the woods toward the Fletcher house.

He would have liked to take a break, like Kade said. Curl up on the couch and watch some crappy TV, Sparky between them to make sure their skin didn't accidentally brush.

But Felicity had pulled him aside at the wake in the twenty seconds her mom let her out of her sight to tell Theo that the Fletchers were dangerous, and they were planning something.

Which meant it was time for Theo to have a chat with Aaron's parents. He hadn't told Kade where he was going. He would've insisted on coming along, and Theo didn't want to put Kade anywhere near danger. He was safer at home with Sparky.

Theo brushed the twigs off his clothes and knocked.

Footsteps reached the front hall. It was Aaron. Theo could recognize his footsteps even before he got super hearing.

The door opened. Aaron was still wearing his funeral suit, the top button undone. His hair was limp, barely any gel left in it. When Theo had left the wake—his mom watching disapprovingly from the corner—Aaron had been telling one of the caterers the *proper* way to make devilled eggs, rubbing his hands through his hair in a way Theo hadn't seen since they were in grade school.

"Oh," Aaron said, gloved hands flexing at his sides. "Hey again. Guess the gang's all here."

"What?"

"Felicity's here," Aaron explained. "Her mom, too. Our parents went off for some weird whisper-conference in the living room. They told us to go catch up. Like I wanna *catch up* with the girl who broke my heart, like, four days ago, who I've just been forced to be around all morning."

Theo nodded until he figured out something to say. It took a while.

"How are you doing with that?"

Aaron rolled his eyes. "Better than you've been doing. However shitty my week's been, yours is worse. It's fine, I'll get her back."

He bit his lip. Theo hadn't seen him do that since grade school, either.

"Hey," Theo said. He cocked his head, listening to see if anyone was walking by. No one was, because his house—much like Theo's and Felicity's, and every house this close to the cliffs—had so much land around it that it took a full minute to get to a real street. The only people who 'walked by' were people who meant to be there, or people who were going for a stroll through the woods.

Theo lowered his voice anyway. "When you dated Kade—"

Aaron scoffed. "We didn't *date*."

Theo ignored it. "Was it before you dated Liss? Or during?"

"Before," Aaron said instantly. He paused. "Mostly. I was a dumb kid, okay?"

"Sure, two *whole* years ago!" Theo forced himself to lower his voice. The numbness was retreating, replaced by that big, satisfying anger he'd felt when he was charging Felicity at the funeral. Hot and clean and *purposeful*.

Theo shook his head in disgust. "You are such an asshole."

Aaron shrugged. "Okay. That's my *thing*. That's always been my thing, it's been *our* thing, before you started getting all..."

He stopped, raising gloved hands to his hair again. He winced as he pulled his injured hand through the limp, gel-less strands.

Theo frowned. There was something peeking out

from the bandages. Dark and thin, like someone had drawn on his wrist in strange black ink. Then Aaron put his hands into his pockets and Theo lost sight of it.

"Never mind," Aaron said. "Shouldn't have said that. Especially not today. I'm...sorry."

Theo rolled his shoulder uncomfortably. "What happened to *apologizing is for the weak*, like your dad always says?"

Aaron rolled his eyes again. He looked embarrassed. "Yeah, well. Liss keeps talking about, like...rotten fruit and legacies and shit."

Theo glanced down at Aaron's hand, glove and bandage and strange sickly black lines all hidden in his pocket. The faint stench of decay.

"Rotten fruit?'

"Yeah. Apple never falls far from the tree, whatever."

Theo frowned. "Your parents aren't a rotten tree."

"Neither are yours!" Aaron laughed, the sound short and brittle. "I don't know what she's talking about. Anyway, she's still in the kitchen. Won't shut up about gingerbread houses for some reason."

Aaron stepped back to let Theo through. Theo followed, thinking about every ugly glimpse he'd gotten of the Fletchers—the yelling and the threats and the innocent comments that couldn't have been that innocent at all, the way they made Aaron flush with shame. The house suddenly felt sinister and full of secrets. Felicity's hidden necklace; Theo's parents watching him across the room as Theo lied to the nurses how he got hypothermia in spring. Was every family so full of secrets?

Theo stopped. "Where are the others?"

He knew, of course. He could smell them from here, if he breathed deep and focused hard: rich cologne and even richer perfume, none of it played down for the occasion.

Aaron looked over his shoulder, already heading for the kitchen. "Did you *seriously* come here to see my parents?"

Theo shrugged.

Aaron stared at him in disbelief. He curled his lip like he was going to make a snide comment, then forcibly straightened it.

"Still in the living room," he said slowly. "Am I allowed to come, or is this *another* private chat?"

Theo clapped him on the shoulder. "Go keep Felicity company."

Aaron flinched. Barely, but visibly. He wet his lips, and Theo could see another comment begging to claw up his throat about how *weird* all this was, what was so important they couldn't they tell him, he didn't want to go and keep his ex-girlfriend company.

Then Aaron nodded and headed wordlessly for the kitchen.

Theo strode down the hall, too focused to care whether Aaron was watching him. His feet moved automatically through the rooms he'd spent so much time in since he was a boy, but the home was suddenly harsh and unfamiliar.

There was no water on the living room table, which was strange. The first thing the Fletchers did for guests was put out a pitcher of ice water with the slim, fancy glasses they used for company.

Mrs. Fletcher sat on the nicer couch, her posture uncharacteristically terrible as she leaned over to whisper to Beverly Sloan. Beverly was an uncomfortable distance away on the opposite couch, sitting perfectly straight instead of leaning in to hear Mrs. Fletcher. Mr. Fletcher was nowhere to be seen.

"...better early than late," Mrs. Fletcher finished.

Beverly caught sight of Theo at the door. Her hand curled into a fist against her dress. It looked like a signal.

Mrs. Fletcher jerked up. She spotted Theo and stood, giving him a hasty smile. "Theo! We didn't expect to see you again so soon. How are you doing?"

Beverly said nothing. She just stared at him from the couch, her dark brows creasing together. Theo wondered if she wore that sun pendant underneath her sleek dress.

"You should have let me know you were coming," Mrs. Fletcher continued, twisting her hands together in front of her. "We would've made something for you."

Beverly gave her a steely look. Theo had always

found her intimidating, even when he was a kid. Felicity was *fun* to offset her sharpness. Beverly was all blade, nothing to soften her edges. Carol said she used to have a sense of humor. She used to drink coffee with Carol when Felicity came over for playdates. Then her husband died, and there was no more coffee and no laughter.

"We all know I couldn't eat it," Theo said. "Unless somebody's offering up their wrist."

The room went silent. A grandfather clock ticked in the center of the back wall, positioned perfectly between the two women on opposite couches.

"Where's Mr. Fletcher?" Theo asked.

"He's picking up antibiotics from the drugstore," Mrs. Fletcher said, too fast. Her smile turned desperate. She waved towards the couch. "Why don't you take a seat?"

Theo didn't move. "Why haven't you told Aaron?"

"I..." Mrs. Fletcher stared down at the stack of unused coasters sitting in a stained-glass jar on the table. "I don't..."

Beverly sighed tightly and crossed her legs. "I'm going to stop you right there, Theo. We can't talk about it."

Theo gritted his blunt teeth. "We're on the same *side*. We *all* don't want me letting Cyth out of their cage. We *all* want to find my sire and take revenge for my dad's—for my dad. He was your friend, I *know* you want that."

He looked at Mrs. Fletcher for the last part. Calling Beverly Sloan and Victor Fairgood *friends* was a stretch. But whatever they were, they had all known each other for the better part of twenty years. That had to count for something.

Theo had to stop his hands from shaking as he continued, "My dad knew who my sire was. Who was it?"

Mrs. Fletcher gave him an anxious smile. "We really don't—"

Beverly cut her off. "Felicity's been listening at doorways again, hasn't she?"

Theo didn't answer. He could smell Felicity's floral perfume coming closer.

"And that's not all she's been doing," Beverly continued. The hint of a smile crossed her severe face. "That girl's loyalties have always been...skewed."

A singsong voice came down the hall. "I heard my name! Is someone badmouthing me? Say it to my face, cowards."

Felicity pushed the door open, hair swinging, holding a champagne glass full of something that smelled significantly stronger than champagne.

She placed her chin on Theo's shoulder. "Hello, sad boy. How're you feeling?"

"Great," Theo said dryly. "Thanks."

She winked at him, then turned to the women perched on the couches. "Are we spilling everything? It's about time. Tell him about the small car, ball of tar, tall bar thing. Sidenote: you need to *enunciate* when you talk, Mom."

"Felicity," Beverly said, voice low. "This is *not* the time."

"Then when *is* the time, Mom?" Felicity grinned, cheeks red with anger. "This is *bullshit*. Theo's been going through hell, and we've been—what? Plotting against him?"

"We've been—" Beverly's jaw snapped shut. She looked pointedly up at Mrs. Fletcher, who had been in the middle of reaching for her knee. Everyone stared at Mrs. Fletcher's outstretched hand, frozen over Beverly's dark dress like a warning.

Beverly gave Mrs. Fletcher a stern look. "I'm sorry. What did *you* think I was about to say?"

Mrs. Fletcher yanked her hand back. "Nothing!"

"Do you think I'm an idiot?"

"No!" Mrs. Fletcher laughed nervously, fiddling with the top button of her blouse. "Of course not. I...you've just...expressed frustration...about..."

She trailed off. She seemed to be putting a lot of thought into the wording, like it was any use speaking in code in front of Felicity and Theo now.

Felicity groaned. "Mom! Cut the shit! Theo told me everything."

"Everything," Beverly deadpanned. "Why don't you enlighten us?"

"I would *love* to," Felicity announced, and started listing on her fingers. "The stories about the founding of the town are real. You've been training me to kill vampires since I was a toddler. *Theo's* a vampire, but not the kind we kill, and his sire wants Theo to get his vampire wife out of her burning coffin and Theo's dad somehow found out who someone was, and—"

She gasped, turning to Theo so fast her hair smacked him in the shoulder. "Oh my god, did he find out who your *sire* was? *That's* why he killed your dad?"

Theo nodded stiffly.

"Oh shit," Felicity said, dazed. She let out a peal of horrified laughter, took another slug of not-champagne and whirled back on her mother. "Guys! That's his *dad*, how could you not *tell* him that?"

"Felicity." Beverly sighed.

The door flew open. Everyone fell silent as Aaron came in, hair flopping over his eyes.

"Okay," Aaron said flatly. Everyone but Beverly avoided his gaze. "Not suspicious at all. Do you want me to leave, so you can continue your totally normal conversation—" He paused, looking around the room. "Where's Dad?"

"He's picking up your antibiotics," Mrs. Sloan said hastily.

Aaron's gloved hand curled into a careful fist. "No, he isn't. He got those yesterday."

Mrs. Fletcher smiled at her son with increasing intensity, a muscle flexing in her jaw.

"No," she said, strained. "You're mistaken."

Aaron scoffed. "I think I know what pills I took this

morning, *Mom*. Sorry for not going along with whatever you're trying to talk these guys into, *Mom*. Maybe I'd cooperate if I was actually in on the lie, *Mom*."

The living room was silent. Mrs. Fletcher kept staring at her son like if she just did it hard enough, she could get him to take it back.

"What?" Aaron snapped. "Seriously, just *tell* me! Did you guys kill someone last year and now everybody's sworn to secrecy? Is Felicity in on it?"

His voice kept rising, but Theo wasn't looking at him anymore. He was too busy watching Beverly. While Mrs. Fletcher was still smiling in panic at her son, Beverly stared pointedly at Theo. Like she wanted to say something important, but couldn't.

He frowned at her. *What?*

She shook her head. Her stare intensified, her dark eyes drilling into him.

Aaron's cry reached a crescendo. "What the HELL is going on in this house?"

"*Aaron*," Mrs. Fletcher yelled. "That's *enough*."

Aaron's shoulders rose. He wasn't used to his mom yelling at him. His dad was the loud one in the family.

"Yeowch," Felicity muttered, clicking her teeth against the edge of her glass.

Mrs. Fletcher patted her blouse down.

"So sorry about that," she said with another placating smile that reminded Theo of his own mom, always putting appearances first. "Theo. I'm very sorry for your loss. But I'm afraid we really can't say anything."

Beverly asked, "How's your car crash friend doing?"

Mrs. Fletcher's head snapped around to look at her. She gave Beverly a small, rigid headshake.

"I hope he's alright," Beverly continued, ignoring her. "I saw him vomit all over the grass. Lucky he missed your shoes."

"He's fine," Theo said warily.

Beverly hummed. "Is he?"

A cold chill washed over Theo. He thought of Kade lazing on his couch, Sparky on his lap. Laughing at something on the TV. Not paying attention to who might be sneaking in the back door.

Theo marched forward and took Mrs. Fletcher's arms. "Where's your husband?"

"I..." she stammered. "I...he's out."

"Where?" Theo demanded.

"He wouldn't say," Mrs. Fletcher whispered.

"Uh," Aaron said uncertainly. "Theo, what the hell is happening? Let go of my mom. Mom?"

Felicity shushed him. Her hand darted toward her pocket, and for the first time Theo noticed a heavy weight inside the material, pulling it down. On the other couch, Beverly made another fisted hand signal at Mrs. Fletcher, the same one as before: *stop*.

Theo shook Mrs. Fletcher. "Is he going to Kade's house?"

Mrs. Fletcher shook her head. "We didn't...nobody, not in generations..."

She bit her tongue hard. She didn't have to say it. The panic in her eyes was confirmation enough.

"Theo," Aaron said. "What are you doing, man?"

"Ask your mom," Theo snapped.

Then he ran.

THE DOOR SLAMMED SHUT.

Kade's eyes flew open. He was sitting on the couch. The living room was suffocatingly warm. He reached to tug his blanket off and was met with fur instead, Sparky tilting her muzzle up to lick his face.

"Alright, calm down," Kade told her, smiling reflexively even as someone else's emotions drained out of him: horror, pain, blinding fear. Another doozy of a dream-memory Kade didn't remember after he woke up. Whoever that man had been, Kade hoped his pain ended fast.

Sundance bustled through the front door, a plastic shopping bag dangling off her good arm. She'd bought more cream.

"Car's getting towed," she informed him. "And we're not getting fined for destruction of public property."

"Whoo-hoo," said Kade, filled with guilt.

Sundance restocked the fridge. "I'm gonna go down to the car place and put down a deposit on the first car that doesn't look like it'll shit itself before it hits one hundred miles."

She shoved the plastic bag into their plastic bag holder—another plastic bag—and moved toward the couch, reaching out like she was going to pet Sparky or maybe even touch Kade's head. She did that sometimes, rubbing his stubbled scalp, and he twisted away even though he loved it.

But she didn't touch either of them. She just hovered there for a moment, then thumped the couch like a punctuation mark at the end of sentence.

"Right," she said. "I just need to find some more endless goddamn paperwork, then I'll be off."

Kade nodded. He still felt guilty, even though she was being so nice about it. She didn't yell at him much anymore, not after that self-induced hospital visit in freshman year that they didn't talk about.

"I'll be sewing in my room," he called as she headed down the hall. She liked to know where he was after he'd done something especially stupid, and it comforted her to know he was doing his art projects rather than, say, drinking alone in the woods.

Kade nudged Sparky until she climbed off him, then headed into his room. He didn't even get to sit at his sewing machine before he knocked a needle off his desk. It went pinging across the room, lost in the worn carpet.

"Shit," he said, looking down at Sparky. "Hey. Yeah, you. Out of my room while I sort this out. No, use my bed, don't walk over there, that's where the sharp shit is."

Sparky jumped nimbly onto his bed and then toward the door. She gave him one last questioning look, head tilted adorably.

Kade waved at her. "Go! If you get a needle stuck in your paw because of me I'll kill myself."

She cocked her head further. Then she walked out, Kade rushing behind her to close the door.

"Alright," he muttered as he spun to face the danger zone. Silver in a wash of gray. He was definitely getting stabbed.

Behind the door, Sparky whined.

"Give me a second," Kade called. "I just gotta—"

A soft noise made him stop. Low and sliding. The hair at the back of his neck stood up. He turned—

—and was immediately shoved up against his drawers, a meaty hand clamped over his mouth. Mr. Fletcher stared down at him, eyes hard and determined. He held a blade against Kade's throat. It wasn't a fancy hunting knife like the Fletchers were so fond of. It was a box cutter, the hilt plastic and cheap.

Kade tried to push him away. But Mr. Fletcher was too strong, his bulk pressing Kade hard into the wood. The more Kade writhed, the harder he pressed.

Sparky barked from the hallway.

"The more you struggle," Mr. Fletcher said unsteadily. "The worse this is gonna be."

He reached up and pinched Kade's nose shut, his palm covering his mouth. The box cutter pressed harder into Kade's neck.

"I'm going to do this until you pass out," Mr. Fletcher told him, face twisted in disgust. "Then I'm going to cut you. You won't feel it."

Kade whimpered. A tear slid down his cheek. Sparky was barking in earnest now, scrabbling against the door.

Mr. Fletcher sighed. "I'm sorry, okay? This was never going to end well for you. At least this way might save a lot of people."

Kade bucked uselessly against his grip. He couldn't suck in a breath. His vision was already tunneling. Still, he struggled. He couldn't let Sundance come back and find him dead, just like she'd been fearing for so long. He promised her she wouldn't outlive him. He *promised*.

And Theo. Beautiful, stubborn Theo barreling head-first into the next thing so he wouldn't have to think. He'd asked Kade over the summer if he still wanted to die, prompted when Theo talked about their homework load in junior year and Kade said he'd rather jump off the cliffs near Theo's house.

Kade didn't remember what he'd replied. Another joke to ward him off. But he remembered what Theo had said to him after: *Well, you better stay alive. We're together in this.*

Kade didn't want to die. Not like this, held down and struggling while spots bloomed in his vision. He couldn't move—but that couldn't stop Kade "Monster" Renfield. Time to do something he'd been threatening since his classmates started barking at him.

He peeled his lips back from his teeth. Then he pincered a small wedge of Mr. Fletcher's palm and bit down as hard as he could.

"Shit," Mr. Fletcher spat. "Get off!"

Kade hung on. He didn't have much flesh in his mouth, but that just made it easier to bite. He could already taste blood.

"Goddammit," Mr. Fletcher bellowed. He wrenched his hand back.

Kade kneed him in the stomach. The only useful thing his dad ever taught him: if you want somebody to go still, get them in the stomach. Knock the wind out of them.

Mr. Fletcher wheezed and stumbled backward. He raised his knife hand, slashing out.

The blade caught Kade across the shoulder.

He yelped. It was quickly drowned out by Mr. Fletcher, who suddenly shrieked in pain and collapsed sideways. He'd stepped on the needle Kade had been searching for. It had shot straight through his shoe and into the meaty part of his heel.

Sparky barked wildly. The door vibrated with blows as she threw herself against it.

Kade ran for it. Mr. Fletcher tackled him, slamming him into the carpet and dropping the box cutter.

"Goddamn booby trapped," Mr. Fletcher snarled, scrabbling to get a grip on the blade.

"Stay *still*," Mr. Fletcher barked.

Kade lunged forward, latching his teeth into Mr. Fletcher's ear.

Mr. Fletcher howled. Sparky joined in.

The bedroom window shattered.

Theo streaked through it, his shoe catching on the window frame and tearing out a chunk of wood. He landed on all fours on the carpet and bounded forward to tear Mr. Fletcher off Kade.

"WHAT THE HELL IS WRONG WITH YOU?" he yelled, holding Mr. Fletcher up in the air by his neck. "THE RITUAL'S NOT UNTIL SPRING! WE HAVE TIME! YOU DON'T JUST GO FROM ZERO TO MURDER, YOU CRAZY SHIT!"

Mr. Fletcher gurgled. His shoes scrabbled at the ground, hands clawing at Theo's tight grip around his throat.

Kade pushed himself up shakily. "Theo—"

Theo slammed Mr. Fletcher into the wall, making the man cry out as his head bounced roughly against it.

"You don't touch him," Theo growled around his fangs. "Got that? *None* of you touch him. He's *mine*."

"Theo," Kade said weakly, mind reeling with *he's mine he's mine he's mine*. "You might wanna put the guy down."

Theo dragged Mr. Fletcher back and slammed him

into the wall again. Once. Twice. Three times. The man's head lolled, his eyes falling shut.

"THEO," Kade yelled.

Theo stopped. He turned to Kade, eyes liquid black, fangs sharp and dangerous.

He loosened his grip. Mr. Fletcher fell into a limp heap on Kade's floor.

"Hoooly shit," Kade whispered.

"He's alive," Theo said distractedly, stalking up to Kade and lifting his hands like he was going to do something impossible, like touch his face. He faltered in midair and gripped Kade's sleeve instead, just above the cut.

"I'm fine," Kade said.

"You're *not*," Theo replied, glaring worriedly at the wound. He looked up and paused. He stared at Kade's bloody mouth.

Kade licked blood off his teeth with a wince. "I bit him. Twice."

Theo nodded. He stood very still, gaze roving over Kade like he didn't trust he was right there. He was still gripping Kade's sleeve, his fingers a solid weight through the fabric.

Kade's breath hitched. Theo was watching him so intently, like he was about to say something important.

"Answer your *phone*," Theo said desperately. Then he let Sparky in.

"It's on silent," Kade said, dazed. He tried to

remember where his phone even was right now. Back on the couch?

Sparky bounded into the room, whimpering. She made a beeline straight to Kade, licking his hand and going onto her hind legs to lick his injured arm.

"*Ow*," Kade said. "Sparky, are *you* a vampire?"

Sparky licked his face with her bloody tongue. He pushed her off, petting her ears while she whined and curled around his legs.

"I'm okay," he assured her. "I'm good."

Theo stared at him from the doorway. His funeral clothes were covered in dirt and twigs. There was a dead leaf in his hair. His eyes flickered: black, brown, black again. He looked devastated.

"What?" Kade asked, stricken with a horrible dread. "Oh shit, what is it? Did you find out more terrible crap while you were gone? You have to tell me."

Theo shook his head. He blurred forward so fast that Kade gasped. Then Theo was standing in front of him, black tears gathering in the corners of his eyes.

"Nothing terrible," he said. "Just...glad you're still here."

Then he did something truly shocking: he shuffled forward and rested his head on Kade's clothed shoulder. Just the tip of his forehead, pillowed with his own curls.

Kade stood still, arm throbbing, jaw aching, dripping blood on the carpet. He didn't put his arms around Theo. He didn't dare. After a few seconds he realized

Theo was breathing with him, their chests moving in unison.

Sparky whined, still nuzzled around his legs.

"I'm okay," Kade whispered. Then, to Theo: "Are *you* okay?"

Theo didn't respond. He lifted his head off Kade's shoulder. For a heart-stopping moment Kade thought Theo was staring at his mouth. Then he remembered the blood on his teeth.

"Right," Kade said, swallowing the foul liquid until he could only taste spit. "Sorry."

Theo blinked. His eyes were brown again. "What?"

Someone knocked on the front door.

Kade jolted back, swearing. In the heat of the moment, he'd almost forgotten about the unconscious adult passed out in his room.

"Oh shit. Shit, *shit*! We gotta get him out before Sundance sees! Wake him up!"

"It's not her," Theo said, instead of calling Kade an idiot for thinking his aunt might knock on her own door. "It's Felicity."

Kade stopped. "What the hell is she doing here? Make her leave!"

"I...I think it might be fine, actually? I think she's on our side."

Kade gestured to the slash on his arm. "Or maybe she's here to finish the job!"

Theo's jaw flexed. Then, like he was admitting something very shameful: "I trust her."

Kade glared. He wanted to bring up Hawthorn—a man they *both* trusted—who had tied Kade to a tree and slashed Theo's chest to ribbons. But Theo was looking at him so determinedly, and Kade was still shaking from adrenaline, and Felicity *had* asked him to take care of Theo.

Kade groaned. "Ugh! Fine. Bring her in. But make sure she's cool first!"

"Got it," Theo said.

FELICITY WAS POSING when Theo opened the front door. One toned arm draped against the doorframe, smiling like she was at a photoshoot. She'd changed into a sundress, and she smelled like soap and strange wine.

"Fancy seeing *you* here," she crooned. She waved down at Sparky, who growled. "Hi, beast."

Theo sighed, pushing Sparky behind him. "Is anyone with you?"

"Can't you tell with your vampire senses? Mommy's on the roof of Mr. McGuilicudy's house with a sniper rifle." She stopped, snorting. "It's just me, dipshit. Mom stormed out after you left. She was really pissed at Mrs. Fletcher."

She shoved past him, looking around the living room which was open into the kitchen. "Sooo what was the big deal? Where's Monster?"

"His name is Kade," Theo said. "Don't call him that again."

She gave him a surprised look. It even looked genuine.

"I always thought he liked it," she admitted. "He bared his teeth often enough. Oh hi, Kade! You look—oh. Shit."

Theo turned to see Kade appear from the hallway, a shirt wrapped around his injured arm. The fabric was already soaked in blood.

Theo gestured at Felicity. "Cool enough?"

"Enough," Kade said, sounding almost as tired as Theo. "Come on. I guess."

Kade led her into his room. Both of them kept giving Theo looks—Kade wary, Felicity gleeful to hide her growing nerves. Theo ignored them. He didn't want to deal with any of this. He wanted to go back to laying his head on Kade's shoulder, feeling his warm weight. Solid. Undeniable. He'd tried to tune into Kade while he ran here, but he couldn't concentrate enough to even tell whether Kade was *alive*. He'd spent the whole sprint over here thinking he might be too late, that he'd arrive and find Kade impaled with a silver crossbow bolt, even though that wouldn't make sense. You didn't need silver to kill a human. You didn't need anything. You could do it with your hands, with a little effort. But Theo imagined it on the run through the woods as dirt and branches caught in his hair: Kade sprawled out on his bed, gray eyes half-lidded and staring, unseeing, at the ceiling. A bright spot of crimson on his chest where the arrow struck him. Like a bird shot out of the sky.

"This is getting kind of ominous," Felicity said, voice getting higher and higher as Kade pushed his door open. "Like, am I gonna walk in and find—oh SHIT."

She froze, staring down at Mr. Fletcher's unconscious body.

"He's alive," Theo said.

Relief flooded her face. "Oh my god. *Lead* with that, I thought I was on shovel duty!" She smacked Theo in the chest and took a few cautious steps toward Mr. Fletcher, eyeing his bloody ear.

Sparky tried to get in the room. Theo pushed her back with his foot and closed the door in her face.

"Stay," he told her, ignoring those big sad eyes.

Felicity nudged Mr. Fletcher's inert body with her foot. Then she squinted. Trying to see if he was breathing, Theo realized.

"He *is* alive," he insisted. "Look! His chest moved!"

Felicity squinted some more. Kade looked over at Theo, concerned.

"He has a *heartbeat*," Theo said. He turned to Kade. "Do you have any rope? Or sturdy scarves? I want to tie him up before he comes to."

"What?" said Felicity and Kade in unison, both their faces scrunching up in such similar confusion that Theo frowned.

"Nobody's telling us what we want to know," Theo explained. "So we're going to make him. Scarf time, then I heal Kade's arm."

He looked at Kade expectantly. Kade threw up his good hand, then turned, grumbling, to his drawers.

Theo tied Mr. Fletcher's hands with an ugly knitted scarf that Kade had been meaning to throw out. Then he fetched Felicity's water bottle from the couch and headed into the kitchen.

Sparky nosed at his elbow, jumping up to put his front paws on the sink.

"Don't," he told her, pushing her down. He lowered his voice, letting irritation leak into it. "I expected better from you, you know. You didn't protect him."

She cocked her head with a whine.

"He could've *died*," Theo said, hand shaking around the water bottle. "He could have died because you didn't try hard enough. You get that, right? You're a *bad dog*."

She dropped to the floor, ears plastered to her head. A tremor shook through her body, from her soft head to her back paws, still puppy-huge.

"*Don't*," Theo snapped. "You're not getting out of this just because—"

He heard Felicity's quick step behind him and fell silent.

"Oookay," Felicity said. "Is that my water bottle?"

Theo jerked his head at Sparky. "Go to Kade. Go on."

Sparky slunk off, tail between her legs. Theo fought down the wave of rage and deep guilt as she vanished into the hallway.

"Kade needs to stay hydrated," he told Felicity. "With all the blood loss."

"Right," Felicity said. "Of course."

"I'm gonna need to bite him soon," Theo explained. "And he's already bleeding. So."

Felicity gave him a pointed look. It was her *'you're being an idiot'* look, which Felicity gave a lot of people and was very good at.

Theo screwed the water bottle lid back into place. "What?"

Felicity sighed. "Bite *me*, dipshit."

Theo screwed up his nose.

"What? Is my blood not good enough for you?"

"No, it's..." Theo trailed off. It made sense. He wouldn't burn her. "Are you sure?"

Felicity pursed her pale lips. "Are you hungry?"

He nodded.

She held out her wrist. It was flushed where Kade was pale, elegant where Kade was gangly. Theo took it, thinking of the mole at the base of Kade's neck.

He raised it to his mouth and bit down. Blood gushed over his tongue, hot and filling. It was better than deer. Better than rabbit, better than badger, better than squirrel.

It wasn't as good as Kade. Not even close.

Felicity grunted in pain. It quickly turned into a sigh

and she leaned heavily against the counter as the venom took hold. A lazy grin spread over her face, eyelids fluttering.

Theo felt uncomfortable. He pulled back, rubbing his thumb over the holes until they faded into clear skin.

Felicity's eyes fluttered open and she gave an ecstatic giggle. Her pupils were huge.

"Holy shit," she whispered. "If that's what it feels like, no *wonder* Kade is hooked."

Theo's newly full stomach squirmed the way it did every time he remembered Kade was addicted to his venom. It made him feel gross. Kade had too many habits that hurt him. Theo didn't want to be one of them.

Felicity followed him back into the bedroom, twirling the water bottle. Kade was sitting on his bed, watching Mr. Fletcher and holding his injured arm out awkwardly so it didn't drip on the sheets. Sparky sat beside him, head on his lap.

Theo nodded at Sparky. "Out."

She slunk out, looking just as miserable as last time. Luckily Kade was too busy watching Mr. Fletcher to notice.

"Fletcher keeps making awake noises," Kade said. Then he nodded at his bloody arm. "Okay. You can heal me, but then you *have* to bite me. You were going to do it before, and you're looking really—"

"I already bit Felicity."

Kade stopped. "Oh."

"You're already bleeding."

"Right," Kade said, looking at the blood dripping down his arm. "No. Yeah. That makes sense."

Theo tried to think of a way to make that hurt look leave Kade's eyes. *I only bit her wrist. I'd rather bite you.*

"You taste better." It felt like the worst option as soon as he said it.

"Ouch!" Felicity laughed, flopping down on Kade's bed next to him and flinging the water bottle into his lap. "I'm sorry, I didn't know you two were bite-exclusive. What's that in vampire culture—promise rings?"

Theo ignored her, sitting down a sensible distance from Kade. "Ready?"

Kade hesitated. Then he took the bloody shirt off his arm.

The wound was deep. Even freshly fed, Theo's mouth watered. It wasn't just that Kade was the other part of the ritual. It wasn't that they were bound together. Kade tasted so good because he was *Kade*. His strangeness and sweetness: the parts he hid behind all that spiky darkness. It didn't matter that they were two halves of a ritual. Even if they weren't, he'd still be able to pick Kade's heartbeat out of a crowded gym.

"You can," Kade mumbled.

Theo looked up. "What?"

Kade nodded at the cut. "Be a waste if you didn't."

Theo glanced at Felicity, who was watching them

with her pointy chin in her hands, her gaze curious and eager.

He pressed his tongue along the wound. Kade let out a whimper.

Cauterize, Theo thought dreamily as he pulled back to see the stripey burn that had covered the cut. He pressed his fingers over it next, another burn over the top of the old one, then both started to fade. When Theo lifted his hand, Kade's arm was blood-smeared and whole.

Kade rubbed the bloody shirt over it. "You can suck it. Shut *up*," he added as Felicity tittered next to him. "The shirt, you can suck the *shirt*."

Theo thought about it. If he was alone, he would have hunched over that shirt and sucked Kade's lukewarm blood right out of the fabric. But he wasn't, so he crossed the room and knelt in front of the unconscious Mr. Fletcher.

"Awake noises?" he asked Kade.

"Like..." Kade grimaced. "Groaning? He moved a little, then slumped over again."

Theo concentrated. He couldn't tell if Mr. Fletcher had more blood in his brain than usual, or if it was swelling, or any other danger signs he should look for after someone had their head bashed into the wall hard enough to knock them out.

He pulled Mr. Fletcher's eyelids back. One pupil was blown.

"Crap," Theo muttered. He laid his hands on Mr.

Fletcher's head and focused. His palms tingled, fingers fizzing with power.

Mr. Fletcher's eyes fluttered open. His pupil was mostly back to normal.

Theo waited. First the confusion set in. Then the panic. Mr. Fletcher yanked at his hands, which were tied behind his back. He gritted his teeth in a smile.

"Boys," he said, and then blinked rapidly when he noticed who was sitting next to Kade. "And...Felicity. It's good to see all of you. I think there's been some mistake."

"*I* think you tried to kill me with a box cutter," Kade said.

Mr. Fletcher sighed. "I may have overreacted. You understand. Felicity?"

"I understand that my mom is weird as shit," Felicity said, twirling a strand of hair around her pinkie so hard the skin went white. "I understand that I was trained in gymnastics and archery and *knives* as a child, and no one told me why I had to keep doing it, and everyone said I'd get in *seeerious* trouble if I told anyone about some of the weirder shit we did. I understand that we have this...stupid, grandiose self-importance about ourselves even though as far as *I* can tell, anyone who's alive right now has done screw-all to earn it. I understand that we're in the middle of a shitstorm that everyone's been terrified of for generations and the only one who's told me what we're up against is Theo."

"We *can't*," Mr. Fletcher said. "Felicity. Boys. We *can't* tell you."

Felicity threw her head back and groaned. "Theo, break his fingers."

Theo knew she was joking. Still, he considered it. He could always heal him after.

He didn't particularly want to break Mr. Fletcher's fingers. He wanted to let him go. Send him slinking back to his family. Felicity's blood had given Theo an energy hit, but it didn't lift the mental fog. Today was so damn *long*. He desperately wanted to stop. To sit down on Kade's battered couch and watch some mindless TV like Kade had suggested so many times.

But the guilt was still in him, that deep anger driving him forward. *How dare you? Your father's killer walks free. It could be anyone. You HAVE to do this.*

Theo reached behind Mr. Fletcher's back, grabbed one of his fingers and twisted until it snapped.

Mr. Fletcher screamed.

Kade screamed with him, shooting up off the bed. "Theo! What the shit!"

"I was *joking*," Felicity said weakly, face stuck in a horrified smile.

Mr. Fletcher thrashed, tears tracking into his neat beard. "God," he spat. "*Christ*. I *can't*—"

"Tell us everything you know about my sire," Theo demanded, shoving back the numb horror he'd felt when Mr. Fletcher's finger cracked in his grip. "Then I'll heal you."

Mr. Fletcher shook his head, face twisted in agony. Theo tried to look at him and see nothing but an obstacle between him and finding his sire, the man who had voted on killing him last year, the man who had sat there all summer and watched Theo choke down food he couldn't digest. But he was also the man who gave Theo rides to basketball practice in middle school, let him watch R-rated movies and taught him how to fish. The loudest voice in every room, booming and friendly, and Theo had reduced him to a crying mess on the ground.

"We're on the same *side*," Theo growled. "Please!"

Mr. Fletcher shook his head again. "Couldn't even tell your dad. Don't know how he knew. He just kept coming—"

Theo snapped another finger.

Felicity gasped. Kade paced, rubbing his head anxiously, muttering under his breath. "*What the shit what the shit what the shit.*"

"Small car," Theo recited. "Tall bar, small tar. What was it?"

"Scars," Mr. Fletcher rasped. "Small scars! He has small scars, and he's known your family for years. That's all your dad said."

"*Everybody's* known my family for years," Theo said. "What scars? Where, on his face?"

"I don't know," Mr. Fletcher sobbed. "Victor didn't say. I still don't know how he found out, but he said he needed to make sure. He was going to meet him—"

"Where?"

"At his house. They were going for a walk in the woods, the day he died—"

Theo leaned back. "Mom said he went on that walk alone."

Mr. Fletcher jerked, a pained cry wrenching out of him. Like Theo had broken another finger. Which was strange, because Theo wasn't even touching him now.

He jerked again, shoulders hunching.

Theo frowned, concentrating. There was some-thing...*shifting* inside Mr. Fletcher. Warping. Cracking.

"What's happening?" Theo asked. "I can hear some-thing...*twisting* inside you."

Mr. Fletcher laughed, the noise bright with pain. "*It is our burden to bear*," he recited, wet eyes fixed on the ceiling. "*No one will throw themselves into this terrible fight except us, the chosen, the burdened—*"

He folded in half with a scream. Something had fractured deep inside him, Theo heard it snap.

"What's happening?" Felicity asked, voice high and strained.

"So *stupid*," Mr. Fletcher laughed, shaking with pain and laughter. He coughed, the movement making him flinch. "God. They should've gotten rid of this tradition along with the sword training."

"What tradition?" Theo asked. "Mr. Fletcher?"

"Secret society of hunters," Mr. Fletcher gritted, shuddering. "Emphasis...emphasis on *secret*. Never actu-ally seen this happen. Hoped my parents were lying.

Scaring me into keeping quiet. Nope! I can feel...I can *feel...*"

He spasmed. Another bone cracked inside him, liquids sloshing in places they shouldn't.

"Theo," Kade said urgently. "Theo, what do we do?"

"I don't know," Theo snapped, hovering his hands helplessly over Mr. Fletcher's torso. "There's—it's *inside* him, I don't—"

Mr. Fletcher sagged sideways, forcing his bloodshot eyes open to fix on Theo.

"You have to kill him," he croaked. He coughed, blood and spit landing on Theo's nice shirt. "Before— before spring. There's no getting out. He'll die either way. Don't give them the chance—"

The coughing overtook him. Viscera flowed over his chin. Chunks of pink flesh came out with the blood. Choking on his own organs.

Theo stood, a numb mess of horror and hunger.

Kade gripped the back of his shirt. "What do we do? *What do we do?*"

Theo shook his head. He felt like he was watching this through a screen, like it wasn't happening to him. Vampires, murderous history teachers, secret societies of hunters, dead dads. How could any of this be real?

Mr. Fletcher gave one last cough. Then he slumped over.

No one asked Theo to check for a heartbeat. Mr. Fletcher's glassy eyes were answer enough: the man was dead.

NINETEEN

MILLY HART STARED at Mr. Fletcher's body—ear bitten and bloody, gore dripping down his chin, slumped against Kade's wall between his drawers and his trashcan—for so long that Kade started sweating again.

Finally, Milly said, "You know, my friends and I had a middle-aged woman helping us with our homicidal hometown troubles. I never thought I'd turn into her."

"Homicidal hometown *what?*" Felicity echoed. "Who *are* you?"

"She's cool," Kade assured her. He'd been surprised when Theo suggested they call Milly. For a second he had thought it was just something Theo said to make Kade stop hyperventilating. Then Theo went semi-catatonic while they waited for her, and Kade realized they all wanted an adult here to take over the situation. Theo had had a rollercoaster of a day—his dad's funeral, pulling Kade out of a car wreck, saving Kade from being murdered, interrogating his best friend's dad, and then watching the guy choke to death on his own organs.

Theo was a determined guy, but he was also sixteen and grieving. Sometimes you needed an adult to come in and tell you everything was going to be okay.

Milly cocked her head. She looked...intrigued. A little confused.

She hummed and leaned back. "He said your dad knew the Fletchers were hunters? How did he find out, if they can't tell anyone without dying?"

Theo didn't answer. He was still aiming a thousand-yard stare at Mr. Fletcher's corpse.

Kade nudged him. "Mate."

Theo blinked hard, some of the zombie-ness leaving him. "I don't know. He found something. Or saw something. Maybe he saw me eat a squirrel."

"Great theory," Kade said, muffled around his thumbnail. "Can we *please* get the dead body out of my room before my aunt gets back? Milly, how'd you get rid of dead bodies in your hometown?"

"Oh," Milly said. "Um. Our friend ate them."

Everyone stared at her.

"Like," Kade said. "Their...blood?"

"No, their flesh. They fed the remains to dogs and put the bones in the trash."

Felicity widened her eyes at Kade. *What the hell*, she mouthed.

Kade nodded back. One day he was going to sit

Milly down and have her explain the whole story, start to finish.

Scratching noises drifted from the hallway. Sparky whined to be let in.

Theo gave Milly a hard glare. "She's *not* eating him."

"No," said Milly. "Of course. You're sure we shouldn't tell the hunters?"

"I'm not sure about anything," Theo said. "Except there's a dead body in this house, and it needs to not be here by the time Sundance gets home with a new car."

"Of course," Milly repeated. "Let's keep it simple. Kade, where would I find a bedsheet?"

They wrapped Mr. Fletcher in an old bedsheet Kade had been planning to cut up for scrap fabric. It had been on his to-do list for months. He'd never been happier to be awful at to-do lists.

They went into the woods. Not very far, just twenty minutes, with Theo keeping eyes and ears out for witnesses. Sparky stuck to his side, ears plastered to her head, staring up at Theo like he'd just scolded her. Kade waited for him to give her a reassuring pat, but Theo didn't even look at her as they walked deeper into the woods.

The Renfield house only had one shovel. Kade offered to be the one to wield it, but Theo gave him the tiredest glare imaginable and reminded Kade he was still recovering from blood loss.

Yeah, and you're still recovering from Dead Dad, Kade thought as he watched Theo dig, eyes aimed straight at the ground, mouth tight. Theo had spent days bouncing from task to task, but it seemed like everything was finally catching up to him. His fire was gone, replaced by a weary determination.

Felicity sat down next to Kade. She curled her long arms around her legs and rested her chin on her knees.

Sparky growled from her spot next to Kade.

"Cut it out," said Theo and Kade in unison.

Kade placed a hand on Sparky's flank. Sparky's growls faded, her orange eyes trained on Felicity's pale face.

Felicity poked her tongue out at Sparky and then leaned back to watch Theo shovel.

"Soooo," she said. "This is, like…a Band-Aid. Right? While we sort out sire shit? Because they *all* saw you ran off to chase him."

"And you're going to tell them you found me at Kade's, no harm done," Theo said. He paused to push his sleeves up further, the first time Kade had seen him pause since the shovel first bit into the ground. "And they'll think he went chasing another lead."

Felicity nodded. She still looked shocked, but it was a resigned shock. Like something she'd been dreading had finally come to pass. Kade thought back to her scrapbook, all those scribbles circling the dark photos she'd pasted onto the paper. The strangeness and mystery of growing up in a family full of whispers and knife training and bedtime stories that gave you nightmares.

"Hey," Kade said. "Uh. How did your dad die? And when?"

Felicity snorted, like she was impressed Kade had the balls to ask.

"I was six," she said, gaze fixed on the sheet-wrapped body lying next to the hole. "Brain aneurysm. Nothing anyone could do to stop it. That's what Mom said, anyway. Now I'm thinking..."

She stopped, staring at Mr. Fletcher's body.

"I don't know," she whispered. "I don't know what I think."

Milly turned to them. She had been looking up at the trees since Theo started digging. Not because she was disturbed by the body, but because she liked watching the changing leaves. A few weeks before, she and Theo had talked for half an hour about the deciduous trees native to Lock.

"So the hunters have a spell that stops them from discussing it with outsiders," Milly said.

"Looks like it," Felicity said shakily. She blew a strand of blond hair out of her face. "How are we doing, Theo?"

"Done," Theo said. He climbed out of the hole, funeral suit covered in dirt. He didn't even bother brushing himself down. He just dropped the shovel and picked up the body, sliding it carefully into the hole. It landed with a dull thud.

Felicity stood. Kade stood with her, remembering the funeral director asking if Theo and his mom wanted to say anything over Mr. Fairgood's grave.

No one spoke. Birds sang in the distance. Milly hummed quietly, echoing the tune.

"Well," Theo said. Then he picked up the shovel again.

Kade sighed. "Theo—"

"I can do it," Theo said. Then he started shoveling dirt onto the body. No panting, no sweat, nothing behind his eyes.

Felicity nudged a leaf into the grave with her shoe. "Happy birthday to Aaron, I guess."

Kade swore. He'd forgotten about Aaron's birthday party the following night.

Gaze still on his shovel, Theo said, "Are you going to be able to act normal around him tomorrow?"

"What?" Felicity laughed. "We're not *going*."

Theo eyed her and threw a shovelful of dirt over his shoulder.

Felicity gawked at him. "Theo, holy shit. Your dad's funeral was this *morning*, just say we're at your house watching movies! Ooooh, let's actually do that! Let's watch movies instead of going to my ex-boyfriend's house the day after I helped bury his dad's corpse in the woods!"

"You don't *look* like you're helping." Kade gestured at the two of them sitting on the ground next to the grave while Theo shoveled.

Felicity smacked him in the shoulder. "There's one shovel, jackass! What do you want me to do, use my hands? I have enough calluses as it is!"

Theo dragged the last shovelful of dirt onto the grave. He patted it down. Everyone stood next to him and admired his work.

Kade spoke up first. "This is obviously a grave."

Milly hummed in agreement.

"Like," Kade continued, "the first person who walks by this is gonna call the cops."

Felicity kicked leaves over it.

Theo sighed. "Liss."

"No," said Milly. "That's not a bad idea."

Two minutes later, everybody's hands were dirty (plus Sparky's muzzle), and the grave was covered in leaves.

Kade winced. His nail beds stung, pricked with dirt instead of just his own stupid chewing.

Felicity nudged another leaf over the dirt.

"Still grave-y," she decided.

"I don't care," Theo said, exhaustion visible in every line of his face. "I'm leaving."

He strode toward Kade's house, Sparky cowering at his side.

Kade jogged to catch up, wiping his dirty hands on his jeans. Blood tracked down the right leg from his wounded arm. He'd have to do his washing when he got home. Pick up the glass from the smashed widow, clean blood out of his carpet, *then* do his washing. Make up something to say to Sundance if she walked in on him while the bloodstains were still visible.

"God—" Felicity's words cut off as she tried to walk next to Theo only to be met with another growl from Sparky.

"Quit it," said Theo and Kade in one.

Felicity fell into step next to Kade, the three of them walking in a line, plus Sparky. Milly lagged behind, watching leaves drift down to the forest floor.

"God," Felicity repeated. "I can't believe the funeral was this *morning*. You're having a big day."

Theo didn't answer. Kade wasn't entirely sure he heard her, even with the vampire hearing. He was doing the thousand-yard stare again.

"And it's not even dinnertime," Kade said once into the awkward silence. "If *one* more thing happens, I'm gonna freak out."

Felicity flicked her hair, smacking Kade in the face. He picked hair away from his mouth, wondering if she would mention how he had hyperventilated after Mr. Fletcher died, fat tears rolling down his face.

But she just put her hands in her sundress pockets, uncaring about the grime she was smearing into the gauzy fabric. "Can someone give me a ride home? I scootered over."

"I forgot you used to scooter," Theo said distantly.

"I can drive you," Milly called from behind them, chin still tipped up toward the branches. She watched a rust-colored leaf float down, her mouth twitching in a smile like an afterthought.

"Um," Felicity said. "Thanks. *Who* are you again?"

She fell back to hear Milly's answer. Sparky let out a tiny growl as she walked off.

"Cut it out," Kade said.

Theo plodded along silently beside him. With his filthy suit, dirty hands, and hair smudged with blood and twigs, he looked a little like he'd been in the grave they just left.

Kade nudged him. "Hey. Blood boy. You awake?"

"Always," Theo said defeatedly. Then he said, "I like it better when you call me sunshine."

Kade's cheeks heated. He ducked his head. "I'll try to remember that."

A leaf drifted right in front of Theo's face and stuck to his suit. Kade watched it cling to the dirty fabric and thought back to that deciduous conversation Theo had been on the couch with Milly. Kade hadn't been able to stop smiling as he watched Theo gesture excitedly at his phone, Milly pulling out her own to compare their favorites. It felt like a million years ago.

Kade pulled the leaf off Theo's shirt. "Want to stay over again?"

"Yes," Theo said immediately. He blinked hard. "I don't want to intrude."

Kade scoffed. "You're not. We—Sundance *loves* having you around."

"Sundance," Theo repeated in an exhausted tone

that implied he would rib Kade for it properly if he wasn't half out of his head with grief and shock right now.

Kade bit his lip, remembering Theo's bared teeth as he slammed Mr. Fletcher against the wall. *None of you touch him. He's mine.* Theo staring at him wide-eyed and amazed, like he'd expected to find Kade already dead. Theo dropping his head on Kade's shoulder, the first rest he'd allowed himself since his dad died.

"Maybe I do too," Kade admitted. "Sunshine."

Theo smiled. Just a little. The small, tired smile of a boy walking through the woods with blood on his hands and too much on his shoulders.

Then the smile was gone.

"I should go home," he said dully. "See my mom. She'll be wondering where I am."

"Right," said Kade, heart sinking. "Yeah. Of course."

He picked at Theo's dirty collar. "Maybe borrow some clothes first."

Theo nodded. His gaze was distant again.

Kade's head throbbed. One hard lance of pain, short and sharp, before it dulled into a strange, quiet itch.

He winced. Aspirin, he decided. Pick up glass, clean blood, do washing—then aspirin.

TWENTY

THEO BRAKED FOR A STOP SIGN, struggling to remember which road led back to Aaron's place. He'd been driving these roads for years and walking them for longer, and suddenly he couldn't remember which road took him from Kade's side of town to his own.

He tried not to think about the Google search that had told him this 'grief haze' could last a few months. He was already tired of it.

Kade cleared his throat. He was in the backseat again, a fact he didn't even complain about when Theo directed him toward it.

"Left," Kade said. "If you're wondering."

Theo turned left. The Lexus fell into stilted silence again, and Theo prayed it would last.

"So," Kade said, shattering Theo's hopes immediately. "What'd you get up to since we buried a body?"

"Nothing," Theo said.

This was a lie. He'd spent Friday night doing up the garden—weeding, pruning, watering, climbing onto the roof and pulling off the ivy. He spent Saturday dumping the excess and trying in vain to catch up on the school he'd missed.

The whole day, he kept forgetting the most basic crap. Long division. What season daffodils bloomed. Standing in front of the shoe rack for a good ten seconds trying to remember which were his sneakers and which were his dad's. They hadn't tidied up any of his stuff yet. Hadn't even touched it. The last coffee cup he used was still in the kitchen, growing mold.

Kade asked, "How's your mom?"

"Fine," Theo said. He'd barely seen his mom since he got home. She'd been in the kitchen, making food and then deeming it inedible and throwing it out. Theo had taken some, to be polite, and then he'd had to go into the woods and empty the slippery red velvet cake onto the ground. Hopefully deer could digest cake.

They hadn't really talked until Theo was about to leave for Aaron's party, tearing his bedroom apart to find his popcorn cufflinks: a joke Christmas gift from Aaron. Theo was still pissed at him, but he *did* just bury the guy's dad in a shallow grave, so he wanted to go the extra mile for his birthday.

His mom had knocked on the door, flour in her limp curls, and asked where he was off to. Theo told her, and she pinched her lips as she asked who he was going with.

No one, he lied.

She didn't buy it for a second. *You know how impor-tant it is to be friends with the right kind of people, Theo. That Renfield boy—he might look exciting, in a grimy sort of way, but he's trash. You know that, right?*

He'd told her he knew. Then he'd slunk down to his Lexus to go pick up Kade and take him to the party.

Kade examined his nails in the backseat. He was wearing a less flashy outfit than last time—no fishnets, no skirt, no dark lipstick. Just jeans and the flowy dark shirt with the anatomically correct heart embroidered on the chest. Theo looked at him and tried to remember when he found his chipped nail polish off-putting, his chapped lips something to stay away from and not something he would dream about, if he still dreamed.

He's trash, his mom had said. Theo had agreed so readily. Then he'd snuck off, feeling like he'd just committed a betrayal. He just wasn't sure who he'd betrayed: Kade, or his family.

Sparky sulking didn't help. She kept giving him sad eyes, ears plastered against her head. Licking his hands. Hoping he would relent and call her a good girl again. But every time Theo considered forgiving her, he heard his dad's voice in his head: *you're too easy on that dog. Fair-goods are vicious. Who are you?*

"I'm a Fairgood," Theo mumbled.

Kade looked up from his nails. "Huh?"

Theo gestured at the road. "I'll drop you off here. See you at the party in ten?"

Kade nodded. He adjusted his shirt, which was open at the collar. Moonlight fell across his pale and mouth-watering clavicle.

Theo swallowed, training his gaze back on the road as he pulled over. "What, no complaining?"

Kade shrugged.

"No pointing out that everyone saw you running after me in the woods at Felicity's party? And the whole...*thing* at the funeral? And that my mom saw you come home with me? And that there are rumors all around the school about us being together or you black-mailing me for sex or me blackmailing you for drugs?"

Kade blinked rapidly. He was wearing eyeliner again, the sharp wings making his gray eyes look even bigger than usual.

"I'll start bitching again next week," he said. "This time you get a pass."

He said it too carefully. Theo got the sense he'd been talking to his aunt about being nice to poor, grieving Theo.

"Very mature of you," Theo said.

"Trying something new," Kade replied. He was obvi-ously trying to be calm, but Theo could smell the sweat under his store-bought deodorant. They'd buried a man in the woods yesterday and were headed to his son's birthday party. Whatever Kade's calm was, it was thin and ready to melt at the slightest provocation.

He reached for the door handle.

"Wait," Theo blurted. He'd left Sparky all sad and shaky, he didn't want to do the same to Kade. "Thanks. For coming."

Kade shrugged again. "You asked me to."

Then he got out of the car. Walking ten minutes in the autumn chill to a house party he didn't want to go to, to stand alone in a room full of people who didn't like him, because Theo asked.

The doors were wide open, colored lights and noise spilling out into the dark.

Theo looked through the crowd. The setup was the same as last year—drinks table in the foyer, dancefloor in the living room, a barrier on the stairs to stop people going up to the second floor. The night was young, which usually meant Theo could find Aaron in the kitchen, trying to get away from the noise. He wasn't a crowds guy.

But Aaron wasn't in the kitchen. Theo walked through the crowd, listening as best he could through the din until he heard a girl say Aaron's name.

He tapped her on the shoulder. "Hey. Do you know where Aaron is?"

She turned. It was Skeeter Bass, her scars hidden under a scarf the party was too hot for. She flushed when she saw him, like she was remembering Felicity's mouth on her neck.

"Um," she said, braces glinting underneath the colored lights. "I think he's still dancing? He knocked beer all over my dress. It's my good one, too."

"Dancing," Theo repeated, confused. "You're sure?"

She nodded and pointed into the living room. "Under the main light. He won't let anyone else near it."

Theo followed her gaze.

The main light was broken. It had to be, because it wasn't roving over the walls like the others. It wasn't colored, either, no bright purple or neon green. This was a clear, pale river of light beaming straight down onto the middle of the dancefloor. There was a small gap around it, everyone swaying to stay clear of it as they danced. And in the middle of the gap, basking in the light, stood Aaron.

It wasn't dancing. Not quite. This was more of a demented thrashing, arms waving, legs kicking out. Even his hair gel wasn't enough to make his hair stay in place as he whipped his head around to the beat.

Theo headed through the crowd. It parted easily, everyone giving him distracted, awkward nods as soon as they noticed who it was.

Theo ignored them. "Aaron! Hey!"

Aaron stumbled to a stop. His cheeks were bright, sweat shining on his upper lip. Theo had never seen him dance like that—Aaron's dance moves were strictly limited to the box step or the Cool Guy Shuffle.

Aaron stared at him, dazed. A tuft of brown hair

fell over his sweaty forehead. For a moment Theo thought he was going to get punched, or maybe screamed at.

Then Aaron broke into a wild grin. "Buddy! Hey, what's UP, my man?"

Theo blinked as Aaron yanked him into a hug. "I'm good. Are *you* good, man? Did you take something?"

Aaron shook his head. He stunk of beer and sweat and rot, gloved hands shaking as he stepped back. The black veins above his bandaged hand had gotten worse since the funeral. Thicker and longer, climbing up his arm.

Theo frowned. "Dude, is your hand okay?"

"What?" Aaron glanced down at it and frowned, then shoved it in his pocket. "Don't worry about it. Let's find somewhere we can actually talk."

Theo followed him out of the living room. A few people tried to wish Aaron a happy birthday, but he ignored them, pushing through until he to the base of the stairs in the front hall. It was quieter here, a crossroads for people on their way to the drinks table or the dancefloor.

"Didn't expect to see you dance," Theo said. "Bit early for you."

"I started early," Aaron said. He leaned back against the barrier, eyes widening when it sagged under his weight.

Theo caught his shoulder. "Easy."

"Says you," Aaron said, drooping sideways to lean

against the wall. "Hey! What the *hell* happened with my dad yesterday?"

Theo's stomach fell. He'd hoped they could talk about party things. Birthday things. Breakup things, if it came down to it. Aaron was a natural at avoiding difficult subjects. At most, he'd make a passive-aggressive comment.

Theo said the first thing that came to his head. "Excuse me?"

"Oh, I'm *sorry*," Aaron simpered. "I forgot. We're not talking about it. About any of it! We're not talking about how you barged in all weird demanding to know where my dad was, and no one's seen him since, and Mom won't put in a missing persons report until it's been forty-eight hours. What, did you kill him?"

"Ha ha," Theo said weakly. He looked around for an exit. Where was Kade? Was he here yet?

Aaron rubbed Theo's chest. It was a weird move, nothing close to his usual shoulder slap. "I'm joking. Whatever weird cult shit you guys have going on—"

"There's no cult shit," Theo tried, blinking bright colored lights from his eyes. They'd really mounted them in every room, even in the hallways. Aaron did love a spectacle.

Aaron ignored him, continuing, "...that apparently my girlfriend's mom is also in on—wait, shit. Ex-girlfriend. Whatever. I'm seventeen now! I'm hot, I'm popular, my grades are *good*, goddammit, no matter what my parents say. I'm the second-best guy on the basketball team! Who cares if everyone I love is being super secretive and weird!"

He grabbed Theo by the back of the neck and shook him. Theo had seen Mr. Fletcher do that to his son many times—sometimes in pride, other times in annoyance. It had the power to make Aaron smile like he was on top of the world or cringe like he was under it, just like Theo's dad ruffling his hair. Every time Mr. Fletcher touched his son's neck there was always this moment where Aaron tensed up, unsure if he was being rewarded or punished. So many times, Theo looked at Aaron and saw a mirror.

Aaron jammed their foreheads together, smearing sweat against Theo's curls. "You're still gonna give me a birthday speech, right?"

Theo looked around the hallway at the sparse crowd trickling from one room to the next.

"Um," he said.

"Shit! Forgot your dad's dead. You're let off speech duties. Dead Dad Pass." Aaron rubbed the back of Theo's head and leaned back. "Hey, screw what Liss said. Victor was a good guy. Harsh, but you know, good. You know he hugged me once? Yeah, right before that game you charged out of. Straightened my shirt. Told me he was glad I was around. It was weird. My point is, he was a good guy!"

"Thanks," Theo said slowly, stomach twisting into a hundred guilty knots. "Aaron, I can do a speech."

Aaron blinked hazily. "Seriously? I meant it about the Dead Dad Pass. Liss said to let you do whatever."

"No, no. I'll do it."

"Really?" Aaron grinned at him, and for a moment Theo remembered how much he used to smile back in grade school, before he got his patented Aaron smirk down.

Aaron leaned past Theo and screamed, "TURN THE MUSIC OFF! MUSIC OFF, SPEECH TIME FOR THE BIRTHDAY BOY!"

Theo winced. He looked desperately through the crowd, breathing in deeply. Sweat, spirits, beer, the musk of a hundred teenagers crammed into one space. Then, underneath it: soft smoke, metal, yarn. A heartbeat as quiet as everyone else, moving through the rooms toward Theo.

Kade appeared in the hall, a dark spot of calm in a sea of deafening color. Theo had missed him since he sent him out into the cold autumn air to walk the rest of the way.

He pointed at Kade's empty hands and mimed a drink.

Kade shook his head. "Not tonight," he murmured. He was across the hall, but his words were clear through the quieting music and the dying chatter.

Theo held up one finger.

Kade chuckled. "Never been able to do the one and done thing. When I want something, I want all of it."

Those gray eyes connected with Theo's and held.

Theo clenched his jaw so hard his teeth ached.

A loud clinking dragged him back to the moment. Aaron had found a glass and was banging a random pair of nail clippers against it.

"Everybody shut up," he yelled across the hall as people continued to gather. "My boy's gonna do a speech."

He flung the nail clippers into the crowd. Everybody ducked. The clippers landed on a freshman's arm and fell to the floor.

Then all eyes turned to Theo. Sympathetically, of course. Many of them had been at the funeral. Even if they hadn't, word spread like wildfire in Lock. Everybody knew about Victor Fairgood, lawyer extraordinaire, half of the legendary Fairgood & Fairgood duo, mauled to death by creatures unknown while out on a nature walk.

Theo nodded at them, fighting down a wave of resentment. All his classmates, many of whom he'd never even talked to, gazing up at him like they knew what he was going through. Like they *understood*. There was only one person who even had the potential to understand what Theo was going through, and he was standing at the back of the hall with smudged eyeliner and his hands in his ripped pockets.

"Whoo," someone called. "Go Theo!"

Theo looked over to see Finn Harley—the Night-fowl who excelled at jump shots and absolutely nothing else—raising a fist in solidarity.

Theo gritted his teeth, trying to remember what he'd said in last year's birthday speech. Felicity had been at his side, arm slung around his shoulders in a way that made people whisper.

"Thank you all for coming," Theo began. The only right way to start any speech. "Uh, I met Aaron in grade school. Felicity insisted we needed another person to play tag with, so we grabbed Aaron. And he's never left us alone since."

A nervous titter ran through the crowd.

"Probably not a good idea to bring up the ex," Kade whispered from across the room.

Right, Theo thought. *Damn.*

He cleared his throat. "Anyway. He's been my best guy for most of my life. I can hardly remember a time without him. He, uh. Um."

He looked at Aaron, whose smile was tight and expectant. Almost pleading. They'd been on such rocky ground since Theo got dragged into all this vampire shit, and by extension, into Kade. Theo couldn't look at Aaron without remembering all the times he'd helped Theo with his Math homework, the countless games of basketball they'd played at Aaron's house, how he'd pried a fish hook out of Theo's ear when they were twelve. His careful fingers, that worried gaze as he tugged it free. But he also couldn't stop thinking about Aaron in that parking lot, sneering at Kade with blood in his mouth. Imagining him kissing Kade hard, one hand tight in Kade's frizzy hair, long before Kade shaved it off. Pretending not to know him when Theo came up, ignoring him in the halls...

Theo blinked hard. He looked up at Kade again, who didn't talk to Theo at school unless they were in an empty bathroom. Who didn't even bitch about Theo dropping him ten minutes away so they could arrive at different times.

Theo swallowed. There was a lump in his throat.

"Aaron, uh." He couldn't let his voice break. Everyone was *watching* him. Forget black tears, forget everybody figuring out he was a monster—Theo didn't want them to know he was sad. That he was *weak*.

"Um," he said. *Come up with something. Anything!* But nothing came.

He looked up at Kade, who was watching him with those wide gray eyes. The only concerned face that Theo didn't want to snarl at.

"I'm just really grateful," Theo said, voice rough but steady, "that we're, uh. That we're friends. The last few" —he coughed, caught himself before he could say months—"*days* have been crazy. And he's been so great. Better than I deserve. I don't know what I'd do without him. He's my best friend. He's...he's my person."

Silence. A few scattered claps, two more cheers from people Theo had never spoken to before.

Theo cleared his throat. "Uh, happy seventeenth birthday, man. Love you."

The applause swelled, hands lifted toward the staircase where Aaron was standing beside Theo, stiff as a board.

Theo looked over. Aaron was staring at him. Had been staring at him the whole speech. He'd seen where Theo was looking. He didn't look...betrayed, exactly. Just hurt. The same resigned kind of hurt Felicity showed after they killed Mr. Fletcher: she'd been suspecting something awful was going to happen, and now it finally had.

Theo gave him a quick shoulder slap. "I'm gonna hit the bathroom. See you on the dancefloor?"

Aaron nodded, his eyes dull.

Theo stepped off the bottom stair, shooting Kade a pointed look. *Follow me.*

CHAPTER
TWENTY-ONE

THE ORANGE GLOW of cigarettes was the only light on the porch.

Kade's heart pounded as Theo leaned back, blowing out a stream of smoke. The way Theo had looked at him during that speech—like he was drowning and Kade was a life raft. Like Kade was the only thing holding him afloat. It felt huge. Impossibly huge, the kind you couldn't talk about.

"Thought you might not notice me," Kade said instead. "It was pretty cramped in there."

"If you're around, I can hear you."

"Right. Loud heart." Kade rubbed his chest through his flowy shirt. The embroidered heart veins were rough against his thin fingers. He looked around, trying to think of something safe to say. Other than grass on the lawn and trees looming ahead, there were no plants for him to comment on.

"Hey," Theo said. Something in his voice made Kade's teeth tighten around his cigarette.

"Yeah?"

Theo hesitated. "Aaron gave you a nice first time, right?"

Kade choked. He pulled the cigarette out of his mouth, coughing and spluttering.

Theo clapped him carefully on the back.

"Shit," Kade rasped, eyes watering. "Mate, what the *hell*?"

"I just—" Theo dropped his hand. "I know he can be an asshole. But not in bed. Right? He made it nice for you? I assume it was your first time."

"Of course it was my first time," Kade mumbled, chewing on the end of his cigarette. His cheeks burned. He didn't want to go into how Aaron was his first and currently his only. It depressed him, and more importantly, it was humiliating.

"It was fine," he gritted.

Theo gave him a worried look. At least he didn't seem like he wanted to cry anymore. He had definitely been on the verge of it, back on that staircase with Aaron. Kade wanted the guy to let it out, but not black tears in front of all their classmates.

"Jesus Christ," Kade muttered. He threw up his hands. "It was fine! I knew what I was getting into. It wasn't like I *liked* him."

"Why did you try to kiss him in that parking lot?"

Kade groaned. He hated that Theo could hear his

stupid heartbeat right now, even more damning than his blush.

"I don't know! I wanted him to admit we were... something." He flicked ash to the wood, rubbed it in with his shoe. Hoped it would stain. "And he *never* kissed me, so."

Theo's face twisted. "That's stupid. What is this, the eighties?"

"*Right?* I get his parents are homophobes, but still." Kade tapped the cigarette. There was no ash to get rid of, but he wanted something to look at that wasn't Theo's piercing eyes.

Theo asked, "But you've kissed other people, right? At parties and stuff?"

Kade snorted smoke out of his nose. "Sure. Everyone's lining up to kiss Monster."

Theo's smile faded. Kade tried to come up with a joke, a comment, something mean, *anything* to stop Theo from saying what he was about to say.

"Wait," Theo said. "Have you never had a first kiss?"

"Nope," Kade said. He said it fast, dismissive, hoping like hell Theo would get the hint and change the subject. But Theo just stared at him, looking oddly heartbroken. Like Kade being unkissed was something to cry about.

"You should go back in there," Kade said desperately. "Act normal. Go...dance with some cheerleader."

"Not really in the crowd kind of mood," Theo said, still staring at him. Then he blinked, looking toward the giggling teens at the tree line. It was too far for Kade to see who they were, but he bet Theo could make out every single one of their pores.

Theo took a long breath of smoke. "Could dance out here though," he said, sounding strangely hesitant.

"Oh man. Go for it." Kade flapped a hand at the porch.

"Yeah?"

"Sure." Kade expected Theo to crack a joke, maybe do the Cool Guy Shuffle he'd seen Theo do at parties before, too cool to even try proper dancing. As if Kade had danced anywhere except his room, arms flailing, more jumping than anything else.

But Theo just stared, long enough for Kade to get nervous again. Then he dropped his cigarette, ground it out on the porch with his shoe—and took Kade's shoulders.

Kade startled. "Oh. *Oh*! You mean with me?"

"Why not?" Theo smiled, a little stiff. Nervous. Probably remembering Kade's humiliating unkissed status, hoping Kade wouldn't get the wrong idea. Not that they *could* kiss, even if Theo wanted to. Even if sometimes Kade thought that Theo *might* want to, with all those lingering stares. Laughing at Kade's stupid jokes. Staring at him so intently after he bit him, lips slick with Kade's blood. It was probably just the high. Still, there was this small, stupid hope that remained no matter how hard Kade tried to stamp it out.

He evaluated safe spots to touch. Theo was in a

long-sleeved Henley and slacks. Nothing exposed except his face and his hands, those big soft hands so gentle on Kade's bony shoulders.

"My waist," Theo said.

Kade looked up. "What?"

"Put your hands on my waist," Theo told him.

Slowly, Kade settled his fingers on the soft cotton of Theo's shirt where it was tucked into his slacks. He'd never touched Theo's waist before. He'd touched Aaron's, a few times. The hazy memories paled in comparison to Theo, soft and solid and staring at him like a life raft once again. Like if he let go, he'd float away.

"Okay," Theo said. "Now sway."

Kade's throat clicked. "What, no box step?"

"Just move with me." Theo rocked from side to side, shuffling his feet. Kade followed, heart thumping painfully in his chest. Theo heard it, he had to. He probably heard it louder than the music bleeding out of the house. Some poppy dance song Kade pretended not to like when it came on the radio.

Theo spun them slowly. Kade let him. He couldn't not, they were pressed so close together, as close as they could get without their faces touching. Chest to chest, shoes bumping as they circled each other.

Dancing. Like a real teenager, doing real teenager things. Kade never thought he'd see the day.

He wanted to defuse the tension. Make a joke. But

he couldn't make his tongue work, stunned into silence at the pressure of Theo's strong arms, his face so close and lovely, his eyes devastatingly soft. Then Theo pulled him closer, and Kade's breath hitched as Theo's cheek hovered so close to his own.

Oh god, Kade thought, heart pounding. He pictured Theo smirking as he heard it, not to mention the stench that had to be rising from Kade's sweat. He could feel it dripping down his spine, only stopped by Theo's hand resting on the small of his back.

Kade pulled back, hoping his smile didn't look as vulnerable as he felt. "Golden boy dancing with the Monster. What would your mother say?"

"Ha ha," Theo said, a beat too late. His eyes were fixed on something behind Kade.

Kade winced, desperate not to ruin the moment. "I was joking."

"What? Sorry, I was just looking at the greenhouse." At Kade's confused look, Theo continued: "Remember, I broke into it last year when you were pushing me to scope out the Fletcher house? Me and Aaron joked there would be bodies or ghosts or a drug empire, but there was nothing. Look."

He turned them until Kade was looking at the forest over Theo's shoulder. At the border of it, almost hidden around the back of the house, sat a small, plastic hut that Kade wouldn't even call a greenhouse. After all, you were supposed to be able to see through a greenhouse.

The whole point was to let the light in. Kade couldn't see how any light got through that thick white material.

The padlock was huge and rusty and oddly inviting. A strange shiver ran down Kade's spine. He ignored it, forcing a smile.

"Mysterious plants," he said. "I bet that drove you crazy."

"I did convince myself they were raising secret plants for the government," Theo admitted wistfully.

They twirled another circle around the porch. Kade tried to focus on Theo's proximity, but he found his eyes dragging over Theo's shoulder again, catching on the small dark greenhouse. There was something about it, tucked at the back of the Fletcher house, almost swallowed by trees. Like something out of a fairy story he read as a child, dark and foreboding.

"Theo—" Kade started.

Theo stopped. "Shit."

Kade looked up. Theo was glaring guiltily at something behind them.

Kade turned.

Aaron stood at the edge of the porch. His hair was floppier than Kade had seen it in years, his jaw tight. His injured hand was wrapped around a support beam, bandages peeking out from the glove. Something was wrong with the veins above it. Like blood poisoning, but more...profuse. And *sharp*. It looked like something was trying to cut its way out of Aaron's skin.

Not for the first time, Kade damned his loud heart

for drowning out vampire senses so they didn't notice people sneaking up behind them.

"You walked off in the wrong direction," Aaron said flatly as the boys broke apart. "Just wanted to make sure you didn't get lost. Looks like I'm too late, you're tongue-deep in my leftovers."

"We weren't doing anything," Kade snapped.

"He's not leftovers," Theo said over him. "And he was never *yours*."

Aaron snorted. His tongue moved inside his cheek. For all the crap he had to say about Kade, his gaze was fixed on Theo.

"I don't know what your dad would think about this," Aaron said, voice low.

Theo tensed. "Well he never gets to know, does he? He's *dead*. Somebody killed my dad and I don't know who, Aaron. Excuse me for...for...blowing off some steam!"

Kade felt it like a punch. Aaron had said that once, after they did hand stuff in that same disabled bathroom where he now met Theo for feeding sessions. *We're just blowing off steam together,* he'd said after Kade asked if he wanted to go see a movie. Then he'd given Kade a stern look. *Don't get the wrong idea about this. We're not a thing.*

Aaron laughed again, uncertain. "Your dad...your dad got killed by a *bear*, man. Or are you seriously telling me you believe in all this vampire shit people have been whispering about?"

"Theo," Kade said warningly, but Theo was already stalking forward so fast that Aaron stumbled back.

"You have no clue, huh?" Theo hissed. "Because *no one* will tell you what's going on. Even your girlfriend. Even your mom. Even—"

"Then *tell* me," Aaron blurted. He gripped Theo's shirt, groaning with pain. "For god's sake, *someone* tell me what the hell is going on."

Kade covered his mouth with his hand, whispering so only Theo could hear him. "I don't trust him. Maybe Felicity's keeping her mouth shut, but *I don't trust him*. Especially after we just—"

Aaron whirled toward him. "What are you muttering about?"

"Nothing," Kade said.

Theo's head shot up, eyes wide with shock. Before Kade could ask what was wrong, he saw it: flashing lights. Red and blue. No sirens, just a single cop car pulling up outside the house.

"Ugh," Aaron spat. He rubbed his forehead, flinching when he reached up with his injured hand. "Jesus. Let's get this over with."

He let go of Theo, wobbling as he straightened.

Kade traded a panicked look with Theo. He didn't have to ask—this wasn't noise control. And now he was stuck here, watching as Mrs. Fletcher climbed out of the backseat of the cop car, eyes wet, white-knuckling her purse.

Aaron stopped at the edge of the porch. "Mom? What are you doing?"

Kade squeezed his eyes shut. He didn't want to see this.

A hand touched his shoulder. Kade looked over to see Theo, face tight and grave, nodding toward his car.

Time to go.

CHAPTER
TWENTY-TWO

AARON DIDN'T SHOW up to school on Monday.

Nobody was surprised. Theo heard Sarah Wetterson—mathlete and sympathetic puker—whispering about how weird it was that Theo *did* show up the day after his dad died, and maybe that meant Theo didn't care about his dad very much. It was a good thing his other classmate, Vita Dido—loud, smart, once fit her whole fist in her mouth during biology class—pointed out how serious Theo was about his attendance, because Theo had been about to march across the room to scream at them.

It's so weird, they whispered. *Both their dads in one week. Both mysterious deaths. Maybe someone's killing off the Nightfowl dads.*

They whispered: *Maybe Kade's involved. I saw him follow Theo outside at Aaron's party.*

Theo couldn't take it. The next time he passed Kade in the hall, he dragged him into a bathroom.

"This isn't our usual," Kade said, eyeing the multiple bathroom stalls, the unlockable door and Theo's hand on his sleeve.

Theo let him go, stuffing his hands in his pockets. He still had the lighter, shifting from pants pocket to pants pocket, waiting for Theo to finally hand it over.

"Come over after school?" he asked.

Theo waited for Kade to ask why this couldn't have been a text. Or tease him about whether anyone had seen Theo drag him into the bathroom.

"Why?" Kade asked instead.

"Why what?'

"What's the excuse? You usually have one. Visions, feeding, homework."

Kade crossed his arms tightly over his chest. He was wearing his *WAIT I HAVE ANOTHER BAD IDEA* shirt, the one he'd been wearing when Theo bit him for the first time.

"I need..." Theo swallowed. "I still have your clothes. I have to give them back."

It was even true. The clothes Theo had borrowed were sitting under his bed at home, clean and folded. He'd meant to take them to school today, but he forgot.

He waited for Kade to ask why Theo couldn't bring them to school tomorrow. Or why this was so urgent Kade needed to come around today.

Kade asked, "Am I sneaking in?"

"Mom won't be home until dark."

Kade hitched his backpack higher. It looked like he actually had books in there, as he often had since senior year started.

"See you in your backseat," Kade said, and walked out.

Felicity cornered Theo under the bleachers.

"Not our usual lunch spot," she said as she folded to her knees beside him. "But I'll take it. Can you still eat?"

Theo shook his head.

Felicity made a face. "God. That sucks. I'd kill myself if I could never eat potatoes again."

"Good thing I'm already dead," Theo said flatly.

Felicity snorted. She rested her chin on her knees, winding a strand of shiny blond hair around her finger. She was wearing less makeup than usual. It made her look her age, for once. Ever since she signed the modeling contract, she'd been doing whatever it took to make herself look older. Clothes, makeup, posture. Theo hadn't seen her rest her chin on her knees in a long time. He thought she might've done it while he was burying Mr. Fletcher, but his memory was a little fuzzy. It had been fuzzy all week, actually. So annoying —he had super strength and could fly, but he still got grief fog?

"Soooo," Felicity said into the silence. "How about them Nightfowls?"

"I don't know. Haven't been going to practice."

"Right. Don't want to start flying on the court." Felicity poked a dry wad of gum stuck to the bottom of the bleachers. "*Can* you fly?"

Theo nodded.

"Shit. Seriously?" Felicity grinned. "That's awesome."

"I came here to be alone, Liss."

"Really? You're doing a bad job." Felicity's hand twitched, like she was going to punch him in the shoulder like back when they were kids. Then it fell back to her side. She toyed with her skirt hemline.

"Where's Kade?"

"We don't hang at school."

"Oookay." Felicity smacked her lips. She was wearing the expensive cherry lip gloss Aaron got her for every birthday. "You know that everyone kind of knows, right?"

"Not officially," Theo protested. Then, when Felicity gave him an unimpressed look: "I told my mom we don't hang out, okay?"

Felicity hummed, so high-pitched that Theo winced. "You know how fast gossip spreads. Even with me shutting it down, all your subterfuge and making him ride around in the backseat."

"It sounds bad when you say it like that."

"Is pretty much useless now," Felicity said over him. "You might as well bite the bullet."

"Nope."

Felicity groaned. "Oh my god, who cares if your mom doesn't like *one* person you hang out with?"

"I can't let her down," Theo snapped, so loud that Felicity flinched. Theo cringed. "I...I can't. Okay? It's all I—"

He stopped. He'd been about to say something pathetic.

Felicity finished it for him. "All you have?"

Theo didn't respond. He checked his phone. Ten minutes until they had to head to class.

"I get you're going through a whole thing," Felicity said. "With the murdered dad stuff. But you have me. I don't know if that's a good thing, but you have me."

He frowned at her. Before he could ask why that would be a bad thing, she continued:

"You have...okay, I don't know about Aaron, since we got his dad killed. But you have me. And Kade. Who is actually pretty cool when he's not snarling at you. Even when he is. Kinda wish we started hanging sooner. I tried to invite him to a party last year but he thought I was making fun of him. Which I kinda was, but still."

She paused. Then she reached over and touched his arm. She didn't ask about how muscles worked as a vampire, or say she could lift more than him, like she sometimes did since her gymnast muscles came back over the summer. She just let her hand rest. They weren't good at talking about this kind of stuff, but she could at least give him this.

Theo couldn't look at her. He was pretty sure she understood. The same way Aaron understood: accepting comfort felt like he was doing something wrong. It meant Theo wasn't doing everything perfectly. And if Theo wasn't doing everything perfectly—school, sports, bringing pride to the Fairgood name—then he would get punished. And he'd deserve it. Because Theo only got punished when he was being bad, and Theo wanted to be good. More than anything, Theo wanted to be good.

But sometimes being good meant doing something his parents would disapprove of.

The boys sat on the cliffs near Theo's house, legs dangling off the edge of the place where Kade once planned to jump. The place where Theo had been scooped up to be pried open, his sire's dark blood forced between his lips until he swallowed.

Theo looked out over the lake. It was a *long* drop.

Kade slouched onto his elbows, Theo's borrowed clothes folded on his lap.

"How's Aaron?" he asked, and sucked on a cigarette. He hadn't offered one to Theo.

"Don't know. He hasn't answered my texts. I'd go over, but—"

"Don't wanna get shot with a silver arrow."

Theo nodded. He couldn't stop thinking about the sirens illuminating Aaron's numb face as his mom told him what the police had found in the woods. The horrible familiarity of it. The answering ache in Theo's chest.

"I hate how much I want to see him," Theo admitted. "I don't—I don't even know if I *like* him anymore. But I've known him forever. I know exactly what he's going through. Our dads were kind of similar, you know? All those expectations. All that weight. We used to joke we were the heavyweight twins, carrying all that shit on our shoulders."

Kade blew out a long, slow plume of smoke. "Theo," he said, and his tone made Theo look. He spoke low and hesitantly, like he had something to say but really didn't want to say it.

Kade winced, staring up at the sky. "You know it's, like, *fine* to have weird, complicated feelings about your parents. Nobody's dad is perfect."

"I know," Theo said defensively, thinking about Felicity's disbelieving smile after he denied his parents were bad people. "But my dad was...he was good. He wanted what was best for me."

"Okay," Kade said slowly. "You just...seem kinda freaked out over him disapproving of anything."

"Isn't everyone afraid of letting down their dad?" Theo wiped his hands on his jeans, a leftover habit from when he was human. He had no sweat to wipe away anymore. He felt the lighter in his pocket—the real reason he'd invited Kade over.

"Look," he said in a rush. "I wanted to give this to

you for ages but it was never the right time. Then everything happened, and I got stressed about metaphors—"

Kade sat up, surprised. "Theo?"

"You've been really good to me," Theo said. "Making me laugh. Trying to make me rest. I know I'm bad at it, but it means a lot that you tried."

"Okaaay," Kade said. "Metaphors?"

Theo nodded. "The thing I got you. It helps you die faster. *I* help you die faster. That's my whole thing, right? Killing you?"

Kade stared at him. His gaze darted down to where Theo's hand was worrying his pocket.

"What the hell did you get me?" he asked, incredulous. "Heroin? A *gun*?"

"No," Theo snapped, clenching the lighter so tight he worried it would dent. "I—"

A car rumbled in the distance. Theo turned just in time to watch his mom's convertible emerge from the wooded path, heading toward the house.

"Shit." Kade stood, almost dropping the clothes Theo had folded. He reached for his backpack and stuffed the clothes in. "You said she wasn't home until dark."

"Well, I was wrong," Theo said, watching the convertible pull up the driveway.

Kade slung his backpack on. "Want backup? Or do I run?"

"Don't *run*, that would look so weird!" Theo fell

silent as his mom climbed out of the convertible and made a beeline straight toward the cliffs where they were sitting. Her smile was tight, her curls perfect in a way they hadn't been in days. She wore a white power suit, untouched by the dust and leaves swirling around her as she walked up.

She came to a neat stop in front of them and extended a hand toward Kade. "Hi. I didn't introduce myself properly last time. I'm Carol Fairgood."

"Kade," Kade blurted, grabbing her hand and pumping it hard. "Renfield. Sorry I passed out in your house."

She laughed. "That's no problem. I have to admit, I'm surprised to see you! I was under the impression you wouldn't be coming over again."

Kade flushed. "Right. Sorry. I was just leaving."

He half-turned, like he was going to say goodbye. Then he nodded, fast and tight, eyes averted. Like he didn't want to look at Theo in front of his mom in case she realized something. Realize what, Theo wondered. That they were unwilling members of a vampire ritual? That Theo had danced with him at Aaron's birthday, spinning slow circles around his back porch? That Theo thought about kissing those chapped lips every time Kade laughed, which was a lot more often nowadays? That Theo *couldn't* kiss him unless he wanted Kade to burn?

"Theo," Carol said.

Theo tore his gaze from Kade's retreating figure. He

wanted to snap at her. How dare he want to snap at her? Her husband had just died, she was the only thing he had left.

"Yes," he said, surprised to find his voice was rough.

She nodded at the car in the driveway. "There's a casserole in the front seat, could you take it inside?"

"Sure." He started walking toward it.

"Thanks, hon. It's another one from Russel," she told him as she headed for the house. "Not sure what's in it. He joked that it had a lot of iron, since he cut himself while he was making it. There better not be Russel-blood in that thing, he's far too casual about these things."

Theo hummed distractedly. He glanced at Kade, who was walking toward the woods. Theo hadn't even offered him a ride home.

"He says he's always cutting himself when he's cooking," Carol continued as she reached the front gate. "Maybe that's how he got all those scars."

Theo stopped. He was almost at the convertible. The casserole sat in the passenger's seat, wrapped in steaming foil. Still warm.

"Scars?" Theo repeated. He turned to watch Carol head down the garden path toward the house.

"I always assumed the scars all over his hands were from gardening. Maybe he's just a terrible cook." Carol paused to cup a rose in her palm. Bright red, the ones Theo had pruned over the weekend. She gave it an appreciative sniff and continued, "Funny thing. He went on and on about the blood in this, but I didn't even see a Band-Aid."

Theo's ears rang. Russel's hands, burnished with a hundred tiny scars. Russel coming out of the house as cop cars sat out front. *He knows your family,* Mr. Fletcher had told him.

His first thought was denial. *It can't be him. He's known me his whole life. He taught me how to keep bugs out of the tomatoes. He wouldn't.*

"Weird," Theo croaked. "Hey mom, where does he live again? I want to thank him for all the food."

She turned, giving him a surprised smile. "That's so nice of you. I bet he'll love that. But don't go over right now, he said he was going to visit...I mean, he's going to do something for your dad."

"Do something," Theo repeated.

"That's what he said. I just assumed it was flowers." Carol ran a distracted hand through her curls. "Where's Sparky? She's usually yelling at me by now."

"I locked her in the house," Theo said numbly. He turned, searching for the heartbeat he could hear from a mile away. Kade was almost at the woods, a small figure about to be swallowed up by the trees.

"Mom," Theo said. "Can you actually grab the casserole? I need to go."

Carol frowned. "I'm sorry?"

Theo ran.

TWENTY-THREE

THEO TORE the Lexus through the sleepy streets so fast Kade was glad, for once, to be crouched over in the backseat.

He sat up just enough to see Theo's face in the rearview mirror. Theo's eyes were wide with fury, the steering wheel cracking under his hands.

"Heeeey," Kade said. "You aren't going to run up and, like...stab the guy, right?"

"I'M GOING TO RIP OUT HIS SPINE," Theo yelled.

The Lexus lurched around a corner. Kade slammed into the car door and winced.

"Right," Kade said, holding his twinging arm. "But he has scars. If he has scars, he can't be a vampire! *Your* scars healed when you turned—"

"HAWTHORN HAD TATTOOS," Theo yelled. "WE DON'T KNOW HOW IT WORKS! MR.

FLETCHER SAID HE HAS SCARS, MAYBE THEY'RE SPECIAL MAGIC SCARS HE'S GONNA USE IN THE RITUAL TO DESTROY THE TOWN!"

The Lexus sped around another corner. Kade cried out as he slid once more into the door, funny bone first.

"What?" Theo barked. The car slowed. "What is it? Are you hurt?"

Kade rubbed his elbow, eyes watering. "I'm fine, it's just my arm."

Theo sped up again. The car sailed down the road and pulled up to a shaky stop in front of the tree Kade had crashed into only days before.

Theo surged out of the car. Kade stumbled after him He considered mentioning how useless it was for him to hide in the backseat if he was going to pop out at the same time as Theo, if only to distract Theo from his relentless charge toward the man crouching next to Victor's grave. Russel, Theo had explained on the way over. His gardener. Kade recognized the name—Theo had mentioned him a few times, always trying to sound casual but giving away his fondness.

Kade's heart sank.

The grave was empty. Next to it, Russel rummaged in his pocket.

"Theo," Kade said warily.

Theo ran. Human speed, mostly. He only blurred as he got closer, then grabbed Russel and jerked him up.

Russel grunted. His phone fell out of his hand onto

the dirt-covered grass. One inch to the left and it would've tumbled straight into the empty grave.

"What did you do to my dad?" Theo demanded, clutching Russel by his collar. "What did you *do?*"

Russel's eyes were wide. He wasn't even scrabbling at Theo's hands. He was just staring, confused.

Kade ran up behind them. There was a cheap bouquet of roses next to the empty grave and a bad feeling in Kade's stomach.

"Is he human?" he asked Theo.

Theo's lip curled. "I can hear a heartbeat. Jab him with a fire eye."

Kade dug a knot of fire eye out of his pocket, pressing the vine into Russel's exposed arm. Nothing happened.

Kade grimaced. The guy was wearing shorts with an elastic waistband. He looked like somebody's not-so-cool uncle, tan and fit and slightly balding.

"Theo, I don't think—"

Theo cut him off. "Silver? Got any silver? Any rings?"

Kade hadn't worn jewelry with real silver since the first time Theo came over to his house.

"He's *human*, Theo. It's not him."

Theo gave Russel another shake, teeth bared. Thankfully still blunt—for now.

"The grave is EMPTY," he bellowed, the noise ringing over the graveyard and making both Kade and Russel flinch. "What were you DOING?"

"I-I was about to call the police," Russel stammered. He reached up, scarred hands shaking as they wrapped gently around Theo's wrists. "Theo, everything's going to be okay. I'll call the police, they'll find out who did this."

Theo growled, tightening his grip on Russel's collar.

Russel asked, "What's wrong? I don't understand. Are you okay?"

"Don't ask me that," Theo snapped. "Don't you DARE ask me that. You—you have the scars! And you made blood jokes about the casserole! What did you do to my DAD?"

He shook Russel so hard his head snapped back.

"I...blood jokes..." Russel blinked, dazed. "Theo, what's going on?"

Kade tugged Theo's jacket. "Okay, let's go. Let's *go*, I don't want to bury another body."

"What?" Russel squeaked.

"Nothing," Kade said hastily. He pulled Theo's jacket harder. "Come on, mate."

"No," Theo snarled, voice breaking. "It has to be him. He has to be involved. He's HERE. I won't let him get away!"

"It's not him," Kade insisted. He took a careful step closer, so he was right at Theo's side. If Kade could, he would have twisted Theo's face toward him. As it was, Kade just stood there, touching his shirt.

"You said you could feel it when you saw your sire

again," Kade reminded him. "Can you feel anything now?"

Theo's eyes were glassy, black liquid gathering at the corners. His chin trembled. He wore a deep, desperate anger Kade knew far too well and wished he didn't. The kind of anger that was so big you didn't realize it was something else until you'd already ruined everything.

Kade had ruined a lot of things. He didn't want to help Theo do the same.

He stepped even closer. Hoping, for once, that Theo could hear his thundering heartbeat. Hoping that it drowned out the anger surging through Theo's cold body. That it brought him back here, to Kade.

"Theo," he said. "Can you feel anything?"

Theo jerked his head. Just a little bit. The smallest, most devastated shake.

"No," he croaked. Black tears gleamed in the corners of his eyes. He blinked hard and they were gone. He let go of Russel, shoving him with such force he almost stumbled back into the grave.

Theo stormed off to the car.

Kade gave Russel an apologetic look.

"Please don't tell the cops about this part," he said awkwardly, and ran off after Theo.

Theo drove them to the woods. Then he pulled over and stumbled out, leaving the driver's door hanging open.

Kade got out after him, calling into the trees. "Theo! Hey!"

Theo shuddered to a stop, shoulders trembling. Kade waited for him to pummel chunks out of a tree, like he'd done last week. But he just stood there, shaking.

Then he screamed. A strange, guttural scream that turned inhuman at the end, so high and wailing that Kade had to cover his ears. He'd never heard a more anguished noise. It sounded like something you'd hear in a ghost story right before you died. It made something instinctual prickle deep inside of him, the hairs standing up on the back of his neck. A deer sensing the hunter in the bushes.

Run, whispered the prey animal behind Kade's ribs.

But it was Theo. Kade hadn't run when Theo was in bloody ribbons on the forest floor, Hawthorn looming huge and terrifying over him. He wasn't going to start now.

He slunk forward, leaves crunching under his boots. "Do...do you want a cigarette?"

Theo growled. "No, I don't want a cigarette, Kade! *God*!"

"Well excuse the hell out of me to find SOME-THING to calm you down," Kade snapped. He didn't mean for it to come out angry. But anger had been Kade's go-to armor for a long time. He knew there was something underneath it, dark and quivering, but anger was always easier. Always waiting to strike out, defend, hide the thing underneath it.

Kade took a deep breath. "What would you have done to that guy if I wasn't there, huh, blood boy?"

Theo shook his head. He turned, and Kade was relieved and devastated to see he *still* wasn't crying. Worst week of his life and he hadn't cried yet. Kade had seen him cry last year over the stress of the prophecy, a few stressed tears after being told he was destined to bring so much destruction to their hometown, and now his dad was dead and as far as Kade knew, he hadn't shed one black tear over it.

"You need to stop," Kade begged. "Just—just sit down, watch some shitty TV and *breathe* for five seconds."

"I DON'T NEED TO BREATHE," Theo yelled. "I need to find my sire and kill him. It's the only thing I can think about!"

His breathing hitched. Huge, gulping breaths he didn't need: muscle memory from being alive taking over.

"I failed," Theo rasped. "I—shit, Kade, I failed. Dad asked me to watch over his body. I should've—how could I let him down like that? My mom's gonna *hate* me.'

"She won't hate you! She doesn't even know!"

"She'll find out," Theo said, a terrible faraway look on her face, years of being raised in that house mounting up behind him. "They *always* find out. Dad found out I was dead and Mom is GOING to know, she always knows. She'll find out I failed, and she's gonna *hate* me."

"YOUR MOM IS AN ASSHOLE," Kade screamed.

Later, he would rethink this conversation, go over what he wished he'd said. This was the second biggest thing he wished he could take back. This was the pivotal point where Kade ruined everything, as usual.

"And your dad isn't around to say shit," Kade continued. "He wasn't even nice to you!"

"My dad was *great*," Theo snarled.

Kade laughed, the noise echoing around the trees. The branches were empty, leaves dead at their feet. The birds had flown off when Theo screamed.

"Your dad threatened to rip your hair out in front of the entire SCHOOL," Kade cried. "I heard the rumors, okay? Every time you lost a game or didn't grade well on a test or some stupid shit *everybody* does, you'd come to school exhausted the next day because he'd keep you up all night and punish you if you fell asleep."

Theo stared at him. Kade had never seen him so scared before. Not with Hawthorn, not with Mr. Fletcher choking to death on Kade's grimy carpet.

It took Theo a long time to speak. "Where did you hear that?"

Kade had the bizarre urge to hug him. Carefully, the way he always had to be careful when he touched Theo. As if Kade was a creature made for comfort. As if Theo was made to accept it. As if they weren't made to destroy each other.

"I get it," Kade tried. "I love my mum, but she was screwed up! One time she got so drunk she didn't recognize me when I came home from school. I had to sleep outside."

"Well—" Theo swallowed. The fear was draining from his face, replaced with a steely sharpness. "Well, my dad wasn't like your *wino* mom. My dad was *good*. So what if he was a little rough on me? He wanted me to be the *best*."

"He wanted you to be VICIOUS," Kade yelled. "Jesus. I don't know why he didn't *team up* with your sire!"

"Shut up," Theo snarled, so harsh and sharp that Kade did.

He'd screwed up. He could already feel it in his stomach, that heavy sinking feeling he got when he knew he'd regret it but he was doing it anyway. He just wanted Theo to *understand*, wanted to grip those beautiful curls and stare into those big brown eyes and bleed memory into him: every time he stuck up for his mum after she forgot to pack him lunch or locked him out or got her license suspended, *again*; every time he insisted his dad was great, *really*, he had cool clothes and a big important job and took a lot of business trips and he didn't drink in front of Kade unless it was a birthday or Christmas or he had a really bad day at work. It didn't matter that he slapped Kade around, because he took him to theme parks sometimes and taught him how to play darts and let Kade watch whatever he wanted on TV even when it gave him nightmares. *He's a good person*, he told the cops the last time they brought him in. *He probably didn't know the car parts were stolen, he just made a mistake.*

He'd been such an idiot. And now Theo was looking at him with those same big, betrayed eyes Kade gave everyone who dared suggest there was a chance his parents were maybe, *possibly*, not the best people.

Kade sucked in a breath. "I just—"

"Don't," Theo growled.

Kade shrank back. His prey-animal instincts were starting up again, screaming at him to run. Theo's shoulders were braced and his mouth was set in a sneer, like he was the jock Kade used to avoid in the hallways. Like they'd never traded two words that weren't sharp, never saved each other from a monster, never studied together or buried a body or walked through the woods while Theo pointed out native weeds, telling Kade how they were misunderstood and actually very beautiful and people should stop killing them.

Theo turned around and stalked into the trees.

Kade cleared his throat. There was a lump in it. "Where are you going?"

"For a run."

"What about your car?"

"Don't touch it," Theo snarled. "And don't...don't text me. Okay? Just stay the hell away from me, Kade."

Then he streaked off, tossing up rotting leaves in his wake.

IT WAS sunset when Kade arrived home.

Milly was waiting on the porch steps. She was watching a beetle crawl around her shoes, her hair a thick curtain over her face. A large handbag sat next to her, its strap thick and peeling.

She looked up when she heard Kade coming. "Hello."

"Hey," Kade cleared his throat. "Come on."

If Milly noticed his scratchy voice or puffy eyes, she didn't say anything. She got up, stepping carefully around the beetle she'd been watching.

He led her toward his room, trying not to think about when he'd led Felicity in to gawk at a dead body. Sundance was on the couch in the living room watching

MASH reruns. She tightened her dressing gown when she noticed Kade had someone with her.

"This is Milly," Kade said, barely glancing at her as he rushed past. If he stayed too long she would *definitely* see that he'd been crying on the walk home. "She runs that bookshop I told you about. She's gonna teach me how to play Dungeons & Dragons. Don't wait up."

"Nice to meet you," Sundance called down the hall after them.

"You too," Milly said. She ducked into the bedroom. Kade closed the door behind her. "She seems nice."

"She's great," Kade said distractedly. The sunset shone through his broken window, casting a red glow over the carpet where Mr. Fletcher choked on his last breath.

Kade shuddered and turned to Milly. "You said there was something you wouldn't recommend. To induce the visions."

Milly's shoulders stiffened even more than usual.

"It's...had a lot of bad results." Milly's hand flickered up, as if about to touch her white eye, or maybe the deep scar in her face. Then it clenched, returning to her side. "It would be safer if Theo was here with you."

Grief swam over Kade in a wave. *Stay the hell away from me, Kade.* He didn't know how serious Theo was about that Theo could feed from Felicity. Shit, he could feed from *Milly*, if she was down. Leave Kade to sweat out the withdrawal, which according to Milly was just like regular withdrawal: three to five days' worth of pure physical shit, then months of emotional and psychological shit. Kade would still be locked into the ritual, but he'd be free of needing Theo's teeth in his neck every few days. Theo could stop looking like a kicked puppy every time someone brought up how Kade was a venom junkie.

"Well he's not," Kade snapped. "What are we doing? Blood offering? Sacrificing an animal?"

Please don't let us be sacrificing an animal, he thought. He'd already cried once today.

"Blood offering," Milly said. "But that's only part of it."

She looked around his room, considering. Then she bent down and started shoving his bed.

Kade joined her. The bed scraped over the carpet, revealing dust bunnies that Kade hadn't reached with the vacuum cleaner in years.

Sundance yelled, "Sounds like a very hands-on Dungeons and Dragons-ing!"

"I'm a kinetic learner," Kade screamed back. His heart pounded. He hoped that whatever happened, it wouldn't be loud enough to alert his aunt. He'd kept her out of this mess for this long, and he didn't want that to stop just because he did some vision-inducing ritual in his bedroom.

Milly heaved her handbag onto the bed. She rummaged through it and pulled out the book she'd been translating. It sat heavily on Kade's bed, the golden sun gleaming dully on the black cover.

"Hold this," she instructed.

Kade took it. It was weighed down with something heavier than paper and ink.

Milly took one of Kade's fabric markers from the jar on his desk and bent down. She drew a giant circle on Kade's carpet. She kept herself outside of it the whole time, even though it would have been easier to draw from the middle.

She capped the pen and stood. Orange sunset crept over the carpet, edging into the wonky circle she'd drawn. Milly's head cocked, staring into the circle thoughtfully.

Kade waited, trying not to fiddle with the book's pages. Every book he'd ever owned was rumpled, every test he'd ever handed in creased from Kade's unstoppable fidgeting. It was a bad habit he kept wishing he'd grow out of, like smoking and ruining things.

"Huh," Milly said. She nodded at Kade. "Lie down."

Kade lay down in the circle. He'd have to scrub the marker out of the carpet later. There was a patch of surprising cleanness near the wall where he'd cleaned the blood out of it. He might as well go all in, scrub the whole carpet after this one.

He placed the book on his chest. "What now?"

Milly handed him a pair of embroidery scissors. They were shaped like a bird with blades for a beak. It used to belong to his mother. Kade opened them, remembering how she used to make the bird tweet. She'd tap him on the nose, gently, so she didn't cut him.

"Blood sacrifice," Kade said.

Milly hummed. "Think of it less of a sacrifice and more...opening a door inside you for something to enter."

Kade lowered the scissors. "Milly. If I get possessed—"

"You won't get possessed," Milly said. But she didn't sound entirely sure about it.

Kade frowned.

"You *won't*," she repeated, more solid. "I'll pull you out if things get too intense."

Kade stared up at her. Strange, soft Milly, who smiled like she didn't know how to be warm but she would very much like to be. Who DM'd for her Dungeons & Dragons friends once a week, complete with homemade snacks. Who came from a mysterious place where she made friends she'd kill and die for, friends she *might* have killed and died for, Kade still didn't know the full story beyond a few disturbing details.

Kade nodded tightly and raised the scissors. He dragged the bird's beak over his palm, hissing at the bright line of pain.

"Onto the book," Milly told him.

Kade shivered and lifted his hand over his chest. Blood dripped down his wrist, splattering down onto the embossed golden sun. The gold vanished fast, swallowed by the red. Sunset bled up Kade's legs, touching his stomach, almost at the book lying over his heart.

"Good," Milly said. She sounded worried, and also very far away all of a sudden. "You're doing very well."

Kade's head grew heavy. Something itched at the back of his skull. A barrier. It felt flimsy, like cheesecloth. Like he could put a hand out and push right through.

Kade reached out. The itch in his head intensified—

"Kade," Milly snapped.

Kade dragged his heavy head up just in time to watch Aaron Fletcher come barreling through the broken window, his foot catching on the window frame. He righted himself and swore. Then he froze, staring at the two people who had just watched him break into Kade's bedroom.

A hunting knife glinted in his hand, huge and curved. He was wearing his letterman jacket, which clashed horribly with his leather gloves. His bulk blocked the sunset. Red light streamed around his head like a demented halo.

No one spoke.

A yell drifted in from the hallway. "Everything okay in there?"

Kade swallowed.

Aaron pointed the knife toward him. The threat was clear, even as Aaron's gloved hands shook around the handle.

"Yeah," Kade said, proud of how steady his voice

sounded. He had a lot of practice at telling Sundance everything was fine in the middle of a dire situation. "Just got excited about a dice...thing. Go back to Hawkeye, auntie."

Sundance said something else, muffled through the wall and her turning the volume up. He'd never been more thankful for her shitty hearing. She shouldn't hear what would happen next.

Kade sat up. "Aaron, look—"

"Don't move," Aaron snarled. His usually blank face was twisted, his green eyes shining with unshed tears. Kade hadn't seen him since his birthday party, Aaron's face going slack with awful shock in the police car lights as his mother told him what they'd found. Kade wondered how much they told him. How much his *mother* told him.

"Wait," Kade blurted as Aaron stepped forward. "We didn't kill him!"

Aaron shook his head. His hair was limp, ungelled for the first time in years. Kade hadn't seen it like this even during their short-lived trysts, meeting up in the woods or sneaking into Kade's room to do hurried hand stuff before slinking away. No telling anyone, and no kissing. Like this was the eighties or some shit.

"Don't pull that crap," Aaron hissed. "I know *every-thing*. My lips are sealed, but I know now. I know what has to happen to keep the town safe."

He stopped, jaw working. Like he wanted to say more, but he didn't dare. His hand tightened around the knife blade. He was holding it with his left hand, the gloved grip clumsy.

His right hand hung near his waist. The black lines on his skin had crept even further up his arm, halfway to his elbow. They were darker than they had been a few days ago. Thicker. And...pulsing? Kade's lips curled in horror as he watched them bulge in time with Aaron's fast heartbeat.

"Shit," Kade whispered, hands sweating around the book on his chest. "What the hell is with your hand?"

"What do you think, jackass?" Aaron spat. "You were there!"

He lifted his bad hand like he was going to cradle it protectively to his chest. Then he stopped, forcing it back down. His gaze flickered to Milly, who had been reaching out slowly toward Kade's lamp.

"Don't," he warned.

Milly's hand froze in midair. "They didn't kill him. The spell did."

"His fingers were *broken*," Aaron croaked.

"Aaron," Kade tried, forcing his fuzzy mind back on track. He was missing something important. He'd seen their faces in the vision, just for a second, and it made him realize something terrible. He needed to see them again.

Kade continued, "I know you're going through it, mate, but we need—"

"Don't call me *mate*," Aaron said, accent morphing

into a terrible mockery of Kade's own. "Don't even talk to me. Don't *look* at me."

His face twisted, like he wanted to be angry, then evolved into something deeper, bigger, more unwieldy.

"Did..." he said, and swallowed. "Did Theo...?"

His face crumpled.

Kade saw an in. He held up his hands pleadingly. "Aaron. I swear, none of us meant to hurt him."

It was the wrong thing to say. Kade knew it as soon as it spilled out of his stupid mouth. Aaron's face reformed into anger, shiny and bright, a burning fire cleansing everything else in his body. Making space for the wrath needed for the next act.

He lunged forward.

Kade threw the book at him. It made a thick, muted smack as it connected with Aaron's hip, bouncing off harmlessly.

Shit, Kade thought, scrabbling up. *Maybe I should've gotten into sports. Turns out I* do *need to know how to aim sometimes.*

His lamp sailed through the air, smashing into Aaron's chest and shattering. Milly had ripped it off the table. Half the socket still clung to the plug.

It slowed Aaron, his breath whooshing out of him. Still not enough to stop him. He descended on Kade, shoving him back into the carpet.

He pressed the knife to Kade's throat. It bobbed against the blade, cold fear racing down Kade's spine.

He was lying in the same spot where Mr. Fletcher had held him down. Like father, like son.

Kade flailed at Aaron's face, looking around wildly. Where did the embroidery scissors go?

Aaron reared back, teeth gritted from Kade's clumsy defenses. He raised the knife.

Milly ran behind him and locked her arms around his. Aaron grunted, struggling.

A flash of gold next to Kade's head. He scrabbled for the embroidery scissors. The bird's beak stabbed his thumb before he closed his hand around it properly. He reared up and jabbed the scissors straight through the glove of Aaron's bad hand.

Aaron shrieked. His back bowed in agony. He shoved Milly away, sending her stumbling into Kade's bed.

"Crap," Aaron panted. He yanked the scissors out of his hand. Black liquid oozed down the glove, oily and disgusting. Both boys gagged.

"Oh god," Aaron said, wrinkling his nose.

"What the hell?" Kade said, dazed.

Aaron shuddered. Then he raised the knife again.

Kade panicked. He reached out, closing both hands around Aaron's and squeezing as hard as he could. He expected a pained yell. He *didn't* expect the cracking noises: sharp and grinding, the flesh under the glove giving easily under Kade's touch. It was almost *mushy*. The stench of rot rolled through the bedroom, overpowering.

The boys gagged again.

Milly struggled up and clutched her arm. Her elbow had struck the bedframe hard.

The door burst open.

Sundance stopped and stared: Milly struggling to her feet, Kade on his back, Aaron on top of him with a mangled hand and tears streaming down his face. The terrible stench of rot emanating from Aaron's twisted glove. The knife in his good hand, poised and shaking over Kade.

"What the HELL?" she yelled.

"'S what I said," Kade mumbled.

The haze in his mind intensified. For a moment he thought he might pass out. The world flickered: he was in his bedroom, Aaron on top of him. He was in the woods, falling—

—to the forest floor.

He is going to die.

Not for another year, of course. But he doesn't know that. Everything in him wails that he will die here, now, with so many townsfolk dead around him and a hole in the ground. There is a casket in the middle of it, tied with chains and bucking from Cyth's repeated attempts to free herself.

The boy looks at his vampire, the one who once gave him a forget-me-not. He is tied down several feet away, black tears streaming down his face. He stares at the boy, wide-eyed and pleading.

The lead hunter bellows something in a language long dead and throws in a torch. The coffin erupts into flames.

"This is for my daughter," the lead hunter snarls.

Cyth's lover screams. The other hunters have him pinned to the ground, where he struggles through dozens of ropes knotted with thorny flowers.

"Cyth!" the lover cries. "No!"

The lead hunter yells one last word. The boy will die without knowing what it means.

The ground shudders, drowning out Cyth's shrieking from the burning coffin. Something huge and dark springs up from the hole, and for a moment the boy fears all is lost.

Then the dark thing solidifies. Grows branches. A tree twists over the hole, sealing it closed.

Suddenly the clearing is just a clearing again, the wind dying down. The only vampires left above ground are Cyth's struggling lover and the vampire who once gave the boy a forget-me-not. His *vampire.*

"What did you do?" Cyth's lover screams, his skin smoking from the thorny bindings. "What did you DO?"

"I gave her what she deserved," the lead hunter says. Blood drips from his nostrils onto a sun pendant hanging around his neck. He staggers, catching himself against a tree.

The boy stares across the clearing at his vampire. He isn't moving. Isn't trying to escape. He simply lies there, eyes wet. Staring back at the boy.

The boy wets his lips. He should run. Instead, he finds himself crawling toward his vampire, keeping low in the trees so the hunters won't see him.

Cyth's lover roars. He rips through another rope.

"I will get her back," he screams. "Then we will...we will rain HELL down upon you all!"

The lead hunter laughs. Blood flecks the bark. Someone tries to steady him and he pushes them away.

The boy keeps crawling. He's almost at his vampire now. He has no idea what he will do once he reaches him, but he can't stop. His vampire's eyes get wider and wetter as he watches the boy crawl, like he expects him to stop at any moment. Run off into the woods. Leave him to his fate.

The boy knows he should. And yet.

"You can't let her out," the lead hunter spits. "There's no key to that door. There isn't even a lock."

"Then I will make one," the lover bellows.

He bucks against the thorns. Something cracks deep inside his body. He swells, a pair of wings bursting out of his back and severing what was left of his bindings. The hunters around him scramble for more, but there are none.

The boy panics. Reaches out and grabs his vampire's hand, which is scored with burns.

It is the last time the boy will touch his vampire's skin for a year.

It happens in a blur: his vampire screams a warning. The boy looks back in time to see a blur of wings and teeth flying at him.

The boy and his vampire are ripped into the air, then shoved down onto the dirt below the new tree. It feels like a wagon pressing down on the boy's chest. He cries out in pain, twisting his head to look at his vampire pinned down across from him, eyes huge and helpless.

"You think you're the only one who knows old magics," Cyth's lover growls, pale skin still smoking from the vines. "The door is fresh. I can lick the leftovers."

He trembles with concentration. The dirt below them grows warm, as if the fire below them is seeping through.

The surviving hunters clamor for weapons. Several of them try to help the lead hunter, who is on the ground now, coughing blood.

Too late. The monster's eyes are closed, dead languages falling off his tongue.

"Master," the boy's vampire begs. "Please don't do this."

The monster ignores him. His face flickers, veiny and pale and then back to the cruel beauty the town was used to. The dirt below them burns, until the boy is convinced he is being roasted alive.

He screams as the magic takes hold. His vampire yells his name, but the boy can't hear it. Can't reach for him. Can't do anything but scream and feel the terrible—

—dread.

Oh god, Kade thought as he struggled back to consciousness, eyes cracking open. *Oh god oh god oh god.*

He'd seen their faces. There, in the very last second as the spell took hold. He'd seen the boy's face. He'd seen the boy's vampire pinned to the dirt next to him. More importantly, he'd seen Cyth's lover holding them down, his true face flickering through the fanged, pale monstrosity.

He knew that goddamn face.

"Theo's in danger," Kade slurred, all the vowels blurring together.

Nobody heard him. A tear dripped from Aaron's chin onto Kade's cheek. He

had the knife up again, blade glinting red in the sunset. Sundance jerked forward, arms out like she was going to tackle him.

"THEO'S IN DANGER," Kade yelled.

The knife paused in midair.

"He's in danger," Kade repeated, holding out a hand for his aunt to stop charging. "I swear. I swear on my aunt. He's in danger, we need to save him. Whatever shit you think you need to do with me, save it for after we rescue Theo. *Please*."

Kade watched the doubt flicker through Aaron's agonized eyes. Watched him look up at Milly, who was holding the good fabric scissors she'd stolen from Kade's desk, and Sundance, who was ready to leap on his attacker with her useless teeth bared.

Kade gripped Aaron's letterman jacket.

"Please," he repeated. "For Theo."

Aaron stumbled back, breaking Kade's grip. He glared down at him, his face twisted in loathing as he clutched his ruined hand to his chest.

Sundance jerked toward him. Kade held up a hand. *Not yet,* he mouthed. He was waiting to see if he was right. He always thought Aaron would stab his best friend in the back. But they needed more people on their side, and Aaron was taking a shockingly long time to reply.

"Shit," Aaron whispered. He squeezed his eyes shut. When he opened them, his face was smooth, only his tear-filled eyes betraying how much pain he was in.

"Get up, Monster," he said flatly. "Somebody else has to drive."

CHAPTER
TWENTY-FIVE

Sunset streamed through the curtains, staining Theo's bed crimson.

Theo lay perfectly still and watched the light slowly make its way up his body. *Eating him,* he imagined Kade saying. Kade always came up with weird shit like that. They'd be hanging out and Kade would say a shadow looked like a dragon or that the soap suds were 'kissing his fingers' while he did the dishes, turning boring activities into something new and exciting.

Theo gripped the red sheets. On the floor next to him, Sparky lifted her head.

"I'm fine," he told her. "Quit it."

Sparky whined and dropped her head back to her paws. He hadn't let her on the bed in days.

Theo had run full speed through the woods for half an hour before he stopped feeling like he needed to howl. Broke off some branches and a whole tree in the process from not dodging fast enough.

There was a knock at the bedroom door.

Theo sat up. A speck of bark rolled down his face.

"Come in," Theo said, dusting his hair off for the dozenth time since he got home.

Carol was still wearing her white power suit, even though she would have usually changed into her at-home clothes by now. He supposed she was making up for all the days she'd spent in her PJs.

"I realized we never talked about Sparky," she started.

Theo tensed. Sparky swiveled her head toward him, her orange eyes wide and questioning. Theo was mad at her, but he never wanted to get *rid* of her.

"She's never bitten anyone before," he said. "We're working on her aggression, I really think—"

"She can stay."

Theo stammered to a stop. "What?"

"She can stay," Carol repeated, and smiled. It was soft and apologetic. "This week has made me realize what's important, and that I...I've barely seen you. I was thinking you could show me what you've been doing in the garden."

Theo's chest constricted with panic. He'd been so careful to do it at night, or when she was away.

"I don't know what you mean," he tried.

"Parents know, honey." She didn't say it like she usually did, tense and warning. She said it like an olive branch. An outstretched hand, waiting for him to take it.

"I'm sorry," Theo said automatically. Even with the soft way she was looking at him, he couldn't back down from a lifetime of habits.

"No. We were too hard on you. It's...a harmless habit." She cleared her throat and flashed her teeth in a hopeful smile. "I'll see you down there? I just need to change."

Theo nodded dumbly.

"Great." Carol walked over and pressed a kiss to his forehead, something she hadn't done since he was very young. She ran a hand through his hair, ruffling it with such clear love in her eyes that Theo had to fight not to lean into her touch. They hadn't mentioned his dad once, but with Carol standing over him ruffling her hair just like he used to, they didn't need to.

Then her hand was gone. She left the room with another smile, looking relieved and even a little excited.

Theo sat there, scalp tingling. Sparky got up and nosed at his knee, thumping her tail curiously.

"Thanks for not growling at her," Theo said. He swallowed the lump in his throat and stroked Sparky's head. "Maybe you really are getting less aggressive."

Sparky's tongue lolled out happily. She nosed at Theo's wrist, pleased to be petted after days of half-hearted scratches or flat-out dismissals. Theo felt guilty, watching her tail wag faster. She hadn't *meant* to let Kade get hurt. She was just a dog, and she was doing her best. Maybe he was too hard on her. Maybe—

A scream echoed through the house.

Theo went rigid. "Mom?"

No answer. Theo and Sparky leapt up in unison. They both bolted for the door, Theo almost tripping over Sparky in his haste. He could hear her heartbeat pulsing hard and fast. She was at the end of the hallway, her breathing strained.

"Mom," Theo called, bursting into the hall. "What's going on?"

Theo froze.

His mom stood at the end of the hall, her back pressed against the wall.

Theo's sire loomed over her. Its wings were folded tight against its body, head scraping the ceiling. It was staring straight at Theo, straight *into* him.

Theo shuddered. That horrible knowledge sank into his bones: *I am his*.

"Don't—" His voice broke. "Don't you dare touch her."

The creature cocked its head. A pointy ear twitched.

"*Or what?*" it asked. Its voice sounded like rocks rubbing together.

"I'm gonna kill you," Theo whispered. His hands shook. Hawthorn would have killed him if Kade hadn't been there with a distraction and a crochet needle. Cheech's ax was hidden in the depths of Theo's closet, wrapped in newspaper. If he tried to run back for it—

His sire's arm shot out, grabbing his mom by the wrist and blurring down the stairs.

Theo blurred after them, a cry wrenching from his throat. Sparky followed, tripping over her puppy-large paws.

His sire was waiting for him in the living room. It had one arm around Carol, squashing her to its pale chest. She squirmed, beating at its long, thin arm.

"Theo," she croaked, tears in her eyes.

"It's fine," Theo tried. "Everything's going to be fine."

Sparky growled. Her ears were plastered back against her head. She crouched low and barked.

The creature cocked its head at Theo again. *I wanted to see what you would do,* it had said back in the woods. Would he snap his mother's neck in front of him out of...what? Pure curiosity?

"*So,*" the creature said. Its arm tightened around Carol's waist, making her gasp. "*What next, my——?*"

It stopped. Its head twitched toward the front door just in time for Theo to hear the footsteps.

The front door banged open. Kade's voice rang down the hallway, filling Theo with hope and terrible dread.

"THEO! It's him!" Kade skidded to a stop in the living room doorway, gray eyes blowing wide with terror as he took in the creature in the corner of the room.

Aaron stumbled in after him, sweating and pained, cradling a mangled hand and a hunting knife to his chest. Theo couldn't stop himself from gagging—Aaron's hand was bent and twisted, the skin black with rot, black veins creeping up toward his elbow. It stunk like decay. There was a hint of bone poking out from Aaron's pinkie.

Aaron gasped when he saw the sire, color draining from his tanned face. His good hand tightened around the knife blade. He looked at Theo and curled his lip in disgust.

Theo's stomach sank. He didn't have to ask: Aaron *knew* about him.

The creature's wings snapped out. It dropped Carol to the ground and launched itself at the boys in the hallway, slamming Aaron into the wall and snatching Kade by the shirt collar.

Aaron slumped to the ground, groaning, eyes lolling behind his lids. His head drooped toward his lap.

Kade yelped as the creature flew up toward the ceiling.

Sparky growled. She ran at the creature and crouched low, ready to jump.

The creature's raspy voice rang through the room: "*Lie down.*"

Sparky shuddered. She looked back at Theo, liquid black flickering through her eyes.

Theo shook his head. "Get up," he demanded.

She shuddered a second time. The liquid black swam through her eyes until the orange was gone. She lay down.

Kade yelped as he dangled from the monster's grip. "Theo! Shit! It's—"

The creature covered Kade's mouth.

Then it began to change: the hand over Kade's mouth first, claws melting into blunt fingers. Then its arm, and then its chest. Finally, its face. A man stared down at Theo, hovering high in the middle of the living room. He was dressed in a button-down and slacks, the same clothes Theo had seen him wear for the past sixteen years.

Victor Fairgood inclined his head. A curly strand of blond hair fell over his face.

"Theo," he said gently. "It's good to see you."

FOR ONE STUPID, childish moment, Theo felt a stab of joy.

Then reality sunk in. That bone-deep knowledge was back, telling him something Theo used to be proud of: *I am his.*

Theo shook his head. "Dad...how...I saw your *body.* You..."

He looked at his mom, who was wiping tears off her cheeks. She caught him looking and grinned, a wild laugh bubbling out of her.

"Isn't he magnificent?" she said, gazing up at Victor. There was a light in her eyes, a naked and near-holy devotion he'd never seen before. Like he could ask her to draw a knife across her carotid artery and she would ask how deep.

Theo kept shaking his head. He couldn't stop. Next to him, Sparky whined. Her whole body shook.

"I saw a body," Theo croaked.

"You saw *a* body," Victor corrected, still holding a squirming Kade by the shirt as he hovered high in the air. "You snuck in to see Lemmings, of course you'd sneak in to see me. Especially after that note I left."

"I've seen you eat," Theo tried, trying to remember the sparse family dinners his father had attended. "You're...you don't eat much, but I've seen it."

"Yes, and I've seen *you* eat at every one of the Fletchers' foul dinners this summer."

"Baby pictures," Theo whispered. "I saw...baby pictures..."

"You saw *someone's* baby pictures." Victor gave him a look, almost pitying. "Theo, really. You're being a little slow about this, son."

"You're my sire," Theo said numbly. He thought back to the terrifying movement in the dark, being crushed to that creature's steely chest. The agony of teeth in his neck, the sheer terror of the fall. Drowning. His dad had let him *drown*. His dad had been the one who *dropped* him, who slit his wrist and shoved his vile blood into Theo's mouth and forced him to swallow.

Over by the wall, Aaron groaned. He tried to push himself up, then slid right back down. The hunting knife clattered to the polished wood.

"I don't want to hurt you," Victor continued. "You're very special to me. You know that. But I can't risk anyone ruining my plans. Come with me, my boy."

He said it softly, like he wasn't holding Kade

aloft by the collar with a hand over his mouth. Kade writhed in his grip, face red with effort. Theo could hear him grunting, inhaling desperately through his nose. That hand over his mouth was pressed *tight*.

"Theo," Victor said expectantly. Theo got the feeling he would hold out a hand, if they weren't both currently occupied.

Theo wet his lips. His voice came out tiny and pathetic, like a small boy afraid of getting in trouble. "I can't."

Victor sighed. "It's just until the time is right. Then you can come back."

"And kill Kade?"

Victor's lips thinned. Something very old curled up inside of Theo. *Prey animal,* he thought hazily. Kade had that on a crop top somewhere. Theo had watched him stitch the words into the fabric.

"I was always worried you were too soft," Victor said. "But when the time comes, you remember who you are. You're one of us. Always have been. And Fairgoods are..."

He trailed off, waiting. Kade kicked him in the shin. Victor didn't look at him, too busy staring Theo down, eyes full of terrible understanding. Like he knew everything Theo was feeling right now.

He raised his eyebrows expectantly.

"Vicious," Theo whispered.

Victor smiled. "Come up here."

Theo looked pleadingly at his mom. She gestured up at her husband hovering over them.

"Go on, honey," she told him.

I thought you wanted to see the garden, Theo thought. Then he rose into the air, feeling more monstrous than he ever had with his teeth in Kade's neck. It wasn't a long way up, but it felt like a lifetime. A lifetime of tripping classmates in halls and panicking when he lost a game or failed a test or people dared to comfort him, afraid his parents would find out.

Victor held Kade out. "Feed. You're looking peaky."

Theo reached out numbly. His hand curled in Kade's shirt.

Victor dropped his hand from Kade's mouth as he handed him over.

Theo waited for Kade to speak, but he didn't. He'd stopped squirming as soon as Theo reached for him. He just stared, eyes wet, as Theo held him up.

Sparky yipped. Her muscles quivered, front legs jerking up.

Victor shushed her. "Stay."

She lay back down.

Be the prey or be the knife, Theo thought. He thought of crouching behind a bush with his father, hands sweaty and small around a rifle, willing a deer to run. He thought about Kade's eyes, shiny and gray and beautiful, just like when he'd left him there in the woods. Theo had told him to stay away and he'd come to save Theo anyway.

Kade curled a hand around Theo's sleeve. Theo could hear his heart hammering in his chest, feel his heat through his shirt. Kade was shaking.

Shaky guy, Theo thought. *Loud heart.*

He flew so fast he blurred. When he stopped, he was at the wall with Aaron, standing protectively in front of Kade. He stooped and grabbed the hunting knife from where it had fallen next to a half-conscious Aaron. Then he planted his feet. Waiting for something he couldn't dare to imagine.

Irritation flickered over Victor's face. He floated to the ground. Carol was there waiting for him. She slipped her hand into his.

"Why did you leave the note about your body?" Theo whispered. "Why did you try and make me hurt Russel?"

"I told you," Victor said impatiently. "I wanted to see what you'd do. I *was* hoping you would kill the gardener. For me."

He took a step forward.

Theo spread his arm in front of Kade protectively. "I thought you wanted me to *join* the vampires!"

"I want you to join *me*," Victor corrected, eyes gleaming. "I thought if I raised you this time—your whole life, not just after you were dead—I could instill some better instincts. And if that failed, I would win you over through that—" His lip curled. "That *soft* heart. But I failed on both counts. You picked him over your family, again."

Theo stared at him. "What are you *talking* about?"

"Ah," Victor said. "The Sloans didn't tell you, then?"

Kade tugged on his sleeve. "Theo."

Victor cut him off. "He is not worth throwing your family away for. He's *nothing*, Theo. A means to an end. To be used and consumed."

"You shut up about him," Theo whispered. He couldn't raise his voice. If this were one of the stories Kade liked, he would be shouting. Declaring his rebellion proudly. But here he was, cowering over Kade, like if he just made himself small enough, they would vanish from this place.

Victor sighed again, squeezing his wife's hand absentmindedly. "Is this going to be a fight? I hope not. I hope I can just...take him away. And you'll come with me. And when the time comes, you'll do what your birthright demands."

"You're not gonna touch him," Theo managed.

Beside him, Aaron groaned. His head lolled sideways, staring at Theo. There was blood on the back of his head, Theo could smell it over his rotting hand.

Theo turned back to his dad. The front door wasn't far. Just down the hallway and around a corner. He could make it out with both boys if he ran fast enough.

"Dad," he tried. The word shattered in his throat. "Just let us go."

Victor's face hardened. Like this was the final straw. Betrayal was one thing, but *begging*—begging was weak. *Soft*. Everything he'd tried to train out of Theo.

Victor dropped his wife's hand.

Kade tugged the back of Theo's shirt. "Theo—"

Theo cut him off. "Any ideas?"

Kade's mouth moved wordlessly. He gave Theo another pointed look, like he wanted to speak but didn't want Victor to overhear. Near the stairs, Sparky whined again.

"I want you to know," Victor began, lifting once more into the air. "You did this to yourself."

He flew at Theo.

Theo charged. They crashed together in midair. Theo flailed out with the knife—too slow. Even with Victor's hands on his throat, Theo didn't want to stab him.

Victor wrenched the knife from his grip and threw it backward into the living room.

Kade ran for it. Aaron stumbled up, fell, stumbled up again. There was a bloodstain on the wall where he'd been lying.

"My love," Victor said, hand around Theo's throat.

"On it," Carol called.

Theo watched her run for the knife. Watched her and Kade wrestle for it, watched Aaron clumsily tackle her. She stomped on his mangled hand and he screamed, so agonized that Theo flinched.

He clawed at his dad's hand. Kicked out. Victor was unrelenting, hand tightening on Theo's throat.

"This could have been easy," Victor said. "This could

still be easy. You're a Fairgood. You don't have to turn your back on that."

Theo kicked again. It was like kicking a wall of stone.

Victor sighed. He flew them upward, shoving Theo up on the ceiling Theo dusted once a month since he was twelve with a feather-duster strapped to a broom. As Victor pressed him into it, plaster cracking around Theo's head, Theo realized that he hadn't dusted as well as he thought.

Below them, Kade and Carol struggled over a knife. Aaron had his good arm locked around Carol's leg, tears streaming down his face, on the verge of passing out. Carol fumbled for a vase perched on the living room table and smashed it into Kade's torso.

Victor slammed Theo into the ceiling three more times. Theo's head cracked against it, pain exploding through his skull. Plaster rained down onto the knife fight below them. Kade had the knife now. Carol held a piece of shattered vase.

Theo scrabbled at Victor's grip around his neck. "*Dad.*"

"I had such high hopes," Victor said over him. He dug his fingers into Theo's shoulders, ten bright holes of pain that made Theo howl. He lifted a hand to grip Theo's hair tight enough to rip out a human's scalp.

"Sixteen years," he continued. "What a waste."

He yanked Theo down, flipping them over. Then he

flew full speed into the ground. Floorboards cracked around Theo's body.

Theo twisted. Kade and Carol had stopped circling each other long enough to gape. Aaron used this opportunity to flop over and bite Carol's ankle. She kicked him and he fell back, barely conscious.

Victor cracked a fist into Theo's face, snapping his head sideways. He slammed Theo into the ground again. The floorboards cracked and cracked. Theo felt black blood fill his mouth and thought of foundations, of roots, of rot.

"Mom," Theo croaked over a split lip. "Help."

She crouched in front of Kade, holding a piece of shattered vase. Blood dripped down her fingers, the sharp edges cutting into her palm.

"I wish I could, honey," she said, eyes on the knife in Kade's shaking hand. "But I'm the reincarnation of lady Cyth. When we let her out, I'll absorb her and get all my old memories back. Isn't that wonderful?"

"Reincarnation," Theo repeated, head ringing from being slammed into a hard surface. There was plaster in his scalp, soft woodchips from running over a tree, varnished woodchips from the floorboards. "That's not a thing. Is it a thing? Kade?"

Kade said something, but it was lost in Theo's ringing ears as his father slammed him into the ground again.

Theo stared up into a pair of brown eyes so like his own and found he couldn't say anything. The despair was so vast, the betrayal so deep. He couldn't see a way out of this. He was doomed, it had him when he was born. There was no escape.

Victor started, "Now. This is your last chance to reconsider. Are you going to be a good boy and accept your fate, or will you continue this charade?"

Theo squirmed. His cheek was swelling, he could feel it. His cheek bled into his mouth, black blood down his throat. He swallowed it back.

"I won't let you take him," he whispered.

Victor sighed. He raised a hand over his head—

Then he jerked.

Theo looked down. A knife stuck out of Victor's stomach. Someone had shoved it straight through his back and out the other side.

A familiar voice rang through the living room. "A little low."

"Shut up, mom," Felicity barked.

Theo looked up.

Felicity stood in the living room doorway, a throwing knife gleaming in her hand. There were more in her belt. She was wearing cargo pants he'd never seen before and a zipped-up leather jacket he'd bought her for her birthday last year.

Beverly Sloan stood beside her, a flamethrower heavy in her arms.

"Remember," she told Felicity. "Be *careful*."

Felicity screamed and ran. She threw two knives,

dragging more out from her belt. One landed in Victor's shoulder, the other in his stomach.

"CAREFUL," her mom repeated, but Felicity wasn't listening. She leapt up, all gymnast grace, ready to leap onto Victor's chest.

Victor didn't even stand. He just struck out, the way one would strike an annoying fly. Felicity went spinning sideways, landing on the floor next to Aaron with a dull thud.

Now Victor stood. He brought Theo with him, closing his hand once more around Theo's neck.

"Beverly," he said, eyeing the flamethrower in her hands. "Always a pleasure."

Beverly curled her lip. "You son of a bitch. This whole time—this *whole time*. Carol, you crazy bitch."

Carol blew hair out of her eyes. She'd earned a cut across her collarbone since Theo last looked at her.

She started, "I am the beloved—"

Beverly cut her off. "Leave. *Now*."

Victor laughed. It was low and almost pleasant, and Theo shuddered to hear it. It meant he was about to take someone down. "If you think you can take me out with that little matchstick, you're sorely mistaken."

She lifted the flamethrower. Not at Victor, like Theo had expected. But at Kade and Carol, still circling with their blades.

"I don't," she said. "This is for them."

Felicity sat up, cradling her elbow. "Mom!"

Beverly shushed her. She stared Victor down, elegant hands perfectly steady around the flamethrower.

Victor cocked his head. He looked at Theo dangling from his grip. Then at Kade with the hunting knife, Aaron semi-conscious at his feet. At Felicity reaching for another throwing knife.

He didn't look impressed. But then he looked at his wife, bleeding and clutching a shard from her favorite vase. She stared back at him, eyes wide and reverent.

Victor's jaw clenched. He gave Beverly a tight smile.

"Until next time," he told her. He looked at Theo, who was still squirming with a hand locked around his throat. He let go slowly, one finger at a time.

Theo dropped to the ground.

"What a waste," Victor said quietly. He motioned toward his wife, who ran after him, still holding the vase shard. She slipped her other hand into his. Before Theo could wonder if she would look at him, Victor's hand blurred around her waist and they were gone. A breeze blew through Theo's hair with the force of it. The front door banged open.

Theo blinked at the space where his parents had been standing. Woodchips and blood.

Sparky ran to him, licking his hand and jumping up.

Theo pushed her off. Then he lurched over, pulling Kade behind him once more.

He turned to Beverly. "We're not dangerous."

"Cool it," she told him, dropping the flamethrower

to her side. "I'm not going to kill you. The Fletchers, however—"

Kade cut in. "Uh, guys? Aaron's having a seizure."

Theo turned. Aaron was lying on the ground. Felicity held his head with her one good arm. He was spasming, eyes rolling in his head. Foam dribbled out one corner of his mouth. A wet spot spread down his jeans.

"Shit," Theo heard himself say. He dropped to his knees next to Aaron and grabbed his head. For a moment nothing happened. Aaron continued to jerk against the floor. Sparky whined, nosing at Aaron's twitching hand.

"What's happening?" Beverly asked. "Why isn't it working? Do you need to bite him first?"

Kade squeezed Theo's shoulder. "You need to concentrate. Remember?"

"Right," Theo mumbled. He closed his eyes, trying to break through his haze. His head hurt. The room span. Finally, he felt the buzz in his fingers.

Aaron's jerking slowed. He stilled, heartbeat slowing. His eyes fluttered open.

"Hi," said Theo.

Aaron punched him. Theo's head barely moved, too out of it to remember to move with the impact.

Sparky growled.

"*Don't*," Theo warned her.

Sparky's jaw snapped shut. She dropped back to the ground and trembled.

Aaron fell back, groaning. His rotted hand was still mangled, and now his good hand was hurt, too. His thumb sat at a strange angle, already swelling.

"Good job, asshole," Felicity barked, holding her injured arm carefully. "Now you have TWO busted hands!"

Aaron struggled to his feet. He wiped furiously at his cheeks, wet with tears and foam.

"This doesn't mean we're even," he spat.

"His dad's dead too, asshole," Kade told him. He was holding his shoulder, bleeding where Carol jabbed him.

"Dead dad club," Felicity said, dazed. "We should make shirts."

Theo stood. The room wheeled around him. His skull was cracked, he could hear bones shifting.

"Aaron," he said. "Let me heal your goddamn hands."

Aaron recoiled. "Get off me! Don't *ever* touch me again. You're..."

He stumbled back, almost falling into the hole Theo had made with his body. Then he righted himself and ran out.

Felicity said something to her mom. Theo didn't hear it. He was pretty sure he was going into shock. When he zoned back in, Kade was kneeling in front of him, shaking him lightly. Sparky sat next to him, watching Theo anxiously.

"Oh thank god," Kade said. "I thought you were in some...vampire trance or something. Are you okay?"

Theo shook his head and swallowed the black blood in his mouth. His cheek was still bleeding.

"My entire life is a lie," Theo said.

He waited for Kade to wince. Maybe make a joke to make Theo feel better. But Kade just stared at him, gray eyes full of terrible recognition. Like he understood. It should have made Theo angry. Should've made him snap at him, the same way he'd been snapping at anyone who dared suggest they knew how he felt. But as Theo sat there next to the hole his father had made with Theo's body, plaster dripping down from the ceiling, he couldn't muster anything but exhaustion. Maybe Kade did know how he felt. Maybe their messed-up link that led Theo to find Kade tied up at the tree went both ways. Maybe Theo's cold heart was leaking and Kade was catching the drops. He hoped not. No one should have to feel like this.

Theo asked, "How did you know to come?"

"I had a vision."

"You saw my dad?"

"Yeah," Kade said uncertainly. "And, uh...um..."

Beverly spoke up. She had been examining her daughter's injured elbow.

"You two should see something," she said.

CHAPTER
TWENTY-SEVEN

FIVE MONTHS after Theo Fairgood died, he sat on the cliffs next to his house and watched the sun go down. He had a pair of Kade's fabric scissors and an old photograph from the Sloan house in his lap.

Beverly Sloan had sent Felicity to get the photograph she'd stolen from the Cheech house, then left the house. Just to be safe. Felicity had come downstairs with a dazed look on her face, clutching the elbow she hadn't let Theo heal on the way over.

It's, uh... She'd trailed off. *No wonder she didn't want me to see it.*

That was last week. Theo had spent every night since then lying on Kade's couch, looking at the faded photograph.

A gentle breeze ruffled Theo's hair, carrying a scent Theo knew better than any other.

"Hey," he said as Kade sat down next to him. "Where's Sparky?"

"Left her at home," Kade replied, sliding his legs carefully over the cliff edge. He looked at the sunset turning the water orange, then gestured at the fabric scissors. "Could've taken my shitty pair, by the way. Are you gonna cut it up?"

He gestured at the photo in Theo's hand.

"Nope," Theo said.

"Oh. Alright." Kade averted his eyes.

Theo hadn't seen Kade look at the photo much. He got it out of Kade's drawer at night, then slipped it back before Kade woke up. He hadn't seen Kade touch that drawer in the last week, except to show Sundance, who had peered at it for two full minutes before announcing that she was going to take a long, *long* walk.

It was a small photo. Black and white and faded with age. There was a burn at the corner that was so old it didn't smell like ash anymore. Two boys stared out from the frame. When Theo had first looked at the photograph sitting in Felicity's palm, he had felt a strange tunneling sensation. Like time was flimsy and he was putting a hand through it, reaching down through the layers. Like all of this had happened already and would happen again.

It was *them*. Theo on the right, dressed in a Victorian-style suit. His curls were smoothed back, his posture straight and proper as he stared the camera down. Kade stood on the left. He was wearing a puffy white shirt and suspenders, his dark hair in a knot on top of his head. It was undeniably them, down to the stubborn curl escaping over Theo's forehead and the mole on Kade's neck.

The boys looked relaxed, almost happy. It matched the writing on the back—small and smudged and spidery, a lot like Kade's. *A pair of fools* it said. *1833.*

Theo rubbed the burned edge of the photo. "I can't tell if he's dead yet," he told Kade. "I keep looking at… at *him*. I can't tell."

"Can't tell by looking at you, either." Kade rocked sideways, nudging him. They were both in full sleeves again, long pants and socks. Kade wore a scarf. Both had gloves: Kade's were black leather, Theo's the bobbly yellow ones Kade had given him last year. It was one of the only things he'd taken from the house before he moved in with Kade.

Temporarily, of course. Just while he figured out what to do next. Even though both Kade and Sundance told him he could stay however long he wanted.

"He's dead," Kade continued. "They—we—*they* only start spending time together after he's dead."

Theo nodded, shoving the photo in his pocket.

Kade cleared his throat. "Are you going to forgive Sparky anytime soon? She looks *so* sad when she climbs into my bed at night."

"I forgive her," Theo replied, frowning. He'd shoved his face in Sparky's fur that first night, shaking, whispering what a good dog she was, despite everything.

"She's not sad about *me*," Theo continued. "She's sad that she obeyed...that she obeyed Victor."

"Oh. Then why is she sleeping with me?"

Theo thought about lying. It felt useless at this point.

"Because I told her to keep you safe," he admitted.

Kade looked away again, cheeks heating.

Theo's mouth watered.

Kade cleared his throat. "So what did you come out here for? You can see the sunset from my house, too. If you go on the roof. You can chill with the wisteria, I know how much you love that stuff."

Kade eyed the dizzying drop. Then, as if thinking better of it, he shuffled back from the cliff edge, bringing his legs with him. The Kade of a few months ago might have made a game of it, dangling his legs so wildly Theo would threaten to pull him back. But today's Kade didn't do this. He looked tired.

Theo could relate. He'd never wanted to sleep more than he had in the last month.

"I wanted to try something," Theo said. He reached over and picked up the fabric scissors.

Kade sucked in a nervous breath.

"Relax," Theo told him. He reached up to his head, taking one of his blond curls and cutting it at the base. Then he let the curl go and watched it drift over the sunset-heavy lake.

Kade's breath left him in a whoosh. "Shit, sunshine. You freaked me out. *I* can do that."

Theo hesitated. Then he handed the scissors over.

Kade took them, fitting his gloved hands easily through the handle. "All of it?"

Theo nodded, throat thick.

Kade cut another curl. Then another. Blond strands drifted out over the lake, curl after curl after curl. An endless forest of hair drifting off the cliff and landing in the water.

Theo's eyes itched. "Is it working?"

Kade snipped another curl off and let the breeze catch it.

"Kade," Theo said. "Is it working?"

Kade didn't answer.

Theo reached up and ran his hands through his hair. His perfectly intact curls, which had stayed the same length since he died. The same curls as his dad, the same as his mom if she dyed and curled it like she had been doing for the past two decades. The hair Victor had ruffled so many times while Theo tensed, waiting for his grip to turn tight.

"It's pretty cool actually," Kade said, too fast. "Like —holy vampire powers, batman. Immediate hair growth. Doctors hate him—oh shit."

The first sob made Theo curl over, shaking with it. Cold black tears rolled down his cheeks.

"Shit," Kade repeated. He dropped the scissors and rubbed a gloved hand into Theo's back, voice soothing and a little panicked. "You're okay. *We're* okay. Everything's gonna be fine."

Theo wanted to laugh. But he couldn't do anything except sob, deep and desperate, dropping his head against Kade's fabric-clad shoulder.

He wasn't sure how long he cried. Long enough to stain Kade's shirt black, the fabric sticking oily and black to his skin. Long enough for the sun to almost disappear into the horizon.

Kade glanced over the cliff Theo was dangling his legs over. "God. I'm glad you're finally letting it out, but could we do this further away from the cliff? C'mere, sunshine."

He guided Theo as he crawled back from the edge until Kade's shoulders relaxed.

"There we go," Kade said again. He reached up like he was going to pull Theo's head back to his shoulder. Then he stopped, flexing his hand in midair. He'd tucked his sleeves into his gloves. It looked silly, but it meant there was less chance of accidental skin contact.

Kade ran a cautious hand through Theo's hair, pulling out unattached strands left behind from the failed haircut.

"Tell me about plants," he said.

Theo snorted bitterly, wiping his cheeks. Sundance had assured him he'd feel better after a good cry. He felt like a cored apple.

"I can tell you about a flower," he rasped. He dug in his pocket and brought out the lighter he'd meant to give Kade that day in the woods.

Kade took it and held it up to the light. The metal

glinted: a snake baring its fangs one side, its tail turning into flowers on the other.

"It'll help me die faster," Kade said, remembering. "You know I don't have to use this to smoke, right? I can...light fires for, like, s'mores. I can light candles."

He smiled. The small, pleased curl of his mouth made Theo wonder how anybody could ever be scared of him. This jagged boy who embroidered a mouse in the pocket of his ripped jeans so he could look inside and see a little buddy. Who stayed up late to fix his aunt's work shirt and brought cheap steak to mix into Sparky's kibble.

"He looks like a fun guy," Kade said, tapping the snarling snake. "What are the flowers?"

Theo twisted the lighter, knitted gloves brushing Kade's leather ones.

"We call it the fang orchid," Theo explained. "It looks like a snake, so animals will think it's dangerous. But it isn't."

Kade ducked his head. The blush was back. Theo watched it bloom, hungry for things beyond blood.

"Thanks, sunshine," Kade said softly. He ran his gloved thumb over the snake's face, trailing it all the way over the other side to meet the flower petals.

"I promise not to lose it like my last three lighters," Kade continued, and tucked it into his pocket. Theo was tempted to leave it like that—let Kade walk him home, sit him on the couch and watch mindless TV like they'd been doing every day since he moved in. But

Theo wanted to tell him. There was nothing holding him back anymore.

"Kade," he said, and swallowed. "You know how you said I wouldn't kiss you even if I could?"

Kade froze. His shoulders lifted back up, like Theo had just dragged them back toward the cliff and forced Kade to look over the terrifying drop. Then he steeled himself.

"Uh," Kade said. "Yeah? Why?"

"I was surprised when you said that," Theo admitted. "I thought it was obvious. Especially after this summer. I'm really crazy about you. Not because I need your blood or because we're…"

He touched his pocket to feel the photograph tucked inside.

"Trapped together," he finished. "I'm crazy about you because you're sweet. And smart. And caring. You're so soft under all those spikes. You try to hide it because so many people give you shit for it, but I see you, and you're…you're *so* beautiful, man."

Kade's eyes were wide. His lips parted, pink and chapped and making Theo ache.

"I'd kiss you every day if I could," Theo admitted. "Every day."

Kade's heart skipped a beat. Theo heard it: a short, sharp pause before it slammed into action again, beating in double time. Kade looked exactly how Theo pictured when he'd imagined this over the last few weeks: dazed, pleased, disbelieving. Then, finally, drowning everything else out: devastated.

Theo expected it to stop there. They couldn't be together, not in the way they both wanted. But Kade's face changed into something steely and determined.

"Kiss me now."

Theo stared at him. "It'd hurt."

"It hurts when you don't kiss me," Kade said, and grinned. It wobbled at the edges. He pulled off his scarf, the same one he'd used to hide his burns before they figured out Theo could heal them. He turned around, the back of his neck pale and unblemished and waiting.

Theo leaned in.

Kade's neck blistered the second Theo kissed it. Still he lingered, basking in Kade's metallic softness and listening to Kade's breath hitch.

Finally he leaned back. The kiss mark was raw and shiny on Kade's neck. Theo started pulling off his glove, ready to heal it.

Kade caught his arm. "Don't. I want to keep it."

Theo looked at the leather covering Kade's hand. Somewhere under there was that burn from the forest after they fought Hawthorn. *A keepsake,* he'd told Theo a few nights ago when Theo ran into him in the kitchen. *I wanted proof you'd touched me. Even if it hurt.*

Kade pushed himself up with a sigh. "Come on. Let's get out of here."

Theo stood, glancing back at the house where it had all happened. There was still a hole in the ceiling where

Victor had shoved him into the plaster. Another hole in the floorboards. Theo had only been back in the house once, and that was to rescue his plants.

"Theo," Kade prompted. He took Theo's hand, rough leather against knitted wool.

"Right," Theo said. "Coming."

They set off toward the woods. Theo watched the scorch mark gleam on the back of Kade's neck, thinking of burn cream and lumpy couches and doting dogs, but mostly of kisses.

He was going to kiss Kade. The decision sunk deep, making a home in his bones: even if it was the last thing he ever did, Theo would find a way to kiss that boy without hurting him.

SPECIAL THANKS

Thank you so much for reading VENOM BOUND! You can grab the last book in the trilogy, SOUL BURN, on Amazon, B&N and KU.

If you want to support me, please leave a review on Goodreads, Amazon and any social media of your choice.

You can get updates on my upcoming books by subscribing to my newsletter! Sign up by visiting my website at isbelleauthor.com. (by signing up you also get a free sapphic novella!)

You can find her on Tiktok @i.s.belle_writes or on Instagram @isbelleauthor.

ACKNOWLEDGMENTS

First off, let's give it up for my Kickstarter backers! I was blown away for the support this early-access campaign got. Let's go down the line:

Eden Mason, Milo N, Ashley Binder, Victoria P, Ary, Michelle B., Briar, Valentine, Ashleigh Wolfe, Bee Marie Chase, Lisa Herrick, Ayanna W, Ayla Peyrot, Ember, Maggie Callow, Persephone Embers, Katie Olive, Lucy Holland, Maddie Murray, Xander Beck, Kym Saunders, Hann K, Paige L, Katherine Nichols, JJ, Korvus F. M., Effy, Franchesca Caram, Michael Anthony, You, Steffi Happy, Mal M., Rowan Knight, Craig Esser, Marie C, Caitlyn Manning, Faith Dam, Gabriel De Jesus, Eric McCurry, kishaya wicks, Jor-Jor, Jess Autiero, Sophia, Maya Tohill, Jessica Williamson, DangerDays, Hailey Robinson, Clarissa, Finn, Virginia Queen, Gwyny Rankin, Stuart Turnbull, Jordie, Rafa Apolo, Stephanie Lucas, Raul Alonso, Breaker Chittenden, Millie, Phoenix, Gee Rothvoss, Fergus (the dear kitty cat), Jessi Heimer, C F Chan, Ashliicat, Noal, Urna Mukherjee, Nico, Lily Schnur, Rachiel Rosser, Chris Mobley, Rebekah Roennfeldt, Jack Schiller, Mish

Phillips, Tara W, Tiffany Culver, Tayva Case, Dead Fish Books.

And of course my formatter, Edward Giordano, my cover artist Nani (shinirikaya on Insta), my editor Catriona Turner, and lastly my wonderful betas, Chloe Spencer and Eleanor B!

ABOUT THE AUTHOR

I. S. Belle writes Young Adult and New Adult books that are sometimes spooky, often romantic, and always gay.

She works in a bookstore in New Zealand and stops to pat dogs in the street. If you have a dog and your local bookshop allows pets - for the love of booksellers, please bring them in.

She has a Creative Writing Masters from the International Institute of Modern Letters. You can find her on Tiktok @i.s.belle_writes or on Instagram @isbelleauthor.

ALSO BY I. S. BELLE

I. S. Belle

LGBT+ Young Adult Fiction

BABYLOVE SERIES

BABYLOVE

SUGARSNAP

SWEETHEARTS

ZOMBABE

ZOMBABE

HONEYBLOODS SERIES

HONEYBLOODS

HONEYBITES

HONEYCRAVES

BLOOD TETHERED SERIES

BLOOD TETHERED

VENOM BOUND

SOUL BURN

GIRLS NIGHT

GIRLS NIGHT